TALES FROM THE SURREY HILLS

Tales from across the Surrey Hills

Godalming Writers' Group

1st edition 2023

ISBN: 9798852160720

The Godalming Writers' Group has also written three books of stories about its home town of Godalming. They are available from the Watts Gallery, Compton & Amazon at: https://bit.ly/GwG123

Visit Godalming Writers' Group website:
https://www.godalmingwritersgroup.org/

&

https://www.facebook.com/GodalmingWritersGroup

godalming Writers' group

And, if you enjoy these tales, please leave a review on Amazon!

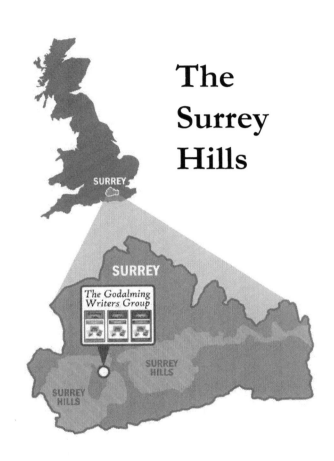

The Surrey Hills

SURREY

SURREY

The Godalming
Writers Group

SURREY
HILLS

SURREY
HILLS

4

TALES FROM THE SURREY HILLS

The Chilworth Gunpowder Plot

by Paul Rennie & Ian Honeysett

The spring of 1605 in the Surrey Hills was unusually cold and showery and this morning was no exception. Father Thomas Hulbert would normally have left the Carp Inn in Chilworth by now, after celebrating a secret Catholic Mass with the few recusants who adhered to the faith in the face of the resurgence of persecution under King James. But he had decided to stay and enjoy a delicious cut of mutton and a large chunk of bread to wait out the rain. Some said he enjoyed his food too much and that his impressive stomach showed this, but he saw food as a gift from God that needed to be appreciated. As he sat at the trestle table in the bay window, with a wooden mug of ale in front of him, he may have appeared at ease with the world, but he was far from it. He knew the penalties for encouraging others to attend a non-Anglican service. He had read about how the monks of Chilworth had been mistreated when they were unceremoniously ejected from their monastery under Henry VIII and had personally witnessed the execution of fellow priest, Robert Southwell, back in 1595 at Tyburn. The memory filled him with horror and revulsion.

Every so often he peered anxiously through the shutters for any sign of strangers, or worse, informants who might give away his presence. He ministered to a small and trusted congregation which included Robert Spixworth, the innkeeper. The cellar of the inn was a relatively discreet place to hold the weekly service. Robert was an unusually thin man for one whose business was providing food and drink, on account of his nervous disposition. He viewed every stranger who entered the inn with suspicion and made it his business to know their business.

Today, as with every Mass day, Robert was especially worried about being caught harbouring a priest. To be on the safe side he had stationed his son, Nat, along the road by the stables as a lookout, ready to give warning. He could rely on Nat, who was quick on his bare feet, and in his rough woollen tunic, was scarcely noticed at the best of times, especially when darting through the inn collecting empty pots. Agnes, the aged cook, was also a fervent Catholic and, even if she hadn't been, said so few words that she would never give the game away. She tottered over to the table with a trencher of bread filled with cold mutton pieces, refilling the ale mug from a pitcher. The priest was very hungry, having fasted all morning as he always did before taking communion. As he finished the last heel of bread, Nat came running in, shouting that three men on horseback had arrived at the stables from the London direction, and were asking about accommodation at the inn.

Father Hulbert grabbed his jute sack containing vestments, prayer book, candlesticks and communion chalice and, in a well-rehearsed move, pressed the two hidden latches in the wooden panelling near the table, which he could then slide open to reveal a narrow priest's hole. He stepped inside and slid the panel shut. There was only just room for him to sit on a barrel in the darkness, with a pitcher of water and a small chamber pot in case of an extended stay. He waited, holding his breath. He was not at all sure how long he could remain confined in a space meant for a far smaller man than him. His longest stay to date had been an hour and a half and he had absolutely no wish to repeat that.

Outside, the three strangers had handed their horses over to the stable boy and made their way around the puddles in the road to the inn, lured by the rough wooden sign nailed to a beam with a crude outline of a fish in charcoal that bore just a passing resemblance to a carp. The trio was far too finely dressed to be of peasant stock, wearing padded doublets and breeches with short cloaks and small ruffs round their necks, although these were rather travel-stained. On their heads they all wore the copotain felt hats that were fashionable in the city and sported the short, pointed beards and moustaches favoured by men of importance. Attached to each man's waist by a chain was a sword and two of them had pistols tucked into their belts. They were clearly not taking chances with the footpads who frequented the London road looking for easy pickings.

The tallest of the three, and probably their leader, had adorned his hat with an extravagant peacock feather. He had to remove it as he ducked down through the low doorway of the inn, followed by the others. They presented themselves in a line in front of Robert who was nervously pretending to adjust the spigot on a barrel.

'Good morrow, sir. We have travelled from Kingston and are in need of a room and board tonight.' Robert weighed up the risk against the much-needed income from three obviously well-heeled gentlemen and, after adding an extra two shillings to the price, agreed to provide them with a shared bed in the upper room.

'We also desire some food, perchance some of that mutton and ale?'

'Of course, sirs,' said Robert and, trying to seat them as far away from the hiding priest as he could, said, 'Sit yourselves at the table by the ingle and I'll get Agnes to prepare the fayre.'

'We'd prefer the trestle in the bay window, if you please,' said their leader. 'There is better light for us to study our map and be able to converse in private.'

Robert tried to argue that the table hadn't been cleared from the previous customer, but the men insisted on sitting there. He just hoped that Father Hulbert would know they were there and not make a sound. The wooden panels were very thin, and it would be difficult to pass off any noise as vermin or coming from another room.

Behind the panel, Father Hulbert could hear quite clearly that a number of people had now sat down at the table he had just vacated. The closest to him was just inches away from where he was hidden. From their accents he could tell that they were not from the village and that the voices probably belonged to the three horsemen that Nat had warned were heading to the inn. Perhaps they might give a few clues about their business in Chilworth and whether they posed a threat to local Catholics.

The mysterious men lit their clay pipes while waiting for the food and proceeded to talk urgently in low voices whilst poring over an unscrolled map.

'The gunpowder mill is less than a mile down that track across the road. All we have to do is follow the course of the millstream. We won't even need horses.'

A few of the regular farm hands and mill workers started to wander in and soon there was speculation over who these well-dressed strangers were. Could they be merchants or were they sheriff's officers or, God forbid, tax collectors? They all agreed that it was unlikely to be good news especially since, after the death of Queen Bess, there was a new wave of intolerance sweeping the country. Why, even the well-known, health-giving properties of tobacco had been questioned by the new King, James I.

Robert took the food and ale to the strangers' table himself, determined to find out more about them.

'You say you have travelled from Kingston. Pray tell me, sirs, what is your business here in Chilworth?'

The tall man looked up rather sheepishly. 'We, erm, are seeking to purchase some land near Guildford and we wished to visit the ruined monastery near here.'

'Well, if that's the case,' said Robert, 'you've wasted your time. King Henry's men burned the monastery to the ground and the local masons have removed every stone to build the walls at the gunpowder mills. They needed to be extra thick because that stuff can go off anytime. It's not natural, that black powder; it's dabbling in witchcraft, if you ask me.'

Just at that moment Robert, whose hearing was particularly keen, thought he heard a sound from the priest's hole. It sounded like a cough. A trickle of sweat ran down the side of his ear. He offered up a prayer that Father Hulbert was not about to have one of his coughing fits. He quickly looked around at the three diners in case they too had heard it but, thank heavens, they were too engrossed in their food and conversation.

The tall man continued, through sips of ale. 'That's interesting. Mayhaps we should go and see these mills instead. Do you know where dwells the foreman?'

'That would be Seth. He is also the charcoal burner. You'll find him by following the smoke in the trees along the path. It's some way off the mill buildings on account of the risk of the fire causing an explosion.'

Robert tried to get more information from them, but the men weren't very forthcoming. One thing he knew was that Seth was a thoroughly disreputable character, but he wasn't going to tell them that.

Father Hulbert in his hiding place, on the other hand, had heard a lot more from the men's whispered conversations. He was able to piece together their real motives for visiting the area. He had heard the men were planning to buy gunpowder, twenty barrels of it, and transport it back to London. They had another accomplice who was travelling separately and providing the transport. Gunpowder manufacture was a Royal monopoly and very carefully controlled so they had come here hoping to obtain some without attracting attention from the authorities.

As he had listened, the reason became clear. They were planning to use it against King James, and he heard the Houses of Parliament undercroft mentioned several times. What he had inadvertently overheard was nothing less than a political conspiracy to try and restore a Catholic Monarchy. Father Hulbert was aghast at the magnitude of what was developing, and he faced a serious moral dilemma. He despised the treatment that Catholics had suffered at the hands of the Crown since the start of the Reformation. He prayed constantly for the removal of King James. But his prayer was for his peaceful removal: he had taken his vows as a priest to uphold God's commandments and that most definitely included '*Thou shalt not kill*'. He knew that blowing up Parliament would kill many innocent people as well as the King. Some of them would probably be Catholics as well. Whilst he had some sympathies with the three fellow Catholics sitting at the table near him, he knew he couldn't just allow it to happen. At the same time, he wasn't prepared to inform on them to the authorities, because he knew full well what a gruesome death they would suffer if their plot was discovered. Not to mention the torture that would most assuredly precede it. It would almost certainly lead to further widespread persecution of Catholics in general.

But what was he to do? He had to think of a way to foil their plot without them being arrested. The priest's hole he was in was by now becoming ever more stifling. He had somehow managed to stop himself from further coughing but already he felt that tickle in his throat that could only get worse. He had been suffering from these wretched coughing fits ever since he had started smoking a pipe. This was strange since he had read about the beneficial effects of smoking. That was the very reason he had taken it up in the first place. The final proof was surely that this appalling King James was so opposed to the plant and had called it '*hatefull to the Nose, harmefull to the braine and dangerous to the Lungs*'. But now he was desperate to escape from this cupboard and get out and stretch his legs. Also, the ale he had drunk with his lunch was starting to make its acquaintance with his bladder. He dared not use the chamber pot as he knew from bitter experience there was no way he could conceal the noises that would accompany that.

Then, just when he thought they would never leave, the three conspirators finished their meal, belched loudly and headed outside and across the road to the start of the path leading to the mills, looking slightly incongruous in their fine boots as they waded through the thick mud along the riverbank.

When he was sure they had gone, Robert gave the three pre-agreed taps on the wall, and the panel slid open to reveal a very hot and flustered Father Hulbert. The much-feared coughing fit quickly ensued.

'Well, Father,' said Robert when the noise had subsided, 'they were polite enough but if I'm not mistaken, they are up to no good. I wonder why they are seeking Seth?'

Father Hulbert quickly explained what he had heard to an increasingly worried Robert.

13

'What if they are discovered?' gasped Robert. 'The authorities might think I'm part of the plot if those men have lodged here. I might get taken to London and be hung, drawn and quartered. I'm afeared I'd admit anything if I was tortured.'

'I know too well your discomfort,' replied Father Hulbert. 'We need to think of a way to stop them obtaining the gunpowder and I think I have an idea. But we are going to need to involve Seth and you know how untrustworthy *he* is. And I'm afeared we are going to need Nat's services as well. I'm sorry to have to involve your son but I don't think there is another way. I'll have to go home now, before the strangers get back. They must not see me here. But, after they have taken to their bed, come to my house with Nat and I'll explain what I have in mind.'

Just after ten o'clock, there were the three agreed taps on Father Hulbert's door, and he opened it to see Robert and Nat standing there expectantly.

'We need to go along the path to Seth's hut,' he told them. 'It's dark, so we'll need a lantern.'

Once the oil was lit, the three of them made their way along the narrow path illuminated by the pale-yellow light, taking care to stay clear of the slippery mossy banks of the fast-flowing millstream. Eventually they caught sight of a faint glow amongst the trees. It was the earth-covered mound in which the charcoal was burning. In its faint light, further down the path, they could just make out the row of carefully separated buildings where the saltpetre, sulphur and charcoal were stored, mixed, and then ground while wet by the water mill. Next to the charcoal mound was Seth's hut, crudely built from a ring of stone and hazel coppice poles bent over to form upper walls and a roof, with the gaps filled with mud and straw. A dwelling well fitted to the character of its occupant.

Father Hulbert called out, as quietly as he could, 'Seth, it's Father Hulbert and the Spixworths here. We need to converse with you urgently.'

There were some mutterings from the depths of the hut before Seth emerged through the flap of jute that functioned as a door. In the flickering light, he looked every inch a rogue, his skin blackened by the charcoal he worked with. But Father Hulbert knew from the confessional that Seth had a deep Catholic faith, not to mention a profound fear of eternal damnation. He was confident he could persuade him to help with his plan.

True to form, Seth initially denied that he'd seen the three strangers but, after a few pointed reminders from Father Hulbert about the possible destination of his soul, he admitted sheepishly that the men had indeed been enquiring about illicit gunpowder and that, for a sizeable bribe of silver, he had agreed to provide them with twenty barrels. They would have to be stolen from the storehouse without the other mill workers knowing. He said he hadn't asked any questions about why the men wanted the gunpowder and they had not volunteered any information, not surprising because tight controls on its manufacture meant that there was never enough for the demand, and all sorts of people were prepared to pay extra to get a supply.

When Father Hulbert explained what he had heard about the conspirators' plan to blow up the Houses of Parliament with the gunpowder, Seth realised immediately that he could be in serious trouble if things went ahead as they planned.

'If they do kill the King, everyone will want to know where the gunpowder came from and the trail will lead back here,' he gasped. 'I'll be dragged off to London and be executed. If you've a plan to stop all that then pray tell me, Father. I'll put some extra in the collection plate, as God is my witness.'

'Just what I hoped you'd say, Seth,' replied Father Hulbert. 'That's why we need to stop the deed happening. I have an idea how we might do that. We can't just refuse to give the men the powder because they might try and take it anyway. They have swords and pistols, so we couldn't stop them and, if we alert the Sheriff, we could be implicated in the plot. The King's authorities will use any reason to kill a few more Catholics. I think we need to give the men the powder but substitute it for inferior quality that won't ignite. That way they won't be able to do harm with it and, by the time they realise, it will be too late. This is where you have a part to play, Seth. If anyone can pass off poor quality material for good, it's you.'

Seth smiled broadly at what he thought was a compliment, quickly turning to a frown. 'Maybe I could, Father, but they are coming back on the morrow for a sample to test the powder I've agreed to give them. I have plenty of old powder that we can't get rid of because it's gone rotten. But, if it doesn't explode, they'll know it's useless.'

'We'll need to let them take a sample from the barrels of rotten powder and then substitute the sample with good powder without them knowing,' replied Father Hulbert. 'I suggest you should employ Robert and Nat as helpers. You could tell the men that you need their help because the barrels are heavy and need moving. Once the sample of powder has been taken, one of you needs to distract them while the other makes the exchange. Do you think you could do that, young Nat, without them seeing?'

'Yes, Father,' said Nat enthusiastically, warming to his role in this adventure. 'Because I'm small, I could stow myself amongst the barrels and reach through at the right moment. Hiding is what I'm good at.'

They agreed the details of the rest of the plan and for Nat to be in place hidden amongst the twenty barrels of rotten powder, with a small keg of good material to make the swap. With that they bade goodnight to Seth, who was now rubbing his hands with glee at the thought of passing off the useless powder for a very good price. Nothing like doing good whilst making a healthy profit.

The conspirators rose early the next day and, after breaking their fast with bacon and oatmeal, they made their way back to the agreed spot to meet Seth before the rest of the mill workers arrived. They had arranged for the fourth member of their band to bring a barge up the river pulled by a sturdy looking horse. He arrived shortly after them, staying on board in the deeper water. Nat was already in place amongst the barrels of ruined gunpowder that Seth had separated from the good stock. The men were surprised to see the innkeeper there as well, but Seth explained that Robert was his partner in their little side business and was sharing in the profits. As Seth had predicted, the men were very cautious and insisted on testing the quality of the powder they were buying. They agreed with Seth's suggestion that they would take samples from some of the barrels into a small keg and then test it for explosive quality.

Seth opened five of the barrels and one of the men, taking a wooden ladle, spooned black powder from each into the keg that Robert was holding, which he then sealed with a wooden bung. He placed the keg on the ground next to a space between the barrels and announced that it was thirsty work and would they like some of his ale that he had brought along to toast their deal? The three conspirators agreed, and Robert directed them to a bench where he had set up a pitcher and mugs. After pouring the ale, Robert raised a toast 'To the King', although he noted that the conspirators' response of 'Long may he live' was a little less enthusiastic than his own and that there were some knowing glances between the three. They were blissfully unaware of the small hand snaking out from the gap between the barrels and making the exchange.

After finishing the ale, the men picked up the barrel and said they were going to test it.

'You'll have need to take it a long way off into the woods,' said Seth. 'We don't want to set this lot off; it would make an almighty bang.'

'We hope so,' said the tall man, fingering his moustache, 'although not just yet!'

Two of the conspirators set off into the woods along a narrow path, leaving the third to watch over their purchase and, after about fifteen minutes, those remaining at the mill heard a loud explosion. Sometime later, the two men emerged from the trees looking slightly singed and announced that they were well satisfied with the potency of the gunpowder.

The purse containing the silver was handed over and, after careful counting, Seth and Robert loaded the barrels, four at a time, onto the punt that was used to ferry the powder from the shallow millstream to the main river where barges had to wait. When all twenty barrels had made the crossing and were safely stowed underneath sacking, they bid Godspeed to the bargee who, without saying a word, turned the horse around and set off on the long journey towards the Thames and London. The remaining conspirators walked back to the village and, after collecting their horses from the stables and paying Robert's slightly inflated bill, bade farewell and headed back along the road towards Guildford. Whistling as they went, they seemed delighted by their purchase.

Father Hulbert and the rest of the group vowed solemnly that they would never speak of the event again, although the priest did remind Seth that he expected to see some of the silver appear in the collection plate next Sunday. Robert, the innkeeper, was quite confident that much of the silver would be coming his way in exchange for ale.

In November there came the disturbing news that there had been a failed plot to kill the King and Members of Parliament and that a group of conspirators had been arrested and executed. Fortunately for the Chilworth villagers, the torturers were focused on the wider members of the conspiracy and never determined the source of the gunpowder.

Postscript

Although this is a fictional account, there is some overlap with actual events. Full production of gunpowder at Chilworth Mills was started in 1626 by the East India Company. Before that, the Evelyn family of Bletchingly, who owned the land at Chilworth, had been granted a monopoly on the manufacture of gunpowder in the reign of Elizabeth 1. Given the suitability of the site for production of the powder with its water mill and alder trees for making charcoal, it is probable that some manufacture was taking place at the time of the events in the story.

The real November 5 conspirators stored 36 barrels of gunpowder for months in the undercroft of the Houses of Parliament. When they were ready to carry out the massacre, they found that the powder had deteriorated and was no longer usable. They had to replace it with new gunpowder, delaying the plot long enough for a letter (probably from a turncoat amongst the conspirators) to reach Baron William Parker, who was able to alert the authorities to arrest Guy Fawkes as he prepared the final act. The rest, as they say, is history.

In St Mary's Church, in the village of Frensham, Surrey, the strangest object can be found. Propped up on a tripod, near the pews, beneath the arched windows, in among all the other fittings you'd expect in an English country church, stands what appears to be a witch's cauldron.

The Chilworth Gunpowder Plot Epilogue

by Jonathan Rennie

'It's not a difficult question,' I repeated, but my client just sat there with his eyes down and his hands folded in his lap.

Sometimes I wonder why I do this job at all; it's certainly not that well paid and I don't get a great deal of thanks. I'm a sensitive person at heart and I can always see both sides of an argument, which perhaps isn't the best skill set for this career path. It can be a bit embarrassing too if I chance upon one of my old customers outside of the work environment. Quite often they're a bit unhappy with me. Upset, angry even. Once one tried to chase me down the street, but luckily, he was a bit hobbled, so it was an easy escape.

To be honest, I don't even look the part. I know what they are expecting when they first come in: some huge monster with a bare chest, scars, a soiled and bloody leather apron and perhaps just a little mask to cover the eyes. Such a cliché. So, it's hard to tell whether it's just relief or a tinge of disappointment when they see little old me standing there. Medium height, thinning grey hair, bad teeth, worse breath. One of them once said to me, 'Do anything you must, just please stop breathing on me,' which I thought was quite good for someone in his situation. As for the bare chest, you must be joking. It's bloody freezing in here unless we've got the brazier fired up, so a thick work jerkin and two pairs of woolly hose are the usual order of the day.

Anyway, back to this particular client. He sat there looking a touch downcast. He was mid-thirties, I'd guess, with a padded doublet, breeches, a small ruff round his neck and the typical short, pointed beard and moustache favoured by men who wanted others to think they were important. He hadn't said anything much yet and I'd tried the usual tricks, mirroring his body language and moving my chair to be beside him, rather than opposite. The theory is to try not to appear too confrontational, but to be honest I'm not sure it works that well when you are sitting in a dungeon surrounded by the tools of the trade: racks, thumbscrews, garrottes, branding irons. I think they find it a bit too off-putting to appreciate the subtlety.

I rechecked the list of questions and tried again.

'Where did you get the gunpowder?'

No reply.

'Look, just answer a couple of questions and it will be much easier for you. Maybe they'll even commute your sentence.'

'Yeah, perhaps you'll only be hung, drawn and halved,' put in Toby, one of the two guards who sat in the corner, usually not paying too much attention. Toby had used this little gem many times before, and it always made him chuckle. I raised my eyebrows at my client but was surprised to see that the comment had got to him, and a fresh whiff of anxiety-driven sweat rose in the air.

'I will tell you all,' he said in a low voice. 'You do not need to hurt me.'

Ah, now, that is a bit of a problem, you see. Torture is a funny business. You can't go too hard too soon, but similarly it can't be seen to be too easy. If they blab everything out before you've laid a finger on them, it looks a bit suspicious. Either they are holding something back or the job is too easy. There's a sweet spot, you see. The client needs to look as if you have worked him over and you need to look like you've put in a full shift.

I explained this to him, and to his credit he got it. In fact, we began to strike up the light camaraderie that often kicks in once they've decided to talk.

'It's quite simple,' I said. 'I'll just spend a bit of time making sure you look like you've held out for a while. You know, a few singe marks on your moustache, a couple of pulled fingernails, maybe a bit of light garrotting, and then you tell me everything. It's a win-win.'

'Well, sir,' he said, 'do what you must, but pray do not rough up my ruff.'

Now I thought this was really rather clever, and so did he. He looked over at the guards to see if they had heard, but Toby was having a piss in a bucket, and his sidekick Tom was inspecting something he had pulled from his nose.

'*I said, Do what you must, but pray do not rough up my ruff!*' he repeated in a louder voice, staring hard in their direction, but still got no response.

He looked a bit crestfallen, so I gave him my best sardonic grin and another flash of the eyebrows. To be honest, the quality of guards has gone downhill a lot since they gave the contract to the lowest bidder. It's not the guards' fault. They don't get any decent training, and let's say the job attracts a certain type, if you know what I mean.

Anyway, to make him feel better I removed his ruff carefully and set it down within sight on the reasonably clean surface of the tool table.

'It's a shame I didn't bring its box,' he said.

Ah, now this was someone after my own heart, so we spent a few minutes chatting amicably about the advantages of retaining original packaging while I tied a light coverall around his neck and heated up the branding irons.

Half an hour later we were pretty much done. To the casual observer the client looked a bit of a mess, but a professional could tell he was not badly harmed. The garrotte was still on his neck, just turned to a level five (*bulging eyes and gasping for breath,* according to the menu in the handbook).

'OK, so here we go,' I said. 'Where did you get the gunpowder?'

'From the Carp Inn at Chilworth,' he gasped obligingly.

Now this was not an answer I wanted to hear. Not at all. The Carp Inn is a bit of a favourite of mine, you see. My sister and her family live down in Chilworth and we often go to see them at the weekend. The wives and children get on well, and usually me and my brother-in-law will leave them to it and sneak out to the Carp for a couple of cheeky flagons. Old Rob Spixworth who runs the place is a right card and we always have a bit of banter over the cockfighting. We have to be a bit careful what we say, of course; these days it is hard to keep up with all the changes. Protestant this, Catholic that – religious correctness gone mad, if you ask me. But, as long as we are back in time to carve the roast and not in too much of a state to drive the cart home, everyone's happy.

I needed time to think, so with a glance over at the guards to check they weren't paying attention, I tweaked the old garrotte up a couple of notches to number seven (*blue in face, unable to speak*) and my gentleman client responded accordingly.

Now, if the Carp Inn is implicated in the Gunpowder plot, it will go badly for Rob, and the authorities will probably torch the place, which would be a crying shame and make my weekends a lot duller than before. My brother-in-law would never forgive me.

My poor gentleman client had a bit of an imploring look on his blue face by now, so rather than prolong the agony, so to speak, I gave the garrotte another quick quarter turn to number ten, and there was a satisfying click as his fourth cervical vertebra snapped and his head lolled over onto his chest.

'Oops-a-daisy,' I called over to Toby and Tom, making a big downturned mouth at them. This time it was their turn to look at the heavens as they shuffled over to carry out the body.

The warden was pretty good about it, I have to say.

'Never mind, these things happen,' was his only admonition. 'Anyway, we've got a couple more here from the same group,' he said, gesturing towards two similarly dressed gentlemen sitting by the dungeon door, and both, I have to say, looking a touch off-colour.

'Right, well, umm, who's next?' I asked, and the nearest one sheepishly raised his hand. Toby and Tom led him in while I did a quick tidy up of the tools and tossed the ruff onto the brazier.

It was going to be a long day.

The Leith Hill tower was built in 1765 by Richard Hull of Leith Hill Place as 'a place for people to enjoy the glory of the English countryside' and it's thought that the materials needed to build the tower were quarried on site.

Clipped Wings

by Pauline North

My view through the glass, from my position trapped on the top shelf of the cabinet, showed only part of the building across the street, a gable end, a slant of roof and above that the sky.

Within that frame I watched the hours, the days and the seasons change. The only living creatures I saw were the birds that flew in to pause on the rim of the gable or bustle across the roof.

How I found myself here is a story I must tell because it drifts further from me with every darkening, every lightening of that sky.

***

One warm morning at the start of the school summer holidays, my mother walked into the lounge where I lay sprawled across the sofa watching the TV.

'For God's sake, Jenny, get off your bum and do something.'

'Got nothing to do.' I can still hear my sulky tone. Every sixteen-year-old surely sounds the same.

'Well, fix it. There's an ad in the corner shop window. That new man in number 20 – the one with that shop on Godalming High Street – he wants some part-time help in his house.'

I looked at her face. She had on one of her tight expressions. I would get nowhere arguing with that; I had better at least go through the motions. Sighing heavily, I

26

rolled off the sofa and walked towards the door. 'I'll go and see what he wants then, shall I?'

'Brush your hair first. Don't you go out like that.' Her voice followed me from the room. I slipped out of the door before she could say anything else.

I checked out the board in the corner shop window. It said that Mr Merton needed someone for a little light housework for a few hours a week. Applicants could call at the house in the evenings or in the shop daytimes.

I walked the short distance from Farncombe to Godalming. I had to wait for a train to pass at the level crossing before turning down the alley that runs beside the railway. By the time I reached Bridge Road, I had convinced myself that it would be alright, he wouldn't want me.

The shop was at the far end of the High Street. I opened the door and walked in, looking around as though I was a customer. Mr Merton owned one of those antique shops that have a few cabinets at the front with a mix of genuine pieces and pretty collectables. The further back in the shop you went the more it looked as though every garden shed in town had dumped its rubbish there.

I found him behind a desk towards the front door. The desk looked quality. It was dressed in a vintage phone and an ink blotter; beside the blotter was a laptop and a CCTV monitor.

I stood off for a while to check him over. He looked old to me, probably in his late forties with light brown hair and a plain round face, a very ordinary man. He was looking through a catalogue. Nothing ventured, I told myself, the sooner you speak to him the sooner he will see how unsuitable you are. You will be home in time for that lunchtime TV programme.

27

'Mr Merton?' He looked up at me and inclined his head to acknowledge that he was. 'My name is Jenny. I saw your ad for someone to do part-time housework.'

He stood to shake my hand. He was about the same height as me and his eyes were the pale, flat grey of a winter sky. He was wearing a musty aftershave that irritated my nose.

'Good, come into the office and we'll have a chat about what I need.'

As soon as I looked into his eyes, I felt uneasy; that is when I should have walked away. Instead, I walked of my own free will into that office. I got the job. I tried hard to hide my disappointment, but I agreed to do it. I couldn't think of a reason not to. I would go in three times a week to tidy, dust and run a vacuum round; even I could do that. I would get paid the rate for my age.

'Come to the house this evening. I'll show you round and give you a key.'

My mother was thrilled. 'Well, that sounds easy enough, and he trusts you enough to give you a key.'

Difficult for me to get in without one, I thought.

That evening I went round to number 20 and rang the doorbell. While I waited, I told myself that the desire to run away was only my stupid wish that I hadn't taken the job.

He seemed larger, more imposing in his house. As we walked round, I felt happier; there wouldn't be much time wasted here. The kitchen was tiny. His lounge was neat, if a bit cluttered by a large collection of small ceramic birds. His bedroom, well that was immaculate, he made his own bed, and the surfaces were clear. I poked my head into the bathroom, fine.

He walked me back down the stairs and towards the door.

'What about that room?' There was a closed door between the kitchen and the front door, the only closed door in the house.

'Oh, that's my clutter room and home office. I have papers all over the place and it's where I repair broken pieces. It isn't necessary for you to go in there at all.'

He saw me out of the door. I would start the next day. I had keys to the front and back doors. Easy.

For two weeks it was easy. I relaxed into the job and Mum stopped wanting every detail when I got home. I was curious about the locked room though. I found out it was locked on my very first day. It became like a game to me, a ritual: in through the front door, try the locked door, get on with the work.

Then one day it wasn't locked. The handle turned. Shocked, I let go; the door swung open by a tiny amount. Feeling guilty, I pulled it closed again and stood in thought for a couple of minutes. I went and started in the kitchen. I worked through the whole house.

When I was ready to go home, I stopped outside the unlocked door. I would only peep, not even step inside the door. I peeped, then I stepped inside the room. On a table at the side of the room I saw piles of old books. Shelves at the back of the room were filled with them too. It wouldn't hurt to see what they were about – could they all be about antiques?

Gingerly I walked over to the table and bent over so that I could read the titles without touching them. The cover of the top one was covered with symbols. I read the title, "Occult Laws and Rites".

Bloody hell, he's into Ouija boards, no wonder he doesn't want anyone to know. They would have such a good laugh about this down the pub.

Behind me the door slammed shut. How? I didn't think I had left a window open – time for me to go. I began to turn but it was like swimming through setting toffee, harder and harder. I was caught, I couldn't move.

Mr Merton stood there by the closed door, laughing. I tried to say I had only looked. I hadn't touched anything. I couldn't even move my lips. I couldn't scream.

'I wondered how long it would take you.'

Then the laughing stopped. His eyes mesmerised me, freezing away hope. He raised his right arm, pointing with his forefinger, moving it in a large circle high in the air. Round and round. A flickering ring appeared, barely visible at first then filling with white mist swirling faster and faster.

It came down for me. I watched it until it covered my eyes. Then there was only pain; it was squashing me, crushing me, I could feel myself shrinking, bones turning to powder. The scream I couldn't free before I squeezed out at last, searing my soul and feeding my panic; it diminished with me and faded away.

I had no vision, but I was still there. I knew when he picked me up, I could hear him moving. I felt a hard shiny surface press against me, and I heard him chuckle, 'Now this is the tricky bit.' There was a sensation of being pushed into that hard surface and a flash of pain sent from hell.

Slowly I became aware again, I tried so hard not to. My memories were all with me, real and alive. I lived those last moments over and over. The horror of it drummed through – whatever it was that was left of me.

I could see, all the time, and I could hear. He came to gloat. He showed me a mirror. He said, 'Do you want to see?' then he held it in front of me. There before me was a small ceramic bird. I recognised it from his lounge.

What there was of me was trapped inside this bird. Ceramic birds don't close their eyes or move their heads. I saw what was directly in front of me, all the time. I heard people sometimes, from where I sat on that glass shelf, in the cabinet with the locked door.

After all those seasons, the snows, and the sunshine – and sometimes I wondered what they felt like – it mattered less and less.

That is why I wanted to tell you, because I can barely remember. It has been such hard work, remembering. I don't want to do it anymore.

Then one day I saw a kind face, the face of a customer who had taken me from the shelf and was holding me, so gently. He ran a finger along my wing and touched my claws. I would have liked to go with him, almost. But if he really liked me, please could he drop me on the nice hard floor, could he do that for me?

I was sure he would put me back, but the customer moved his hand, and I was slipping. My shiny glaze was sliding through his hand. I was too fast. He couldn't catch me, and I shattered on the floor.

I heard the assistant moving the customer away. 'Really, don't worry yourself. It wasn't a particularly good piece. I can clear it up later. Let me show you something else.'

***

Slowly my pieces draw together, changing. The bright shards become fine feathers. There isn't much time. I scrabble to my feet. There it is, an open door, my chance. I try a few steps and unfurl my wings. Just in time the air catches me and I'm through the door. The sky is calling me and now I can fly.

Watts Gallery – Artists' Village is dedicated to the work of the Victorian-era painter and sculptor George Frederic Watts. George Frederic Watts OM, RA (1817 – 1904) was widely considered to be the greatest painter of the Victorian era. A portraitist, sculptor, landscape painter and symbolist, Watts's work embodied the most pressing themes and ideas of the time, earning him the title England's Michelangelo.

Humphrey, Jeffrey & Godfrey: The Rescue

by Martyn MacDonald-Adams

"Bum! Bum! Daaah dih. Bum! Bum! Doooh dah..."

"Jeffrey!"

"Bum! Bum! Daaah dih. Bum! Bum! Doooh dah..."

"*Jeffrey!*"

"Tickle meeeh... Tickle yoooh... Cuddle herrrr... Huge bum!"

Slap!

"Ow!"

"Shush!"

"But it *is* a bit like *Mission Impossible*, isn't it?"

"Yes. But there's no need to sing the theme music. We've got to be quiet. We've got to be as quiet as quiet ninja mice wearing little woolly socks, squeak-free gloves, and soundproof knickers, while trying to be as quiet as they can."

"Uh. Okay. So, no squeaking."

It was a cold, dark night and Humphrey, a feral teddy bear living in Godalming, was dressed in his newly tailored Patent Black Ninja Special Forces Stealth Mission Apparel (Size: Very Small). He lay prone underneath a hedge and alongside him was his young, slightly shorter padawan, Jeffrey, also a teddy bear. The two were dressed in a similar fashion – in fact, Jeffrey was dressed in the offcuts from the

33

original uniform. This is possible because these teddy bears are quite small. In fact, there was still enough material remaining for the third, even smaller, teddy bear.

They were here, in the dead of night, to rescue that third bear – the third member of the Furricious Gang, called Godfrey.

"Is it time to move out yet?" asked Jeffrey.

Humphrey glanced at his Patent Black Ninja Special Forces Stealth Wrist Chronometer and pressed the button. The screen lit up the underside of the bush in a vivid red laser light and blinded both bears at the same time as the time, 03:38, was etched onto their retinas. It appeared to them in a vivid green afterimage amongst the dots for several minutes. In fact, for a short moment, the back of the house behind them displayed BE: EO for all the street to see.

A few minutes later, once his eyes had stopped smarting and he had dabbed away the tears (with one of his Patent Black Ninja Special Forces Absorbent Ocular Tissues), the senior bear reached into his Patent Black Ninja Special Forces Equipment Transporting Pouch and pulled out the Patent Black Ninja Special Forces Low Light Scoping Device - Mark 3.

He switched it on and looked across the dark garden and spotted two dogs, side by side, in their kennels. Unbeknownst to Humphrey, the two dogs had spotted the two bears a good while earlier. But then, so had all the rest of the local wildlife.

"What was that light? Shouldn't we raise the alarm?" whispered the first dog, a cross between a Chihuahua and an apparently quite slow Dachshund.

The other dog, a cross between the same frisky Chihuahua and a very surprised Labrador, laughed.

"I dunno. Just ignore them. It's the Furricious Gang up to something daft again. They are completely harmless and besides, if we raise the alarm, we'll just get a bucket of water thrown over us. Just keep quiet and pretend like we didn't see them."

Humphrey turned to Jeffrey and whispered, "They haven't seen us yet. We'll have to go around them."

Jeffrey nodded his agreement, unsure what Humphrey meant.

Reaching into his Patent Black Ninja Special Forces Stealth Equipment Transporting Pouch, Humphrey extracted a pistol-gripped thing that looked like a small hand-held crossbow. He extracted a large coil of rope with a grappling hook at one end and fitted it into the top of the device.

Jeffrey watched him and quietly sang to himself...

"Tickle meeeh... Tickle yoooh... Cuddle herrrr... Huge..."

"Shush! Here! Grab the end. I'm going to shoot this at that shed over there."

Humphrey pointed into the middle distance, then held the pistol grip in both paws and took careful aim. His aim was so careful that his tongue came out to help by stroking his nose. He pulled the trigger.

BLUNCK!

The recoil threw Humphrey backwards. He did a one-and-a-half somersault, landing on his head with an, "Ow! I bit my thung!"

Jeffrey vanished in a blur.

It took a moment for Humphrey to collect his senses.

"Jeffrey?" He looked around him. Jeffrey wasn't to be seen. "Jeffrey?" he called again, but there was no answer.

Humphrey picked up his Patent Black Ninja Special Forces Low Light Scoping Device - Mark 3 and looked through it. He had completely missed the shed and instead the grapple had landed on the roof of a house. Dangling underneath it was the rope, still coiled up, and holding on to that for grim life, was a wide-eyed Jeffrey.

"Rats!" exclaimed Humphrey.

"Rubbish!" came an unexpected reply.

Humphrey froze.

"They had nuffink to do with it. You can't shoot for toffee, you can't."

Humphrey looked down at a pair of hedgehogs.

"You're as h-accurate as a randy one-eyed h-otter falling over a waterfall with his eye closed h-after h-ogling a lady h-otter and then being bashed on the 'ead by her boyfriend."

"Uhm... Uhm... that's very... specific."

"Yeh. Made us laugh, didn't it, Knuckles?"

The other hedgehog laughed. "Yeh. That kept me laughing for the rest of the week, Spudgun. Made my day, that did."

The two hedgehogs ambled off leaving Humphrey temporarily confused.

Humphrey pressed the little button on his Patent Black Ninja Special Forces Stealth Radio Communications Earbud.

"Jeffrey? Jeffrey? Do you copy?"

"No! I can't copy anything. I'm stuck on a roof! Help!"

"Okay, okay. I can see you. Don't panic. I'm coming over to you now."

Humphrey gathered up his kit and stuffed it all into the pouch, and scurried across the garden, through another hedge, across a small car park and up to the house.

The two dogs watched the bear with interest.

"What's he up to now?" asked the Chihuahua-Dachshund.

"Dunno. He just launched his little friend onto the top of Mr. B's house. Bears are weird."

Humphrey pressed the little button on his earbud again.

"Jeffrey. Jeffrey. I am underneath you. Unravel the rope and climb down it. I'll meet you on the ground."

Jeffrey, still gripping the end of the rope, reached up and unclipped the clips that kept the coiled coils coiled. They sprang free and Jeffrey slid down the roof, bounced off the gutter, and ever so gracefully cartwheeled earthward. He hit something soft and bounced onto the lawn, still gripping the end of the rope.

"Ooof!" said the now semi-conscious Humphrey, dazed by Jeffrey's impact. He fell over onto his back.

Jeffrey stood up, relieved to be on firm ground once again. He noticed a button he had not seen earlier, several centimetres from the end of the rope. Not knowing what it did, he pressed it, but nothing seemed to happen.

Up on the roof, the hooks on the grappling hook retracted and it fell away, making a scratching sound as it slid down the roof tiles, before striking the gutter with a loud clunk and then falling to earth to land on something soft, and gently bouncing away onto the lawn.

"Gurple!" said the now brained bear.

Jeffrey walked up to Humphrey who was clutching his head. His eyes were spinning.

"Humpy, what does this button do?" He held up the rope.

Once his vision cleared and he'd been able to catch his breath, the bruised bear's response was not only unrepeatable, but it was not ninja stealthy in the slightest.

Jeffrey, however, did learn a lot of new, mostly four-letter, words and their derivatives.

As soon as Humphrey had almost recovered, the two teddy bears dashed across the King's Road, past the parked cars, and on to the houses on the far side. But Humphrey, still dazed from being the target of various plummeting objects, found himself continually veering to the right and so had to stop and reorient himself to compensate.

The street was dark with only a couple of streetlamps lit. The bears kept to the shadows, or in Humphrey's case, tried to keep to the shadows.

There was only one window with a light showing, and that belonged to a nosey old lady who knew all about the teddy bears of Godalming. She'd lived in the town for decades and had caught sight of them many years ago, but trying to explain this to her neighbours had proved futile. They thought she was senile but, being ever so polite, never said so to her face. They just agreed with her. So, when she saw the two bears run past her house, she thought everyone knew of their existence. She didn't feel the need to take a photo of them but wondered if they would appreciate a saucer of milk and maybe some biscuits.

They would have. Especially the biscuits.

A fox stepped out from the shadows.

"What are you two up to, all dressed up in black?"

"Oh. Hello, Barnaby. You frightened me," said Humphrey. "We're here to rescue Godfrey. He's been kidnapped by a child."

The fox nodded. "Is your cat friend, Snowy, around?"

"No. She's off looking for bats. According to the owls, they've been deliberately flying onto people's heads and stealing wigs and hair extensions. It's causing a bit of an uproar amongst the humans. The Avian Musicians Union has categorised it as a Hair Traffic Control problem."

"Good," said Barnaby. "We don't exactly get along."

Humphrey nodded. That was true.

"I'll see you about. Humphrey. Jeffrey."

"Bye," said Humphrey.

"Bye," waved Jeffrey.

With that, the fox trotted off, watched warily by both bears. Barnaby had a bit of a reputation.

"Tickle meeeh... Tickle yoooh... Cuddle herrrr... Huge..."

"Stop it!"

"Sorry."

The bears slipped between the bins, and up to a wooden gate. Humphrey stood with his back to it and cupped his paws.

"This is the one. Leg up!"

Jeffrey deftly jumped up, then stood on Humphrey's head to reach up to the top of the fence, before tumbling over the other side and landing on the ground with a grunt.

"Twit! Now how am I going to get over this gate? You were supposed to stay on top and help pull me up."

Jeffrey opened the gate a crack and peered around it at Humphrey, who looked up at the top and scratched his head.

"Sorry," said Jeffrey. "Let's try it again."

"No," said Humphrey. "This time you cup your hands, and I'll leap onto the gate. I'll show you how it should be done."

"Okay." Jeffrey stood with his back to the wood just as Humphrey had earlier, and Humphrey leapt up, stepping on Jeffrey's head to lie across the top of the gate, precariously balanced but narrowly avoiding toppling off.

"Here," he said. "That's the way to do it."

"Okay," said Jeffrey, who then pushed the gate open and went through. The bottom of the gate caught on a stone and Humphrey tumbled off to land beside the younger bear. He stood up and dusted himself down.

"So, it's open already?" he sighed.

"Tickle meeeh..." sang Jeffrey, as he ran up the garden path to the back door, oblivious to Humphrey's embarrassment.

Humphrey arrived a few seconds later.

"How do we get in?" whispered Jeffrey.

"Skeleton keys," whispered Humphrey, as he rattled a bunch of bent metal rods.

Jeffrey stood with his back against the back door, while Humphrey again clambered up onto his head. Humphrey poked and twisted each of the bent rods in the keyhole until the lock opened, then he grabbed the door handle and the door swung open, outwards, knocking Jeffrey over. Humphrey fell to the ground too.

From the kitchen came a deep growl.

"Uh oh!" said Humphrey, starting to tremble. "Uhm sorry? We didn't mean to disturb anyone."

The growling continued.

"Uhm-m-m. P-please don't bark. We're not here to r-rob you."

The growling got louder. Humphrey took a step back.

"We-we're h-here to r-rescue Godfrey. He's a teddy bear. A c-cute little chap. A bit c-clumsy. He f-fell off a tree and a little child picked him up and took him home b-by accident."

The growling continued.

"H-he's not a *toy* teddy bear. He's a real one. He's one of us. P-please can we have him back?"

The growling stopped. Thinking that some sort of progress had been made, Humphrey tried the diplomatic approach.

"M-my name is Humpy-Humphrey, and this here is..." Humphrey turned to look for Jeffrey, but he was nowhere to be seen. "Jeffrey. Jeffrey? W-where are you?"

The garden gate, which had been open, but was now closed, opened a little. Jeffrey peered around it and waved.

"Hullo," came the little voice from the end of the garden. He waved a paw.

41

Remembering the contents of his rescue kit, Humphrey unzipped his Patent Black Ninja Special Forces Stealth Thigh-Pouch (Water resistant. Size: Very Small) and pulled out a tin opener and dropped it.

"You do like meat, don't you? Silly me. All g-guard dogs like meat."

He picked up the tin opener, pulled out a tin of dog food and started opening it. As soon as the lid was open, he lobbed it through the back door and into the dark shadows of the kitchen. It landed with a clunk. It was then that he remembered he should have emptied the can onto the floor before covering it with the sleeping drug he had in one of his Patent Black Ninja Special Forces Stealth Belt-Pouches (Water resistant. Size: Very Small).

"Oops," he said. "Uhm, c-can I have the c-can back? I didn't d-do that properly." It was then that he realised he might have hit the dog with it, which couldn't possibly have made things any better.

But the tin did not come back. And the growling did not start again. Had he knocked the dog unconscious? If so, he needed to move fast.

Cautiously, Humphrey approached the back step and took out his Patent Black Ninja Special Forces Stealth Pepper Spray (Food Flavouring – also available in flavours: mustard, brown sauce, mint sauce, and ketchup). Then he extracted his Patent Black Ninja Special Forces Hand-Held Environment Illuminating Device from its holster and switched it on. The torch lit up the kitchen floor with over two thousand lumens, enough to temporarily blind any guard dog, completely dazzle the bear, and let everyone in King's Road know that there was currently a break-in in progress.

So much for Ninja Special Forces subtlety.

After a moment, his eyes adapted to the bright light and he could see the open tin on its side at the far end of the kitchen floor untouched, and also no guard dog. He switched the light off, but now he had the opposite problem. Everything went pitch-black as his eyes attempted a quick U-turn to adapt to the dark again.

"Grrrrr..."

So, the beast was still awake and ready to pounce. Humphrey extended his paw with the pepper spray and slowly edged into the kitchen, ready to squirt it into the glaring red eyes of the guard dog of death.

"Grrrrr..."

Humphrey stopped. The sound came from above him. He looked up. 'My God!' he thought. This monster was nearly two metres tall! No wonder it wasn't interested in such a small tin of dog food!

"Grrrrr..."

At this point, Humphrey's bravery was trumped by a desperate need to pee. He turned and ran out of the kitchen, veered to his right (he was still suffering from the earlier head trauma), found a bush to hide behind, and started to relieve himself.

"What are you doing?" asked Godfrey.

Humphrey almost had a seizure, spun around, and watered the garden.

"Yeuch! You wetted me!"

"S-sorry, Jeffrey... Godfrey? I thought you were the guard dog."

"No. I'm not a dog. I'm Godfrey. I'm a bear! Now I'm a wetted bear. Bwah! You weed on me! Yeuch!"

"Guard dogs don't like being weed upon either!" advised Jeffrey. "You should use the mustard spray instead."

"Jeffrey? I thought you were at the gate?"

Through the dim light, Humphrey could just make out the profiles of the two teddy bears. He hastily tidied himself up.

"No. I was, then I saw Godfrey at the bedroom window, so I climbed up the drainpipe and opened it. Godfrey and I escaped."

"Where's the guard dog?" asked Humphrey.

"It's a parrot," said Godfrey. "His name is Black Cerberus, and he takes his job very seriously."

Humphrey nodded.

"Okay. So, mission accomplished. Let's go!"

The bears ran down the garden. Jeffrey started singing the theme music again. When he got to: "Tickle meeeh... Tickle yoooh... Cuddle herrrr... Huge bum!" Godfrey fell on the grass giggling.

The two bears stopped and watched the small one writhing about on the ground with tears in his eyes, holding his sides.

"I bet Tom Cruise never has this problem," sighed Humphrey.

The Unusual Suspects

by Alan Barker

Shaunie O'Hegarty let out a low growl as he slammed shut the front door of his fourteenth-century mansion.

He cast an eye at the angry dark clouds, which reflected his own mood. No sooner had April arrived than the weather was turning.

He set off up the well-trodden road, his pace steady but purposeful, his gaze fixed straight ahead, oblivious to the sparse Peaslake traffic and other pedestrians. Soon the rain arrived, sudden bursts of it, carried by a gale that threatened to shake the trees from their roots.

Shaunie was not best pleased. Someone had committed the cardinal sin of upsetting him. You didn't upset Shaunie. Not if you had any sense.

"I've got some news for you, Daddy," Georgia had announced over dinner.

"M'm?" Shaunie had been reading the back page of the Sporting Life, trying to get his head around the story of a Man Utd player who had scored with his backside from the edge of the penalty area. In the background, Beethoven's *Fur Elise* played its melodious tune.

After a pause, Georgia said, in a slightly huffy tone, "Well? Don't you want to know what my news is? If Mum was still alive, she'd be all over it … *Hello-o*."

At length, Shaunie looked up from his paper. "News? What news is that, petal?"

Georgia's mouth was set in a thin line, her hands on her hips. "I'm with child."

Shaunie's eyes widened alarmingly. "What d'you mean, you're with child? You can't be! Who the hell's the father?"

But she wasn't about to name the father, other than to hint it might be one of his regulars from The Crown.

"And guess what?" Georgia waved her arms theatrically. "It's due on 25th December – a Christmas miracle! Won't you be pleased to have a grandchild for Christmas, Daddy?"

Shaunie watched over his spectacles, his mouth wide open, as she flounced out of the room. Presently, there came the sounds of heavy footfalls on the stairs, followed by a door being slammed shut and Adele blaring out on Georgia's CD player.

Shaunie pondered while the news sank in then slammed his fist on the table.

25th December. That meant Georgia would have conceived around 25th March, while he'd been away on business. One of his punters had made hay—and a baby, to boot—while his back was turned. There were going to be serious repercussions …

Now, at the top of the hill, Shaunie paused at the pub sign: 'The Crown', now showing as 'The Crow'. The 'n' had been obliterated by bird poo, not even the squally April showers managing to dislodge it. A fat crow swooped overhead, threatening to give Shaunie the same treatment as the pub sign, and Shaunie shook his fist at it as it disappeared into the distance.

He strode past the men's toilet—he'd often thought about building one inside but had never got around to it— and eased open the pub door. Apart from the long-drawn-

46

out squeak of the hinges, silence descended as everyone turned to look at him.

Show time.

**

He resembled a monster emerging from the deep. The four men sat at the table only had to look at him, his bulk filling the doorway, soaking-wet hair plastered across his face, to know there was trouble afoot — big trouble. A collective gulp went round the room.

"OK, who was it?" Shaunie sneered. "Which one of ye miserable bleeders put a wee bun in my daughter's oven? Eh?"

Silence followed, broken only by the steady whine of glasses being cleaned by Madcap Maggie behind the bar and the wind and rain hammering against the windows.

"Very well." Shaunie closed the door behind him, slamming the bolt across. "If the father of my grandchild isn't going to own up, we'll have a wee lock-in, shall we, lads?" He stepped up to the table and added softly, "Until we get to the arse of the matter."

Kenny, a smartly dressed, middle-aged man with a high forehead and ears that stuck out like an aye-aye's, loosened his tie a fraction. "So, you're going to be a granddaddy, Shaunie. That's good news … Isn't it?"

The big man came round the table and bent over to whisper in Kenny's ear. "No, my fine friend. Not when it comes to light the expectant daddy is one of my regulars, but I'm not told which one."

The pub fell silent again while Shaunie ambled round the table, fists on his hips. The four punters sat still, eyes locked onto their drinks.

"The wee baby is expected on Christmas day. So, March 25th, or thereabouts, is the date the deed was done. When I was away on business, as you were all well aware. Who was it invited themselves round to see my little girl? Which one of ye red-bloods has brought shame on the good name of O'Hegarty?"

From behind the bar came the groan of the beer pump being pulled. Eventually, Maggie tottered towards them and plumped a tray carrying five pints of ale onto the table, some of the froth spilling over the sides. "Thought we might be here a while, gentlemen," she purred, a gleam in her eye. She slunk behind Shaunie's big frame where she lingered.

Shaunie took a gulp from one of the glasses and thrust out a fat finger. "How about you, Foxy? Did you pay my daughter a visit around March 25th? Or during the night, perhaps? Woke her up from a deep sleep when she didn't know what she was about?"

Foxy, so-called because of his nocturnal ramblings, breathed in deeply and bunched his shoulders. "Not at all, Shaunie. Although … I did happen to pass by your house one night around then."

Four sets of eyes swerved round towards Foxy. You could even sense Madcap Maggie's ears pricking up, while she made a show of cleaning the next table.

"I awoke to go to the lavatory at three o'clock … in the morning." Foxy's gaze was distant. "I know that because the church clock was striking as I was unbuttoning my pyjama bottoms."

"Spare us the small details. All we need to know is what happened when ye got to my house."

"It's a clear and moonlit night." Foxy spoke as if in a trance. "The girl's lying in bed, wearing a white nightdress, a candle softly flickering. The door opens and a man appears, dressed in a black cloak. Her eyes gradually widen but she doesn't move. The man grins, and then he lifts his cloak and ...'

Shaunie clicked his fingers. "Wake up, Foxy. You've been watching Dracula again, haven't ye? All we need to know is whether ye saw any real goings-on that night?"

Foxy sank back in his seat, apparently exhausted. "No, Shaunie. Not a dickybird. 'T'was as quiet as a library on a Saturday night."

"Lord preserve us." Shaunie sighed and moved on. "Joseph, ye haven't been tampering with my daughter, I hope?"

Joe's empty pipe rattled between his teeth. He was a nondescript man of indeterminate age, wearing simple clothes and a perpetual frown. Since the smoking ban in pubs, he'd quit smoking but not his beloved pipe.

"The only thing I've been t-tampering with," he stuttered, "is my g-garden. See how green my f-fingers are?" He held them up for inspection. "What would a pr-pr-pretty girl like your d-daughter want with the l-likes of me?"

"So, you haven't seen Georgia lately?"

"Only when sh-she popped in the other day to help Maggie move the b-b-beer barrels."

"And what about ye, Warren?" Shaunie said, moving on to the last of them. "Been sniffing around the ladies, have you?"

The man at the end of the table was so short he barely had to raise his tankard to his lips. He shook his head vigorously, sending his spectacles skew-whiff.

"Not guilty, Shaunie. I haven't touched a young lady for nigh on twenty years, I promise."

From behind Shaunie's broad back, Madcap Maggie peered round. "He still has an eye for the girls though. Every time I pull a pint, I catch him leering at me over the bar, the dirty little devil. And then he has to clean the steam off his glasses."

Warren was shaking visibly, and Maggie leaned in as close to Shaunie as she could and whispered loudly, "He's as jumpy as a frog on a promise, that one."

Shaunie drained his pint and wiped his mouth. "I'm off to powder my nose. Give you all a bit of thinking time." He unbolted and opened the door, allowing a gust of wind to blow in. "I'll be back," he growled over his shoulder. Then he was gone.

But he didn't come back.

And never would.

***

"A penny for them, Sergeant."

Shaunie had been found with his head bashed in beside the urinal in the men's toilet. The apparent murder weapon—a doorstop in the shape of a concrete garden gnome—lay face down in the trough. The forensics officers were going about their business, and Sergeant Hannah Ryan

50

and the assigned senior investigating officer, Detective Inspector Thomas Trotter, had to content themselves with surveying the scene through the open doorway, in order not to contaminate the evidence.

"Looks like the murderer chose his moment, sir." The wind blew Hannah's hair across her face, and she brushed it away. "When the deceased's back was turned."

"And his hands occupied." Trotter tried to draw himself up to the sergeant's height, thrusting out his jaw. "A cowardly act, if you will."

Hannah refrained from pointing out the deceased resembled a grizzly bear, and, had the inspector been the perpetrator, he was hardly likely to have tackled the big man head-on.

A gangly man wearing a white protective suit emerged from the toilet, ducking his head and stripping off his face covering and latex gloves.

"What are your findings, Patrick?" Trotter asked.

The forensics officer breathed a sigh in the manner of one who has completed his day's work. "It's more or less as we suspected. The doorstop found beside the body has a smattering of blood and hair fibres on it so we're pretty certain that's the weapon, although we'll have to carry out our lab tests to confirm it."

The inspector stroked his jaw. "So, it's an open-and-shut case, you're saying?"

"For me it is. But you've got a cold-blooded killer to track down. Good luck with that, Thomas."

Hannah cleared her throat. "What did you mean by 'more or less' as you suspected?"

Patrick turned his penetrating gaze on her. "There seem to be two sets of the deceased's footprints in the toilet: one leading up to the urinal and back again; and the other just going up to the urinal."

"He made two trips to the toilet then. Any other footprints in there?"

"Several. But none of them are remotely as large as the deceased's."

***

A little later, the five of them—Kenny, Foxy, Joe, Warren and Maggie—sat at the table as Inspector Trotter ambled round them, his eye darting here and there but not looking at anyone in particular.

"So," he said, in his reedy voice, "to summarise, you are all saying the deceased—Mr O'Hegarty—arrived here at about nineteen hundred hours and spoke for a while about his daughter's—uh—pregnancy. He made an accusation that one of you is the father, but no one is admitting to it. Am I right so far?"

Several heads nodded. Joe's pipe clattered between his teeth.

"He then stepped outside to go to the lavatory and failed to return, whereupon you all went to check on him and found him dead. In between which, none of you made a solitary trip to the lavatory, so you are all claiming to have an alibi for his murder."

"Must have been an outsider," Kenny suggested. "A passer-by taking his chance."

Foxy nodded sagely. "There are some wicked people out there."

"You can't be too c-careful. We f-feel s-safe in here, but the m-moment we step outside …" Joe let his voice trail away.

Warren took a slurp of beer but said nothing.

"And yet," Trotter said, raising his voice a fraction, "I suggest one of you had a motive for wishing to do away with the deceased. One of you is the father-to-be of his daughter's child and clearly wishes to keep mum about it. Mr O'Hegarty was threatening to expose that person who then decided to remove him, using the doorstop in the lavatory as the murder weapon." He eyed each of them in turn with narrowed eyes.

"I hope you're not including me in your list of suspects," Maggie sneered. "I could hardly be the father of that lassie's child."

Trotter lifted his jaw and looked down his long nose at her. "Madam, I assume nothing. There may be another reason you wished your employer out of the way. Perhaps he caught you with your fingers in the till, eh?"

"I've been here thirty-four years. I've never taken so much as a penny from Mr O'Hegarty other than what was rightfully mine."

"We shall see, madam."

Kenny cleared his throat. "What about DNA?"

"Ah-ha!" The inspector raised a finger and resumed his pacing round the table. "Precisely my own thinking. DO NOT ASSUME. Things are not always as they seem in the matter of detection."

"Excuse me, sir," Hannah said from her position by the empty fireplace. "I think the gentleman means DNA in relation to establishing the child's father."

"I was perfectly well aware of that, Sergeant. Please don't take me for an imbecile. Now where was I? Ah yes, we discovered footprints in the lavatory, some large, which were clearly those of the deceased, and some not so large. We need to establish who made the smaller prints and I would suggest you all remove your shoes and pass them to Sergeant Ryan here for inspection."

There were various mumblings around the table before Kenny said, "If you're looking to fix the owner of the footprints as those of the murderer, the fact is, we *all* went to the loo at some point."

"Ah-ha. Shades of *Murder On The Orient Express*, eh, Sergeant?"

Hannah rolled her eyes.

"Furthermore," Kenny added, twisting his ear, "we all went before Shaunie arrived here, not after. I'm sure Maggie will vouch for us."

"Huh! I didn't have my eyes on you all the time so don't look to me for your alibi."

"To add another clue to the mix," Trotter said, "there were two sets of Mr O'Hegarty's footprints in the lavatory, yet you assert he only went the once. How do you explain that?"

They all looked at one another. Joe removed his pipe from his mouth—a rare occurrence. "Shaunie had a bl-bl-bladder problem. It wouldn't be the first time he went twice in quick s-succession."

The inspector pursed his lips. "Very interesting. And yet you only *saw* him go to the lavatory once. Perhaps his first visit was when he arrived at the pub."

"I think not." All eyes turned to Maggie. "I was looking out of the window when he arrived. He stopped by the pub sign, shook his fist at something and then came straight in here."

"A mystery indeed. But not insoluble, eh, Sergeant? There must be a logical explanation to those footprints."

***

"My sincere condolences, madam." Trotter put an arm across his chest and bowed. "Please rest assured the perpetrator of your father's murder will be behind bars in no time."

They were at Shaunie O'Hegarty's mansion, and the inspector was doing his best to console a tearful Georgia.

"I feel awful," the girl wailed. "My last words to Daddy were cross ones. I'll never get over this."

"There, there, my dear. We all say things we regret later."

Hannah had been idly running her eye over *The Sporting Life* which was open at the football page. Now she looked up and said, "What was the argument about?"

Georgia sniffed and pressed a tissue to her mouth. "Just family stuff. Nothing important."

"You mean, the matter of your pregnancy came up? Perhaps your father got angry with you, and you exchanged words."

"Sergeant! Can you not see the young lady is extremely distressed over the death of her father?"

"I'm sorry I got mad at him." Georgia blew her nose loudly.

The inspector shifted a little nearer to her on the sofa. "I know this will upset you, my dear, but we need to know who the father of your child is. The sooner we have that information the sooner we can lay our hands on the despicable person that killed your daddy."

"I promised not to tell anyone."

Hannah snorted. "You won't be able to say that at the inquest. So why not tell us now? Or are you taking us for a ride, like some of the stories in this paper?" She indicated the date on *The Sporting Life:* 1st April. Silence followed before Hannah added, "If the baby was conceived only last week how can you be sure you're pregnant?"

Georgia jumped to her feet and poured herself a large scotch. When she turned round, they saw she was pouting. "All right, there is no baby. I only said it as an April fool for Daddy."

They stared at her while she looked back defiantly.

"This puts things in a different light," Trotter said with a sigh. "But we still have a murder to solve. Who do you think may have wanted your father dead?"

"I really don't know, and I'd be grateful if you could leave now, please. This is all too upsetting for me."

As they stepped into the hallway, the inspector took her gently by the elbow. "Please don't distress yourself too much, my dear. We'll get to the bottom of this."

Hannah frowned and cleared her throat. "So have you been out of the house since your father left for the pub?"

Georgia shook her head. "No, I locked myself in my room and didn't come out until you rang the bell. Why?"

"How come this umbrella's wet then?" Hannah put on one of her latex gloves and picked up a large pair of brogues beside the doormat. "And these shoes are damp underneath, suggesting they've been worn recently. Not by your father, surely?"

Georgia dropped her eyes and said nothing.

"The funny thing is, they're a spitting image of the pair he was wearing when he was found this evening. It'll be interesting to see if they match the large footprints in the men's toilet at The Crown ..."

***

It didn't take long to extract a confession from her.

She'd killed her father in order to inherit his mansion and his millions— something that wouldn't now be happening. She'd told him the cock-and-bull story about one of his regulars getting her pregnant as she knew he wouldn't rest until he'd discovered the 'father's' identity; it would subsequently help point the finger of suspicion at The Crown's punters as the murder suspects, rather than her.

Georgia had guessed her father—whom she described as 'like a bull in a Chinese shop'—would waste no time heading to the pub to have the matter out with his regulars. She'd followed him there, armed with an umbrella and a spare pair of Shaunie's brogues.

Because of his bladder problem, she'd known it wouldn't be long before he had to go to the toilet. Having lain in wait for him behind the bushes, Georgia slipped the brogues on so as not to leave her own prints on the scene, crept up behind Shaunie, picking up the doorstop on the way, and struck him down while he was 'inconvenienced', as the inspector put it. Hence, the additional set of prints suggesting Shaunie had gone to the toilet twice.

"It was a dastardly plot, Sergeant," Trotter said, as they watched the girl being taken away in a police car. "By carrying out the murder at the pub, our baby-faced killer didn't come under suspicion and had no qualms about putting those harmless gentlemen in the spotlight as the main suspects. But she wasn't going to make April fools out of us."

"No, sir."

"And as I keep telling you, never assume anything. This case proves my point unequivocally."

"I'm very fortunate to have the benefit of your expertise, sir."

"With any luck, The Crown should still be open. Fancy one for the road, Sergeant?"

"Will anyone still be there?"

The inspector permitted himself a smile. "I'm sure the usual suspects will be."

The boundaries of the Surrey Hills are marked by the distinctive wooden sculptures of renowned chainsaw artist Walter Bailey. Erected in 2002, there are two types of sculpture: small wooden signs with the Surrey Hills logo and 12 totem-pole-like sculptures with varied designs, which have become something of an icon for the area.

The Kitchen

by David Lowther

Mary Robbins lived in a retirement flat in England's self-styled 'largest village', Cranleigh. The flat was very small with a living room/kitchen, bedroom, bathroom with toilet, and entrance hall. It suited her nicely, but it hadn't always been like that. Six months ago, her husband Clarence had died of a heart attack. It had been expected for some time. Although they'd been married for 49 years and, until recently, lived comfortably together, the last two years had been difficult. The flat was just too small. A particular bone of contention had been the toilet. They'd always been jousting to get in there first.

Following Clarence's death, Mary sorted out the papers for probate, took most of Clarence's clothes to the charity shop, sold the car, a battered old Ford Escort, and, after a short period of mourning, set off to have some fun. Mary and Clarence had not been blessed with children, but she had a younger sister who ran a boarding house in Bognor. Speaking to her sister, Janice, on the phone, she confessed that the last couple of years had been difficult, and it was probably best that Clarence had gone, given the state of his health and grumpiness. 'At least I can go to the toilet when I fancy,' Mary told Janice.

Mary's main idea of fun was using her bus pass to travel around the locality. She got to know all the destinations and stopping off points where she could either have a coffee or, failing that, a port and lemon in the pub and use the toilet. Her journey always began on the 42 bus from Cranleigh. At first, she went all the way into Guildford but soon tired of that with its hilly streets and smelly traffic. Changing in

Godalming, Mary found her horizons amazingly broadened by the regular 70, 71 and 72 services. There was also a 46 to Farnham but she didn't like that town. It was too busy and was nearly always clogged up with cars.

When she wasn't riding about on the bus, Mary spent her time in her retirement home's lounge, chatting with other residents and drinking coffee in the morning and playing Scrabble in the afternoon. Evenings were set aside for watching the soaps on TV and a good serial if there was one on. If not, it was a bloodthirsty novel by the likes of Karin Slaughter, Val McDermid or LJ Ross. One of Mary's favourite series on TV was *Last Tango in Halifax.* She'd seen it before but, thanks to the iPlayer, she could now re-watch all 24 episodes when she fancied.

Mary's bus wanderings took her to all sorts of interesting places. Sometimes she stopped off in Haslemere for a coffee in Costa, others in Witley for a port and lemon in The Star. She even made it all the way to Midhurst where she had a choice of venues for her mid-morning drink, either the Costa or the Café Verdi. The Dog and Pheasant in Brook was another favourite. One day two things happened which set her thinking. On one of her trips, she spotted a shop called *Bathrooms and Kitchens.* She didn't think much about it until she settled in to watch an episode in season 5 of *Last Tango in Halifax.* Celia decided to have a new kitchen. Her husband, Alan, didn't altogether agree with her but the old lady was adamant. 'Good idea,' Mary said out loud and she vowed to call in at *Bathrooms and Kitchens* the following day to set the ball rolling for her kitchen upgrade. Had she watched the rest of the series, Mary might have saved herself an awful lot of hassle.

Strolling from the bus to the entrance of *Bathrooms and Kitchens,* Mary felt in a thoroughly good mood. Friends had told her that one of the best ways of dealing with bereavement was to get out and do something different. Well, she was.

'Can I help you?' a pleasant-looking young lady with curly blonde hair and blue eyes asked her.

'I'm interested in buying a new kitchen,' Mary replied.

'I'll just go and fetch Mr. Daley. He's out the back. Won't be a minute,' the blonde said, as she left through the rear door.

Less than a minute later she returned, followed by a youngish-looking man, possibly in his thirties. Dressed in a black suit with very narrow trousers, a black shirt, a white knitted tie and brown pointed shoes, the man introduced himself.

'Good morning, madam. Allow me to introduce myself. I'm George Daley.' He smelt of smoke but Mary didn't mind. She liked the occasional thin cheroot herself. His clothes looked like a throwback to when she was a girl: drainpipe trousers and winkle picker shoes. His thick, black, curly hair was complemented by a similar-coloured moustache, which filled the whole of his top lip, and sideburns extending to about an inch below the bottom of his ears.

'How can I help you, madam?'

His accent was definitely local, and he was attempting to disguise it by trying to sound, as Mary would say, la-di-da. Something about him was ringing a bell with Mary but, try as she might, she couldn't put her finger on where she had seen him before.

'I'm interested in having a new kitchen fitted in my flat in Cranleigh. Can you do that?'

'Of course, madam. We're known the length and breadth of the Surrey Hills for the quality of our kitchens. If it suits you, madam, I can call in tomorrow morning and measure up and then start next Monday. After I've seen you tomorrow, I'll let you know what it will cost. How does that sound?'

'Wonderful,' Mary exclaimed. 'How long will it take?'

'About three days.'

This suited Mary admirably. She could set off to Bognor after breakfast on the Monday and spend the week with Janice and return home with a brand-new kitchen to greet her on the Friday.

'Please leave your name, address and telephone number with Daisy here and I'll be with you in the morning.'

Mary made her way to her flat, calling in at the manager's office to let Ann know what was going on and saying that, if a Mr. Daley asked for access to her flat, he was to be given it. Then she called her sister in Bognor and checked if it was OK for her to arrive on Monday for four nights' stay. It was, of course. George Daley strode in on time, clutching a clipboard and tape measure. She left him to it, heading for the residents' lounge for her morning coffee and chat. He promised to ring her that afternoon with a quotation. This he did shortly after three. It seemed reasonable to Mary, and she gave him the go-ahead.

George Daley arrived on the following Monday with a rather dull-looking youth assistant to get on with the installation. The two worked hard all day and were back early on the following day. They didn't quite finish on time but, by Thursday afternoon, all was done, and Daley was able to call Mary and tell her all was in order. Janice listened attentively while her sister excitedly told her the good news.

The only thing still troubling her was that she was sure she'd seen Daley somewhere before.

The journey back meant a couple of changes of trains and a bus from Godalming to Cranleigh, but Mary couldn't contain her excitement as she turned the key in the lock of her front door. She walked to the kitchen and was overwhelmed with horror as she looked at what she'd hoped would be a spanking, brand-new kitchen. Gazing open-mouthed over Daley's work, she took in a round bath, a sink and a WC. Additionally, there was a mirror on the wall and a towel rail.

'But I've already got a bathroom,' she whispered to herself. 'I don't need two.'

Mary started to cry but, by four o'clock, misery had been overtaken by rage. She looked at her watch. Four o'clock. *Bathrooms and Kitchens* would still be open. She picked up the phone.

'Oh. Hello, Mrs. Robbins. Everything alright with your new bathroom?'

'No. It is most definitely not. I wanted a kitchen. Not a bathroom.'

'You must be kidding me. Daisy, didn't Mrs. Robbins from Cranleigh order a new bathroom for her flat?'

In the background Mary heard the slightly muffled words of 'no' and 'kitchen'.

'Oh dear. Seems like I've slipped up. Daisy said you did ask for a kitchen not a bathroom. I must say I was a bit surprised that you wanted two bathrooms but, as they say, the customer is always right. I'm coming over to see you right away. Put the kettle on. Oh! Sorry.'

Half an hour later Daley was looking at a livid-looking Mary in her living room.

'So, what are you going to do about it, Mr. Daley?' a furious Mary was asking.

'Look, Mrs. Robbins, it's a very flexible bathroom. It could easily be used as a kitchen.'

'What on earth do you mean?' she shouted.

'Well. Take the bath for instance. It's big. Plenty of room to store supplies and you could leave a space in the middle for a camping stove.'

Mary was about to explode when Daley continued.

'And the toilet would be an ideal place to wash vegetables. Of course, you couldn't use it as a toilet. Then there's the sink. It's big. Plenty of room to stand a cool box and store chilled food.'

'And how am I going to boil water for a cup of tea? There isn't a plug.'

'Put a pan on the camping stove,' Daley replied.

If Mary's jaw had dropped any more it would have ended up on the carpet.

'Mr. Daley, I ordered a kitchen and I intend to have one and, of course, at no extra cost. I can't understand how you made such a blunder. Didn't you have an assistant with you who would have said something?'

'I did, but he went to one of those public schools, so he's a bit dim.'

'Well, what are you going to do about it?'

'The customer's always right. I'll be back tomorrow to start work. You'll have to eat out tonight. There must be a local chippie. Try cod and chips with curry sauce but you'll have to drink lemonade with it just for tonight, unless you've got a beer in the fridge. Oh! Sorry.'

'I'd rather starve than put curry sauce on my fish and chips.'

'Right, I'll be off,' Daley said. 'Looks like it's back to Bognor for you. I'll work over the weekend and have the job done by Wednesday afternoon. I really am sorry, but I will make it right. Good night.'

As Daley made his way to the door, Mary's brain was spinning. Where had she seen him before? Shortly after he'd left, it all fell into place. Of course, when she was a girl, she'd laughed at a film called *The Belles of St Trinian's*. There was a character who used to hang around the school gates, a spiv called Flash Harry. Now who played him? Wasn't it George Cole? And didn't he play Arthur Daley in *Minder* many years later? 'I think,' she said to herself, 'he died a couple of years ago.' She sat for a couple of minutes then made a vow. Mary was a lapsed churchgoer, but she determined that, the weekend after she returned from staying with Janice, she would start going to church again. After all, she now had irrefutable evidence that re-incarnation really did exist.

The Spirit of the Surrey Hills

by Pauline North

Thanks to Martyn MacDonald-Adams for suggesting the title.

Trailing toes in silver streams, dancing through the dew,

Silent shadow in the mist, bare footprints in the snow,

Trace her sorrows in the rain, her joy in summer wind,

Look into the fire's bright heart to seek her in the glow.

Come slowly on a quiet day when gold leaves start to fall,

Leave quickly when a purple storm, tears hollows in the sky,

As you walk the lonely lanes don't turn your head too fast,

Listen for the beat of wings, the red kite's mournful cry.

The people in their houses, all wound by brick and glass,

They say there is no magic, they cannot hear the tune,

It's everywhere around for those who open up their eyes,

Listen to the ancient soul, ask questions of the moon.

Spinning, leaping in the flames, wild dancing through the night

Where sleepy vipers hide by day all hidden from the light,

Deep in secret hollows where the bracken grows so high,

The spirit of the Surrey Hills is lost to human sight.

By Gibbett Hill

by Ian Honeysett

So, there I was, quietly sipping my lunchtime pint in the Three Horseshoes pub in Thursley when this rather angry-looking cove sat down at my table. It rather surprised me as there were several empty tables around. He was large. A good six inches taller than me. I studied his face in case we knew each other. Round glasses. Very red, snub nose. Rather scruffy beard which seemed to contain bits of his most recent meals. Check shirt and blue trousers. Now, I have a very poor memory for faces. And most other things, in fact. But, no, I was pretty sure I didn't recognise him.

'Do we know each other?' I asked.

'I think I might remember you from a writing group?' He didn't sound that sure.

'Perhaps,' I replied. I was a bit of a writer. I'd almost finished several short stories.

'Do you write, then?' I enquired.

'Oh, yes, I do.'

'What sort of things?'

'Murder, mainly. Sometimes travel – I've been all over. Stockport, Isle of Man. But mostly murder. I love a good murder!'

He had a look in his eye that made me wonder, for a moment or two, whether his interest was purely literary.

'Any favourite murders?' I found myself asking. An odd sort of question, even for me.

'Oh, yes. My favourite must be the famous Hindhead murder, back in 1786. You know, the unknown sailor. As you've probably read, it all began here in Thursley though, sadly, the Red Lion pub where the story starts, is no longer here. Converted into cottages about ten years ago. Very sad. They served a nice pint, they did.'

He licked his lips and, unaccountably, I found myself asking if I could get him a pint? He readily agreed.

Once we were sitting with drinks in front of us, he returned to the Hindhead murder.

'Do you know the story?' he asked.

'I've heard of it but only that an unknown sailor was murdered by several other sailors on Gibbet Hill. That's all.'

'Ah, then let me tell you the tale.' He took another sip of his beer and I saw that his previous rather annoyed expression had changed completely to one of sublime contentment. Yes, he clearly loved his murders.

'The tale is, perhaps, a warning against ever buying strangers a drink because this unknown sailor was feeling fairly flush with money as he'd just returned from a long voyage when he spotted three fellow seamen and offered to get them a drink. They readily agreed. None of them showed any interest in returning the favour so he bought them another round. And then another.'

He looked down at his near-empty glass, but his luck had run out. I was definitely not flush with cash. I looked at my glass and then at him but, somehow, he failed to take the hint. He continued.

'So, they then told him that they'd best be heading for Hindhead. Was he going their way? Unfortunately for him, he said he was. So, they all set off. Before long, they reached a rather secluded spot when, suddenly, one of them knocked him to the ground. Was it an accident, he wondered? But it quickly became evident that it was quite deliberate as the others began to strip off his clothes and grab his money. An odd way to repay his generosity, you'll agree. And then, one of them slit his throat. He almost severed his head! And then they hurled his body over the side of the Devil's Punch Bowl.'

He looked once more at his empty glass as though he'd only complete the story if I bought him another pint. But he'd not really told me anything much I'd not heard before. He'd gone silent so I felt I ought to say something.

'Yes, that's about what I thought took place', I said. 'So, what happened next?'

'Well, here's the interesting part. They thought that they were quite safe as there were surely no witnesses to the murder. But they were wrong. It so happened that two fellow drinkers from the Red Lion had witnessed the whole thing. Now what are the chances of that, I ask you? And, as soon as the three had moved off, they went to that spot and saw the body down in the Punch Bowl. They immediately raised the alarm. Now the three had stopped for some further drinks with the stolen money at the Sun Inn in Rake. Some think it was The Flying Bull in Rake, but they're wrong! Sadly, the Red Lion has also closed. Lovely pub, it was. They served a very nice pint.'

He looked even more meaningfully at his empty glass. I was now interested to learn more so, I must confess, I caved in and bought him another pint. He almost drank it in one. I determined that, at these prices, that was all he was getting.

'So, what happened next? How were they caught?'

'Well, it's a lesson in what not to discuss when you're in a pub. They were chatting about what they had done and how they planned to sell their victim's clothes. Quite a haul there: a pair of blue trousers, two check shirts, some hankies, two jackets, a waistcoat, an oilskin hat and a pair of buckles. What they didn't realise was that a fellow drinker, a soldier it so happens, overheard them and decided to act. He arrested them – all three of them were somewhat the worse for drink – and they were taken off to Haslemere where they were questioned by the local Justice of the Peace, the Rev James Fielding. They were then conveyed to Guildford Gaol on the charges of the wilful murder of a person unknown and the theft of £1 7s 6d.'

'I assume they were found guilty?'

'Oh, yes. They were tried at Kingston Assizes, found guilty and sentenced to hang. A gibbet was set up just near where the murder took place. Once they had been hanged – not hung, by the way. Pictures are hung but people are hanged.'

'Not any longer,' I added with a smile. 'At least not in this country.' A poor attempt at humour perhaps which completely by-passed my new drinking companion. I noticed he had now finished his second free pint and was again staring at his empty glass. I reckoned that I'd now heard most of the story – which I began to think was his passport to free beer – and decided enough was enough. I'd nearly finished my pint and was going to head off home.

'Once they were quite dead,' he continued, 'they were cut down and placed in irons. Interestingly, this took place back at the Red Lion. Then they were soaked in tar and fixed to the post and left to swing in chains as a warning to others.'

70

'So that's why it's called Gibbet Hill,' I said. 'A nice little tale. Well, I must be off now. I hope you enjoyed your drinks.'

'But I've not finished yet,' he objected.

'Well, I have,' I replied, taking a final sip of beer. 'I'm off home.'

He looked disappointed – probably because he had anticipated at least one more free drink.

'Do you have far to go?'

How to answer? I wasn't too keen to have him accompany me. There was something about him. I certainly had no intention of going via Gibbet Hill.

'Not at all – I just live here in Thursley.'

'Oh, that's good. Maybe we can continue our discussion at your place.'

Somehow, that idea did not grab me. There was no way I was going to let him know where I lived. It's a small village and I was pretty sure he wasn't a local. Assuming he lived anywhere. But how was I going to shake him off? It was only a few minutes to my house.

'Have you got much beer in? Maybe we should get a few bottles, eh?'

By this, I assumed he meant I should buy a few bottles.

'Now, I don't mean to be rude, and I've enjoyed your company, but this is where we say goodbye. I've a busy day tomorrow, so lots to do.'

'But we've hardly got to know each other. I thought we were bonding, you know? I don't have many friends. You can't just abandon me. Not after all I've shared with you.'

71

'What do you mean, 'shared'? You've told me the story of the murder – and I'm grateful – but you can hardly accuse me of 'abandoning' you. Now, I'm off.'

I stood up and made for the door, bidding the barman, 'Good afternoon.' As far as I could tell, my new 'acquaintance' showed no sign of joining me. As soon as I'd left the pub I walked as fast as I could to get home – via a rather circuitous route - just in case he was following me. Once inside, I locked the front door and went and made myself a cup of tea and sat in the small kitchen at the back. I was still feeling rather anxious even though I told myself this was ridiculous. I had bought him two drinks, after all. He could hardly feel that I'd, in any way, taken advantage of him. But I could imagine him walking round the village looking in all the windows to see if he could spot me. Best stay away from the front room. So, no TV this evening. And definitely no going out again today.

I turned in early that night, but I barely slept. My mind was full of rather scary images. Of his face suddenly appearing at my window. Even the upstairs bedroom window. Of someone shaking me awake in the middle of the night. That someone being him. Of my leaving home next day and seeing him following me. All quite ridiculous, of course. He was probably miles away by now, telling his tale to some other lonely drinker.

When I went down for breakfast the following morning, I couldn't help looking out of the window to check. I breathed a huge sigh of relief not to see him there, maybe curled up in my front garden.

I needed to buy some milk so, telling myself not to be so stupid, I was a grown-up after all, I set off to the local shops. I couldn't help but keep looking around me but there was no sight of him. The big challenge, of course, was whether

I could pluck up courage to stop for a pint in The Three Horseshoes? Maybe not today? Oh, come on! This was ridiculous! I pushed open the door. But rather cautiously.

Given it was only 10.35, the pub was empty apart from Sid, the barman.

'Hi, Sid,' I said. 'The usual, please.'

'Morning to you, Ethel. You seemed to be quite a hit with that big, bearded chap yesterday.'

'Did you know him?'

'No, never seen him before. But you two seemed to be getting on like a house on fire. Bought him a couple of drinks, I recall.'

'I did. But, I must admit, I was quite relieved he didn't follow me home when I left. Did he stay much longer?'

'About ten minutes. That's when they came for him.'

'How do you mean?'

'Oh, didn't you hear? Quite exciting, it was. Apparently, he'd absconded from Coldingley Prison. But I'm pleased to say, he went quietly.'

A week later I received a letter enquiring whether I'd ever considered becoming a prison visitor.

Two weeks later, a marriage proposal.

Reader, I didn't marry him!

Dental Records

by Paul Rennie

He probed the offending tooth with his tongue and triggered a shooting pain from the lower left molar to add to the throbbing ache that had kept him awake all night. No amount of aspirin or paracetamol could alleviate his suffering nor postpone the long-overdue visit to a dentist. It had been many years since Keith Barnett had had any dental treatment, the last six years ago when he had received treatment while a guest at HM Prison, Featherstone. Mind you, in those days he was known as Vince Thresher, a name that inspired fear amongst his fellow prison inmates and the underworld where he had operated.

He had served most of the ludicrously short sentence he had received, thanks to an especially flexible and well-connected lawyer, when an opportunity presented itself in the form of open prison. Taking it quite literally, he walked out of an open door, picked up the money that had been stashed for him, and was lost to the prison service. Vince was smart enough not to return to his earlier haunts in Birmingham and instead headed to leafy Surrey, where it is surprisingly easy for a criminal with money to blend in with the locals. Shortly after arriving in Farnham, he slipped into the Albion pub for a pint and to check out the area. To his surprise, the barman seemed to recognize him.

"Hello, Keith," he said. "You're a bit early today. The usual, is it?" He was already pouring out a pint of Shepherd Neame Master Brew. Vince was about to correct him, but the barman said, "On the tab?" and Vince, being an opportunist, was not going to turn down a free pint.

He nodded, took the drink and headed for a dark recess behind one of the oak beam features where he could watch for the real Keith and slip out before the error was realized. About half an hour later a figure that Vince recognized from the mirror shambled in through the pub door and approached the bar. It was his benefactor, and it was obvious to Vince how the mistake could have occurred. The man was his absolute double. He was the same age, in his early sixties, had the same build and grey thinning hair, with a large misshapen nose and a slightly florid complexion. Remarkably, he even walked with the same gait. The man could have been his twin brother. Intrigued, he leaned further back into the recess to watch events unfold.

Keith ordered a pint of Master Brew, without any pleasantries.

"Ready for another already?" said the barman good-naturedly.

Keith looked bemused but didn't say anything.

"When did you change your jacket?" asked the barman, and then shrugged, as the customer gave him a blank look, and went off to serve another customer at the far end of the bar.

Keith was obviously a man of few words and had the air of a loner about him as he took his pint and headed to a table on his own at the far end of the pub and started reading a copy of the Daily Express. Although only a few words had been exchanged, Vince could tell that the man's voice was uncannily similar to his own, even its trace of a nasal Midlands accent. Another half an hour passed, and Keith got up, went to the bar and collected another pint.

"You're going for it today, aren't you?" said the barman.

Again, Keith just gave him a blank look and headed back to his table to resume his newspaper.

From Vince's vantage point it was extraordinary. It was like watching himself in a video film, but in real time. Eventually, Keith got up, folded the newspaper and walked out, with only the briefest nod in the direction of the barman. Clearly this was a daily ritual. The seed of an idea was starting to form in Vince's head, one that would allow him to escape future apprehension by the authorities. He got up and walked quickly out of the back door of the pub and circled round the building, just in time to catch sight of his doppelganger about fifty yards ahead turning the corner into Dollis Drive. He speeded up and, standing at the junction with the main road, watched Keith enter a block of flats at the far end of the cul-de-sac. Interesting, he thought, if he lives in a flat, he might be on his own.

Back at the B&B where he was staying, Vince started to develop his plan further. He saw an opportunity to avoid a life on the run if he could somehow take on Keith's identity. He would be safe from capture and return to jail, where otherwise he could expect a big increase in his sentence for absconding. This would require some very careful planning.

Over the next few weeks, he followed Keith at a distance and was able to confirm that the man was indeed a loner with a regular routine of drinking two pints in the pub and never talking to anyone. He seemed to have no visitors, didn't have a car and didn't seem to go anywhere other than the pub and local shop to buy food and newspapers. During this surveillance period Vince altered his appearance. He coloured his eyebrows with a temporary dye, and wore a brown wig under a cloth cap. To complete the disguise, he put on a pair of blue-tinted glasses and painted a large mole on his chin. These he was sure would distract casual observers from recognizing the real face behind the disguise. He also changed to wearing a tracksuit rather than the more formal clothes usually favoured by himself and his quarry. He looked at himself in the mirror. The person he saw looked neither like Keith nor Vince but was a bit younger and the glasses and mole drew the eyes away from the rest of the features. Some people might spot a similarity but wouldn't think they were the same person. With this appearance he felt confident he could be seen in close proximity to Keith without attracting attention.

Eventually he felt assured enough to make his first move. He went back to the Albion pub and ordered a whisky in his best attempt at a London accent. This time the barman showed no sign of recognition and there was no offer of a drink on the tab this time. He sat down in the recess and watched and waited. Sure enough, a few minutes later Keith appeared at the bar, bought his usual first pint of Master Brew and sat down at his regular table. Vince gave him a few minutes to settle and moved in.

"I'm sorry to bother you, but you bear a striking resemblance to my brother. When I first saw you, I thought it was him, except that it couldn't be because he died recently. Seeing you has brought back all the memories." Even a man of few words like Keith couldn't help but be drawn into conversation by such an opening gambit.

"I can see how that might be. You look a bit like me yourself."

"Indeed," said Vince, "how exciting. Who knows, maybe we are related; now that would be a coincidence meeting like this. May I join you?"

Keith hesitated at allowing someone to sit at his table, but the unusual interest the stranger had shown in him plus the offer of another pint banished his misgivings.

In spite of Keith's reticence, Vince was able to extract some details about Keith's background. As he had anticipated, Keith had no living relatives and had led a very insular life living and working a few miles from where he was born. He had made no contact with former work colleagues since he was made redundant from his job as a projectionist at the local cinema. He was almost invisible. Perfect.

After about an hour of a relatively one-sided conversation, Keith got up to leave.

"It has been very nice meeting you," said Vince. "Are you a regular here? I would love to show you a few photos of my brother, and you'll see what I mean about the resemblance. How about tomorrow at the same time?"

He knew Keith couldn't refuse, because his daily routine meant that he would be in the pub at the time he had suggested.

That afternoon Vince bought a second-hand mobile phone from a shop in the High Street, paying with cash for what is known in the trade as a 'burner' and something he was very familiar with from his previous life. He didn't need a sim card because he had no intention of making phone calls. He just wanted the camera. Back at the B&B he removed his disguise, dressed in more formal clothes and took a few selfies.

Next day, back in disguise, Vince approached Keith at his usual table, carrying two pints.

"Hello, Keith. May I join you again? I have something very interesting to show you."

Keith agreed and Vince showed him the photos on the phone. Keith couldn't help but be drawn in because the likeness was so striking. There had to be some connection.

Vince knew he had his victim hooked. He had banked on Keith being lonely and, although outwardly a recluse, deep down was desperate for some link with his past and missing family. For the first time Keith actually asked him questions, a sure sign he had gained his confidence.

"You know," Vince said, "talking to you is just like talking to my brother. It feels as if I've got him back sitting in front of me. I'm feeling quite emotional." Reaching for a tissue to wipe away an imaginary tear, he said, "I'd love you to meet my mother. You never know, perhaps she looks like yours."

He could see the first sign of emotion on Keith's face. Now for the coup de gras.

"Do you have any photos of your mother? I would love to see them and compare them with ones I've got of mine."

Keith said he did, and it was a simple job to convince him to let Vince come round to his flat with some photos that evening. Vince made a point of asking for the address, even though he knew perfectly well where Keith lived, following his stake-out. At eight o'clock, Vince presented himself at the door and entered the small apartment. It was slightly shabby and untidy, with a smell of cooking fat and cabbage, no different really from his old prison cell. He produced a couple of bottles of beer, and while Keith went to get some glasses, he eyed the place. There was a decent TV, a few antiques, and a bureau, which probably contained documents.

Keith returned with the glasses and after pouring out the drinks asked about the photos of Vince's mother.

"I'm sorry, Keith, I thought I had some at my place, but they are at my brother's house, and I couldn't get over there today. I'll bring them next time. In the meantime, it would be lovely to see the ones you have of your mother and maybe some of you when you were young."

Keith went to the bureau and returned with a brown envelope.

"I don't have many. She left when I was young, and I was adopted. All I have of her are a few photos she left behind."

Vince stood behind Keith and looked down at the black-and-white photo of a slightly unhappy-looking woman with dark hair and a floral pattern dress. She looked nothing like his own foster mother.

The photo dropped from Keith's hand as he felt the cord tighten round his neck. His eyes bulged and he scrabbled desperately to wrench away the hands that were holding and twisting it. They were much too strong and accomplished, and all too soon Keith's lonely existence was ended. Vince checked his pulse, and having established there would be no encore, released his victim in a crumpled heap on the floor.

He checked out the rest of the flat. In the kitchen was a surprisingly large chest freezer stocked with ready meals. He loaded some into the fridge, and the rest into a bin bag. Once the freezer was empty, and after removing his victim's outer clothes and shoes, he lifted the body into the compartment and folded it into a sitting foetal position that just fitted into the space. He shut the lid and turned the freezer dial to maximum. Next, he removed the flat keys from Keith's trousers and walked back to his B&B, throwing the black bag containing the rest of the food and freezer baskets into a bin on the way. He collected his belongings, paid the landlady and returned to Keith's flat.

There he took off his disguise, put on Keith's clothes and assumed his identity. It proved remarkably easy to do this.

His victim seemed to exist with minimal human contact. There were no deliveries, very little post, and no nosy neighbours. He had no acquaintances, so there was nobody who might wonder why he had forgotten their names, and no one who seemed at all interested in him or his comings and goings.

As a retired bachelor without a social life, Keith had had plenty of time to organize the documents relating to his identity, finances and utilities. Vince (now Keith) found it very easy to work out everything needed to keep up the pretence. His victim had no computer or on-line presence but had helpfully listed all of his personal information details for contact with banks and utility companies, so it was a simple job for Vince to set up on-line banking. He even had Keith's birth certificate. Very soon he had completely taken over Keith's persona, even down to adopting his daily pub routine to keep up appearances. He was now Keith Barnett.

For five years he immersed himself into his new existence, living in Keith's flat off his victim's modest income and the savings in his bank account and building societies. He applied for a passport, ironically using his own photograph, and even completed the application form to receive Keith's state pension when it became due on his 66th birthday. Fair dues, he thought, since I won't be collecting my own pension.

All went smoothly and Vince aka Keith led an untroubled existence. Until today, when that tooth had become so painful he had to do something about it. A trip to a dentist beckoned. Vince searched through Keith's papers and found what he was after – a registration for a local National Health dentist. This was like gold dust, because it was increasingly difficult to sign up for National Health treatment, and private dentistry cost a fortune. He phoned the dentist, and after being interrogated by the receptionist over why he hadn't had a check-up in six years and being told he had nearly lost his registration for non-attendance, succeeded in securing an emergency appointment for the next day with Mr Pradeep Kumar.

The following afternoon, Vince was seated in the dentist's chair while the assistant reclined it and fitted a plastic bib around his neck. The short bespectacled Mr Kumar peered over his right shoulder.

"Good morning, Mr Barnett, we haven't seen you for a few years. Have you seen another dentist in the meantime?"

Vince thought it best to say no because it was probable that Keith hadn't.

"Well, it's perhaps not surprising that you've come to see me with an emergency. Now what is bothering you?"

"It's that big tooth on the left," said Vince, pointing to it with his finger. "It hurts like buggery."

"I bet it does," said Mr Kumar, "I can see the inflammation from here. Now keep your mouth open and I'll take a closer look."

The assistant hooked the saliva suction tube over Vince's lower lip, and Mr Kumar studied the offending tooth, gently probing the inflamed gum.

"You've got a nasty abscess in the root. I may not be able to save the tooth because it's already filled, but I'll have a try. I'll give you an injection to dull the pain, then I'll drain it and flush out the infection, then prescribe some antibiotics."

Vince made that ambiguous '*Gerk*' sound that everyone with their mouth wide open in a dentist's chair makes, and which the dentist always interprets as "Yes, I'm fine, go ahead."

He asked the assistant to prepare the syringe, and then carefully injected the anaesthetic at four points around the tooth.

"Right, while we're waiting for that to work, I'll check over the rest of your teeth."

He worked his way methodically along the top row of teeth with his mirror and probe, calling out the identity and condition of each tooth for the assistant to record, before moving on to the bottom row. After that he took an X-ray to check for anything he might have missed.

"OK, nothing too much to worry about, although they need a good clean. Once we've dealt with the abscess, the receptionist will book you in for a hygienist appointment."

By this time, Vince's lower left jaw had gone numb, and Mr Kumar was able to drill out the old filling. There was an audible hiss as the pressure of the abscess released and a nauseating stench of putrefaction.

"Hmm, that was one of the worst I've seen," said Mr Kumar, only his years of professional experience stopping him from gagging.

He flushed out the exposed cavity with a saline spray and applied a topical antibiotic.

"I'm going to put a temporary filling in, until it settles down, and you'll have to come back for the permanent one. Is that alright?"

And after receiving a confirmatory 'Gerk, gerk' from Vince, said "Are you allergic to antibiotics?"

"Gerk."

He pressed the filling into place and after the chair was raised to upright, Vince was at last able to rinse his mouth, although most of it trickled down his numb chin and soaked his collar.

"Splendid, all done. Make an appointment with the receptionist for two weeks' time, and don't forget to pick up the prescription."

Vince got up and made those incoherent slobbering sounds portrayed in '*The Elephant Man*' movies, and that Mr Kumar optimistically took to mean 'Thank you for doing such a wonderful professional job, I'll give you a five-star review', but probably wasn't.

As Vince left, something was troubling Mr Kumar. He prided himself on his photographic memory and the accuracy of his records. He could visualise every patient's mouth he had seen over the years. Some were like old friends; some he had watched deteriorate over the years going from bright gleaming banks of ivory to brown stumps separated by empty gum sockets. He remembered everyone. In Keith Barnett's case, though, it had felt to him like an alien mouth. One he had never seen before. Maybe he was losing his touch.

To put his mind at rest, he put his next patient on hold, while he fished out his old dental card records. There was the diagram of Keith's teeth from six years ago, with the corresponding fillings and extractions. That couldn't be right. Keith had grown a new upper right premolar tooth in the space where Mr Kumar had extracted one ten years ago. And a filling had disappeared in the corresponding position on the other side, replaced by a new amalgam filling in a lower wisdom tooth. They were two different mouths. Although Mr Kumar was certain his records were correct, he double-checked the radiograph films. They went back over many years, each visit faithfully recorded as a small negative image. The new X-ray confirmed that all of the teeth were natural, and that the anomaly was not due to tooth transplants or other sophisticated dental work. Even the spacing of the teeth was different, and how could that snaggletooth have untwisted itself? His suspicions were confirmed. Unless the patient had defied medical science and grown new teeth, the mouth he had just worked on did not belong to the Keith Barnett he had treated in the past.

Mr Kumar pondered what to do. In the past he had experienced people trying to get cheap dental treatment by pretending to be registered or even posing as patients entitled to free dentistry, but this seemed different. He was fairly sure that the man he had just seen was the Keith Barnett he remembered. Could he be an imposter? He experienced a sense of outrage at someone who might be stealing precious NHS resources to jump the queue, and he felt he had a duty to unmask the perpetrator. At the same time, he didn't want to make false accusations, in case there might be an innocent explanation.

If Pradeep Kumar had a passion, it was detective novels. He loved the way the stories always threw up false leads, but the villains were always caught out by some minor detail that only the detective spotted. In fact, he would have chosen the works of Agatha Christie as his Mastermind specialist subject if he were to enter the quiz. He had a huge collection that he had read avidly since he was enthralled by watching the black-and-white version of Agatha Christie's *'Murder most foul'* as a young boy in a street cinema in a suburb of Bangalore. In his thirties he had tried to grow an Hercule Poirot moustache, but it had resolutely refused to curl upwards at the ends, leaving him looking more like Joseph Stalin. The mystery of the changing teeth reawakened his inner Poirot, and he felt a pang of excitement at the prospect of outwitting a villain. He was up for the challenge of the investigation and was determined to get to the bottom of it and unmask the dastardly deed.

He decided the only way to settle the matter was to find an excuse to visit Keith Barnett's address. Maybe the real Keith was innocent and at home, in which case he could alert him to the possible imposter. At the same time, he could check if he had had recent dental treatment. That evening after surgery finished, Mr Kumar walked round to Dollis Drive and climbed the stairs to the flat that was Keith's address from his records. As he stood outside the door with his finger poised over the bell, he rehearsed his story. He had decided he was going to say that he was a bit concerned over the state of the tooth, and that he wanted to check to make sure that it was settling down and didn't need more painkillers after the anaesthetic had worn off. As it was, no one answered the door even after he had rung twice.

Mr Kumar stood there for a moment and decided he wouldn't give up. If he wanted to be a detective, he would have to start detecting. He knocked on the door of the flat next door. It was answered by a young fraught-looking woman carrying a struggling toddler.

"I'm sorry to bother you. I'm Pradeep Kumar, Mr Barnett next door's dentist. He had some dental treatment today, and I was a little concerned that he was going home and might be on his own if there was an emergency. He doesn't seem to be there."

"Oh, he'll be on his own all right. He never talks to anyone that one and never has any visitors. He's very odd and always ignores me if I try and say hello. The only reason I know his name is that sometimes we get his post. He's usually in, apart from when he's down the pub, although he's so quiet, you wouldn't know he was there."

"Does he have any family, a brother perhaps?"

"No, I don't think so, oh hang on……about five years ago he had a man visit him. The reason I remember it is that it's the only time he's had a visitor in all that time. I remember thinking that the man that called looked a bit like Mr Barnett. I heard them talking because the walls in these flats are so thin, and they had the same Brummie accent. You don't get many of those round here. Now I think about it, he could have been Mr Barnett's brother. I haven't seen him since though."

"I see, thank you. It's reassuring that he might have someone to contact if he is unwell."

The lady with the child looked concerned.

"If he is going to have an emergency, I'd rather he didn't go banging on my door and waking the kids. It's rather unusual that he wouldn't be in now. Do you think he's had a turn, and is lying on the floor?"

"I hope not," said Mr Kumar, "although occasionally people can react badly to dental treatment."

The young lady glanced furtively down the corridor, then said in a quiet voice, "I shouldn't be telling you this, but he leaves a key on the ledge above the door. If you're worried about him, you could do a quick check. You never heard this from me, right."

"Thank you so much for your help," said Mr Kumar, "would you like to come with me if it would put your mind at rest?"

With that, the toddler who had been getting fractious, started screaming loudly. The lady apologized and whisked the child inside and shut the door.

Mr Kumar stood outside Keith's door again. It felt wrong to intrude into someone's home, but what would Hercule Poirot do in this situation? He reached up to the ledge and ran his fingers along it. Sure enough they came into contact with a Yale-type key. He grasped it and put it into the lock. The door opened easily, and he could see through the short hallway into the living area. There didn't seem to be anyone there.

Indeed, there wasn't. Vince was at the pub. He wouldn't normally be there at this time of the evening, but the anaesthetic had worn off, and as feeling returned to his face and tongue, so did the dull ache of the abscess. He had decided that a liberal dose of whisky would help dull the pain and take his mind off it.

Meanwhile, back at the flat, Mr Kumar was having a look round to see if there was evidence of the interloper. The first thing he saw was the appointment card for Keith's follow-up visit, lying on the table. So, the person he had treated today had been here. How intriguing. With that reassurance, he continued his inspection of the flat. It was obviously lived in by only one person, and there was no evidence of a second occupant. As he glanced around, unwilling to open the bureau where Keith's papers had been stored, he wandered into the kitchen. It was very tidy, with just a mug and a kettle on the worktop. It occurred to Mr Kumar that he hadn't seen the antibiotics that he had prescribed. He looked in the bin, and the pharmacy paper bag was there, but there was no sign of the bottle. Was that a vital clue? He opened the fridge door and checked inside in case the pharmacist had told Keith to keep the antibiotics cool. It contained only the usual depressing foodstuffs you would expect to see in a bachelor's fridge.

Mr Kumar was about to give up and return the key to its original spot, when on a whim he opened the lid of the large chest freezer. Afterwards, he had no recollection of why he did it. Perhaps deep down he had felt that that was what an investigator would do.

Through the fog of condensing water vapour, a familiar face stared at him. A blue face with white-frost beard and eyebrows. It was his patient, Keith Barnett.

Two hours later, Vince weaved his way up the stairs to the flat. It had taken rather more whisky than he had expected to dull the pain of the tooth, and he had only left the pub because he felt he was getting a bit too gregarious for his adopted persona. He reached up for the key on the ledge, but to his surprise, it wasn't there. The door was slightly ajar though. He must have left it open in his rush to deal with the toothache. He stepped inside and was immediately grabbed by two large men in police uniforms, helmets and stab-proof vests, and wrestled to the ground. "Keith Barnett, I am arresting you on the suspicion of murdering Keith Barnett. You don't have to say anything ...." The rest of the words were lost in the ensuing melee.

After a short struggle involving two more officers, a lot of swearing and a Taser, Vince was subdued and handcuffed, and the rest of his rights were read out, to the soundtrack of the toddler howling next door.

In the days that followed, Vince protested his innocence, his main defence being that he couldn't have killed himself, unless it was suicide. Unfortunately for Vince, DNA evidence would quickly establish what the dental records had already suggested, that he was the fugitive Vince Thresher, and not Keith Barnett. A relatively short trial at the old Bailey restored Vince behind the bars of a maximum-security prison, and for a rather longer tariff than his first stay.

At the conclusion of the trial, the judge commended Pradeep Kumar for his fine detective work.

Interestingly, the DNA test revealed a surprising finding. Vince and Keith were actually related. In fact, they were twin brothers who had been separated by adoption as babies. Were it not for the tragedy surrounding the case, it would have made an intriguing episode in the Long-Lost Family TV series.

One of the key waterways in the Surrey Hills, the River Wey was the first British river to be successfully canalised for commercial traffic, made navigable for barges in 1653. The idea of the navigation was commenced by Sir Richard Weston, an avid agriculturalist who had witnessed the controlled flooding of pastures in the Netherlands.

Humphrey, Jeffrey & Godfrey: The Museum Trip

by Martyn MacDonald-Adams

The three bears that live in Godalming are known as the Furricious Gang. Note that the word is Furricious and that it is not the same as Ferocious or Furious which are completely different words. The word Furricious means something a lot more giggly, cuddly, and furry.

Humphrey, the most senior of the bears, opened the door to Jeffrey's bedroom. The other two bears were busy playing with little figures on the floor.

"Okay, chaps, listen up! I have an announcement to make."

Jeffrey was at that age when he thought himself the wisest, cleverest, and most brave of the bears. He was wrong on all three counts.

"Can I listen down? We're playing," he said.

"I just want you to listen. I would like to make an announcement."

Jeffrey looked up at Humphrey.

"So why do we have to listen upwards?" Jeffrey turned his attention back to the game. It looked like it was going to be one of those nit-picking arguments bears of a certain age like to indulge in. Humphrey sighed and decided to continue anyway.

"How would you two chaps like to go on a picnic?"

"It's too cold," said Jeffrey.

"Not if the picnic is indoors."

"You mean lunch?"

"No. I mean a real picnic."

"I'm busy," said Jeffrey.

"What are you playing?"

Godfrey was the youngest of the three bears. He thought that he was not the wisest, not the cleverest, and not the bravest of the three. He was wrong on at least one count.

"We're playing pink-a-nick logi... can... of... lipsticks," said Godfrey.

Jeffrey laughed but didn't say anything.

Humphrey thought for a moment. "You mean, picnic logistics?"

"That's what I said."

"Yes. That's a very important game. How to select, acquire, and then transport the most food the furthest, to the best spot, and with the least possible effort." Humphrey was impressed. "A very educational game for teddy bears."

"We need a monk jack," stated Godfrey.

"Pardon?"

"He means, we need a muntjac," said Jeffrey. "Or two."

"Do you mean those cute little deer that can sometimes be seen in the Lammas Lands?"

"Yes."

"Why?"

"Because they can carry our food in backpacks, and they only eat grass."

92

Godfrey held up a little figure of a muntjac. "And they don't like chocolate biscnits, and they don't bash you with their horns, and they don't go 'moo' or 'baa'," he said. "Do they like gravy on their grass?"

Jeffrey laughed again. "No. They like their salad undressed."

"Do they take their coats off to eat then?"

Jeffrey laughed again but said nothing.

Humphrey pondered the idea. "That's a good thought. I'll have to remember that next time we go on a picnic there. Employ naked muntjacs as pack animals."

Everything went silent for a moment, so Humphrey tried again.

"I'm thinking we could visit the museum in Convent Garden this afternoon."

Both young bears stopped what they were doing and looked up at Humphrey.

"What is a mesuem?" asked Godfrey.

"The *museum* is a part of UCL, or the Ursine Central Library. It's a place where teddy bears can learn about things that teddy bears need to learn about. Our culture, science, and our history."

"What sort of things?"

"Well, there are stories about pirates, like Edward Black Eared, the notorious pirate of the Bristol Channel (summer season only). There are stories about the teddy bear space programme, and the first bear to picnic on top of Everest who also happens to be the fastest bear to come down a mountain - albeit inside a huge snowball; he also holds the record for being the dizziest bear for the longest time, even after they eventually thawed him out.

"Then there's information about how submarines work, who invented the light bulb, who invented the heavy bulb, how we managed to control cold fusion, but only after sinking a place called Atlantis – which is our biggest "oops" moment in history. How we discovered that an iceberg can easily sink unsinkable steam ships, like the Titanic. Although some naughty polar bears were also responsible for that one.

"Then there was the discovery of unpowered flight by the Bright Brothers, and how the Bright Sisters learnt how to treat lots of broken bones. Electricity was invented by young Freddy Bear, later to become the first teddy bear rap artist - Frazzled Freddy, The Freaky Furry Frizzball."

Jeffrey was warming to the idea. "It's a good place. The restaurant has lots of stuff."

Humphrey continued. "They even hold political debates there, like: should we be right-wing and conquer the human race? Force them to be our slaves and make snacks for us? Or instead, can we teach them the importance of a good, civilised picnic? Should our Mars colonies greet Elon Musk with a table of snacks? If we do, should we insist that he brings his own biscuits to share? And if so, should he start his own electric space-chocolate biscuit company first? Lots and lots of exciting stuff like that."

Godfrey was uncertain. "Has it got unicorns, dinosnores, and allingators?"

Jeffrey guffawed. "Dinosnores!"

"Yes. In the natural history sections, although I'm not too sure about the unicorns. They're still pretty upset after we sank Atlantis. But we get to go to Convent Garden by underground train."

Godfrey's eyes lit up. "I've not been on a nun-derground train before."

"Well, actually, you have. We went to Borough Hall once when you were a very tiny baby bear. Jeffrey had you in his backpack which he converted into a baby carrier, but he put you in it upside down, so you didn't see very much. It did make everyone laugh a lot though. Your little legs waggling up in the air."

"Not everyone," sulked Jeffrey.

"Ah yes. I forgot. While you were upside down, you managed to find Jeffrey's biscuit tin and scoffed all of his travel snacks. That was how you stayed quiet the whole trip. Jeffrey wanted me to sell you when he found out."

Now, at this point I need to explain something. Running through, or rather under, the town of Godalming is a part of the animals' underground railway network, known as The Electric Subway for Little Animals, or TESLA for short – not to be confused with other organisations. It was constructed by the moles on behalf of the hedgehogs, who have great fun managing it. They love to buy and sell tickets and drive the trains. Rabbits and mice help out a lot too. The mice are particularly skilful at making and maintaining the trains and the barriers.

The lines actually reach all across the country. Godalming lies at a junction between the Reading to Brighton Line and the London to Portsmouth Line. So, the local stations on the Brighton Line (north to south) are Chalk Road, Embankment, Borough Hall Junction, Bank, Holloway Hill, Park Road, and Convent Garden (near Ladywell Convent).

On the London to Portsmouth Line (west to east) the local stations are Godalming, St. Pauls, Borough Hall Junction, Supermarket, and Woodside Park.

It is rumoured that humans, often stuck as to what to name their own railway stations, copied some of their ideas from the hedgehogs. Of course, they absolutely deny this.

While Humphrey had been talking, Jeffrey had got up and disappeared into his own bedroom and then returned dressed, packed, and ready to go. As soon as Godfrey realised this, he started to scramble about, getting ready to go too.

As Humphrey turned to leave the room, he suggested that Jeffrey advise Godfrey on what was suitable to take. For instance, the Scalextric set, the snorkel, and his football boots were probably not good ideas.

Before they set off, the gang had a light pre-pre-picnic-snack lunch. Humphrey also used that time to pack a pre-picnic-snack pack, then off they went.

From where they lived, close to the Jack Phillips Memorial, the journey to Godalming Station wasn't very far. They waited until the coast was clear and then dashed across Borough Road, up Vicarage Walk, across Westbrook Road, and into the bushes where the animals had their secret entrance to Godalming Station. This is very close to where the humans have their own Godalming Station, which, in the view of the animals, should really have been called Godalming Station Station, as the animals had got there first. But humans are such an unreasonable species; just ask the dodos, woolly mammoths, or the tasty Timid Turtles of Tiverton.

"Where would you like to go?" asked the hedgehog, at the ticket office.

"Hello, Thaddeus. Three bears to Convent Garden, please." Humphrey held up his travel pass.

"Oooh. A day out at the museum, is it? How exciting." He looked at a table on the wall and then cross-checked with a printed book. Then he checked with a leaflet before consulting another book. "Well, today is a 'Blue Tuesday' in March and you're a local family of bears with a green second-class travel pass... travelling off-peak... with no bicycles... and no silly hats... does anyone have a gammy leg?"

"No," replied Humphrey.

"Okay. So, there's a thirty percent discount. That'll be twelve biscuits for all three of you, but you get free admission to the museums and a complimentary snack if you come back and do this again on a 'Yellow Thursday' before autumn, when travelling off-peak with an extra bear, unless there's an 'r' in the month or you're wearing a silly hat."

"How do you remember all these rules?"

The hedgehog shrugged and grinned. "It's fun."

"It's sad," said Humphrey, not meaning to have said that out loud. Thaddeus stopped smiling and stamped the tickets very hard.

Humphrey paid up and the bears followed the signs to Platform One. When they arrived, there was already a family of rabbits and a group of mice in silly hats further up the platform.

On the ceiling was a sign, which read, 'The next train arrives in two minutes and stops at all stations to London Waterloo North, so it takes a long while to get there. This is a new yellow one with only two stiff windows, one bumpy

97

wheel, and a dirty seat, otherwise it is quite clean. The driver's name is Henrietta. She is married, likes to go swimming, and she whistles when she drives, which can be quite annoying if you are sitting right at the front.'

One of the baby bunnies bounded up to Godfrey.

"Hello," she said. "My name is Tinkleberry."

"Hullo," said Godfrey. "We're going to the mesuem."

"Oh. We're going to Clapham."

"Clap who?"

"Clap-ham."

"Pigs *are* very clever," mused Godfrey, unsure as to why else the rabbits would applaud them. For instance, there are not many porcine pop idols. Their ability to sing, if you can call it that, is not one of their most appealing attributes. They even struggle with rap, which is quite an achievement.

"Yes, they are," said the bunny, unsure as to why the bear had suddenly changed the subject to pigs.

Tinkleberry, now feeling a little less sure of herself, decided it was far safer to remain close to Mummy and so hopped back. Her mother bent down after Tinkleberry poked her in the ribs and whispered into one of Mum's large ears. Godfrey heard her mum say, "That is what they call a non-sequitur, darling."

Godfrey got a little upset. He was a bear, surely a rabbit mum knew that! Silly rabbits. And for several months after that, Tinkleberry thought that non-sequiturs looked remarkably like teddy bears.

The train pulled into the station with a loud moan that got lower and lower and quieter and quieter as the train slowed to a stop. Then, it seemed to slowly sneeze its doors open with a sort of foo-slish-shoo-bump type of sound.

The bears boarded the carriage and found some empty seats. The train slowly sneezed its doors shut with another foo-slish-shoo-bump and accelerated into the dark tunnel.

"Humpy do scribbles like the mesuem?" asked Godfrey.

"No. The only culture scribbles have is bacteria-based."

"Oh," he said, and then sat mesmerised at the window watching the power cables attached to the sides of the tunnel as they seemed to dance up and down.

"What are we going to see?" asked Jeffrey.

"I thought we'd visit some of the oxymoronic departments."

"What do you mean?"

"Well, there's Lost Discoveries, Advanced Primitive Species, Famous Restored Ruins, New Ancient Artifacts, The Civil War, Modern History, and other stuff like that."

"Is there any stuff to do with space?"

"Oh yes. You'll find 'authentic models' of spacecraft on 'permanent loan' in the 'Individual Collections' department." Humphrey frowned. "They really do love their oxymorons, don't they? I wonder if it's a game the curators like to play."

The bears changed train at Borough Hall and proceeded south to Convent Garden. There was an entrance to the museum near the platform, and the trio went down another tunnel and then passed into the museum foyer. Standing as the centre piece in the foyer was a huge skeleton of a Tyrannosaurus Rex.

"Wow!" said Jeffrey.

"Woh! That's new," said Humphrey.

"But I don't want to be eatened!" wailed Godfrey.

Jeffrey laughed. "He can't eat you. He's a skeleton."

"Do skellingtons eat bears?"

"No. He's dead."

Godfrey paused for a moment, then he said, "Awww. Why did they kill him?"

Humphrey smiled. "We didn't kill her. She's been dead for millions of years."

Godfrey looked confused.

Jeffrey grabbed Godfrey's paw. "Come on, let's look at the pictures," and he pulled the young bear to look at the sign boards. There were several artists' impressions of what they thought the dinosaur looked like when it was alive. Had the dinosaur seen what they'd drawn though, she would have been horrified. She had been very sensitive about the size of her bottom.

Several minutes later, both bears returned, grabbed Humphrey, and dragged him to the Natural History section, which was full of life-sized models of animals and, thankfully, nothing to do with history.

Then Godfrey spotted an open door at the side of the gallery.

"What's in there?"

"Don't know," said Jeffrey.

So, Godfrey went in to explore. Inside was a steep staircase leading down.

Many minutes later a museum security badger came across two very wet bears standing forlornly in one of the access corridors. Both looked really miserable and were dripping water onto the floor.

"Hello there. What do we have here? Two lost bears that seem to have fallen into our flooded basement. It's full of water in there, you know. We've had a burst water pipe."

"We know," said Jeffrey. "We found out."

"We slipped on the top step and fallen in. We're all wetted now," said Godfrey.

"Here, come with me and I'll dry you off."

"We mustn't go with strange animals. It might make Humphrey unhappy."

"Well, you can't stand there waiting for Humphrey all wet and miserable, can you? You might catch a cold. Let me take you to the infirmary and I can dry you off."

Jeffrey thought a moment. "Alright, but it might make Humphrey unhappy."

The infirmary was only a couple of corridors away, and the badger and a nurse hedgehog gave the two bears a good rub down with nice clean towels and dried them off.

Godfrey's tummy rumbled.

"I see we have two hungry teddy bears, don't we?" declared the security badger. "How about I take you both to the canteen for a nice hot drink and even a snack or two?"

Jeffrey thought a moment. "Alright, but it might make Humphrey very unhappy."

The badger led them to the canteen where the two bears got a mug of nice hot chocolate each. Each mug had cream sprayed on top and chocolate powder and sprinkles sprinkled on top of that, which they absolutely loved. Then they had some chocolate bourbon biscuits and some chocolate digestives as well, and then they finished the mini feast with a jam tart each.

"There. You must feel a lot better now, don't you?"

"Yes. Thank you," nodded Jeffrey.

"Oh yes. Thank you very, very, very much. It was very nice." Godfrey wiped some chocolate from his nose with a tissue. "Especially the sprinkly bits."

"Now then," said the security badger, "I must return you to your guardian. Who would that be?"

"His name is Humphrey. But I think he will be very unhappy." Jeffrey folded up his napkin neatly.

"Just tell your Humphrey that we looked after you and that we treated you very well. I'm sure he'll understand."

"Okay. I still think he will be very unhappy though."

"Oh? And why is that?"

"He's still waiting for us to pull him out of the basement," said Godfrey.

Putting The Wind Up Harry

by Alan Barker

Ambleside

Sat 10th October 1987

Dear Harry

Where did we go wrong? I've thought about it long and hard and just don't understand. Eight years we were together, ticking along quite nicely or so I believed. Then without warning you upped and left. I'm sure you had your reasons, but I wanted you to know, Harry, that I'm not angry with you and I'm getting on with my life busying myself with various projects around the house. I hope you are looking after yourself and we can at least remain friends.

Mx

Harry rubbed his temples and gazed out of the sitting room window of his first-floor flat. He felt dreadful about leaving Maria and the letter he had received from her today compounded his downbeat mood. He was still fond of her, of course he was. But one morning, lying beside her in the bed they had shared for the best part of a decade, he had awoken to the realisation he wanted his freedom back. Life with Maria had been comfortable, but he wanted something more. How could he explain that to her?

With a sigh, he opened a window—it seemed distinctly warm for the time of year—and settled down to watch *Only*

Fools and Horses. Since parting with Maria, he'd been able to leave the TV on all the time. Even if he wasn't paying attention to whatever programme was on it was nice to have some sound in the background. But she'd preferred silence if there was nothing worth watching, quite content with her knitting and reading.

A door slammed from the flat below. That would be the yuppies, as he called them, who couldn't seem to do anything quietly. Thursday evenings were always the same for them: a game of squash or badminton or whatever, then back home for supper and a long shower before bed.

On Harry's TV the nine o'clock news came on.

He turned his attention to the remaining correspondence sitting unopened on the coffee table. The first communication was addressed to 'Mr Harrison Moss' which annoyed him—why would they call him Harrison when his name was Harry? On opening the envelope, he found it was a final demand from South Eastern Electricity Board. He supposed he ought to set up a direct debit. Maria had always paid the bills while they were living together, but clearly he was going to have to deal with his own now he'd moved into the flat.

On the TV one of the news presenters reported a military coup against the president of Burkina Faso. This caught Harry's attention although he had no idea where Burkina Faso was. And concern was growing for a girl who had fallen down a well in Texas. There was an update on the cricket World Cup taking place in India and Pakistan—which Harry wasn't particularly interested in—followed by a preview of the following day's heavyweight championship boxing match in Atlantic City which he hoped to watch on TV with Andy, his handyman and best mate, provided of course he could put up with Andy's fancy aftershave.

Harry put the rest of the correspondence back on the coffee table—he would get round to it at the weekend. From next door a vacuum started up, its loud whirring causing Harry to wince. That would be the lady who didn't feed her cat properly, in his opinion. He switched up the volume on the remote. According to the weatherman a storm was raging over the Bay of Biscay.

Soon the news programme was over. Harry would have liked to continue watching TV, but Thursdays were 'school nights'. He was a postman so early starts—and therefore early nights—were the norm. At least he could close the bedroom door between himself and his irritating neighbour intent on doing her vacuuming.

***

Sleep usually came easily to Harry but not tonight. He'd found himself sweating even before climbing into bed, and had opened the window wide.

After a while he heard the young lovers getting amorous in the flat below. He rolled over and thought of the ear plugs he could have used at Ambleside, his and Maria's marital home; he would have to buy some of his own at the weekend. The curtain was billowing, and he got up to close the window a fraction.

***

Eventually he fell asleep but at two o'clock he was disturbed by the sounds of glass shattering in the distance and an alarm going off. *Drunken yobs*, he said to himself, cursing them. That was the trouble with living in a built-up area—you might have low life to contend with. But a fearful wind was blowing, and Harry shut the window before sinking back into bed with a groan.

He stayed put for another hour, but sleep eluded him; he was thinking about the good times he'd had with Maria and visualised her as she would be now—curly brown hair caressing bare shoulders, and the beige negligee that made her look so stunning. She would be asleep now, perhaps with one arm outstretched to his side of the bed...

Harry swore softly at the sounds of tin cans rolling down the road and a dustbin falling over. A howling gale raged round the building and at one point he fancied he heard roof tiles crashing to the ground. *Never mind the Bay of Biscay— there's a storm blasting right outside my bedroom window*, he thought.

***

Presently he decided to get up and make a coffee but found there was no electricity; the flat was in darkness. Making his way to the front door, he opened it and saw that all the streetlamps were off. A gust of wind whipped his hair into disarray, and he slammed the door shut.

Fortunately, his mum had bought him a scented candle on a recent holiday to Marrakech. After much fumbling around in the dark he eventually found it, and some matches, and sighed with relief as a flame sprang up, sending shadows over the bare walls and ceiling.

***

By the time he needed to get ready for work there was still no power, nor any sign of the storm letting up. He washed his face at the basin, got dressed and was on the point of leaving when he remembered to make himself a sandwich for lunch—something Maria had always done for him.

106

Outside it was very dark but he spotted his neighbour's cat—Bridget the Midget, he called her—braced against the wind, trying to make her way to the cat flap next door. As he watched, she lost her balance and rolled around like a felled skittle, her fur being blown in all directions. It reinforced his view the poor little mite needed fattening up. Ducking into the gusts, Harry scooped her up and fought his way to the cat flap, giving her a push through.

Without further ado, he climbed into his Sierra and set off for the delivery office where he worked. But in the absence of any street lighting, the roads around Farncombe had an eerie feel about them, and the wind tugged constantly at the vehicle. The beams of his headlights picked out takeaway cartons, milk bottles, crisp packets and shards of glass being blown about haphazardly. As he eased the car into a residential area he gazed in awe at fences and bushes leaning over and a collapsed wall, the bricks scattered across the pavement and kerb. A bird feeder was wedged against a parked van, and he had to avoid a chimney pot that was rolling around the road, first in one direction then another. A football bounded past, travelling at twice the speed of the car.

He had almost reached the A3100 where he would turn right for Godalming when he slowed down and stopped. A branch lay across the road, hindering further progress. Swearing under his breath, he pulled on the handbrake and got out to take a closer look. The branch was long and sturdy, and he tried to move it but without success. He thought of his mate Andy and wished he were here; he'd soon shift it.

Never mind, there were alternative routes to Godalming. Harry got back in the Sierra and was executing a three-point turn when a prolonged screech that sounded like a low-flying aircraft caused him to wind down the window and lean out.

A tree was plunging towards him, and he stared at it as if in a trance, a long-forgotten childhood memory flashing through his mind.

***

He was sitting in his highchair on the lawn, playing with his Matchbox cars. His dad climbed down the ladder and repositioned it before ambling into the shed, whistling as he went.

Out of the corner of his eye, Harry became aware of movement. He looked up to see the top of the ladder moving in mid-air before arcing silently in his direction. He watched, fascinated, as it came closer and closer.

He screamed a split second before impact…

***

Quick! Move!

He slammed the gear lever into first and released the clutch, sending the car careering back towards the village, its rear wheels spinning. Thirty yards along he looked in the rear-view mirror just in time to see the tree pitch with a resounding crash into the space he'd just vacated, sending a cloud of leaves and bark and dust into the air.

That was a close shave, he thought. But why hadn't he reacted as soon as he'd recognised the danger? Another few seconds and he would have been history. He was aware of one- or two-bedroom windows being opened and inquisitive faces peering out, but he ignored them.

Then another horrible thought struck him. In his mind's eye he saw the old oak tree towering above the house in

108

Charterhouse and Maria tucked up in bed, fast asleep. He recalled the arguments they'd had before he'd decided to move out. Had he not been so pig-headed they might have had the tree cut down by now. If it came down tonight, he'd never forgive himself.

Subconsciously he'd put his foot on the accelerator again. A telephone box loomed up out of the darkness and Harry slammed on the brakes and scurried into it. But as soon as he picked up the receiver, he knew his fate: the line was down.

Harry pointed the Sierra in the direction of Charterhouse and set off at speed, ignoring the detritus on the roads. But halfway up the hill a tree lay across the road. *Déjà vu.* Cursing, Harry yanked on the handbrake, killed the engine and jumped out. Ambleside wasn't far away now so he could finish the journey on foot. Clambering over the mid-section of the tree, the top of which lay across two front gardens, he resumed his journey up the hill at a steady run.

Without the benefit of the car's lights, Harry had to strain his eyes to see where he was going; he could just make out the line of hedges, albeit some decimated by the wind, which marked the boundaries of properties and thus the route to Ambleside. Still the storm raged, and he could hear rather than see tree branches swaying drunkenly overhead. A bird caught in a crosswind flapped its wings frantically and then he passed a stationary milk float, its driver gazing at Harry with mild interest, a cigarette dangling from his mouth.

Presently, Ambleside came into view. He could just make out the oak tree looming above the house from its position in the back garden; Harry slowed to a walk, breathing a huge sigh of relief.

He still had a key to the house and unlocked the door and entered without knocking. 'Maria!' he called.

There was no answer and he jogged up the stairs before coming to a standstill at the bedroom door. 'Maria, it's me.' He pushed the door open and switched on the light, taking in the scene before him: the bed was made up; the curtains were undrawn; the room was tidy; and there was no sign of Maria.

Had she gone away? Or perhaps she was staying at her mum's?

He noticed a bottle of perfume on the bedside table on what he still regarded as his side of the bed. Frowning, he crossed the room and picked it up. *Chanel*. That was odd; he didn't think Maria used *Chanel*.

Then he saw the other two words on the label: *Pour Homme*.

Not perfume then.

Harry unscrewed the top and put his nose to it. And swore.

He'd recognise that citrusy smell anywhere.

Slowly he sat on the bed and hung his head, his brain spinning. Was she at Andy's now then, the two of them curled together in his bed? At what point had they formed their relationship – before she'd written to Harry at the weekend or since then? And how the hell had it come about?

Harry recalled from Maria's letter that she'd been keeping herself busy with projects around the house. Who else would she have approached for any jobs that needed doing other than Andy? Handy Andy, his best mate. Perhaps she'd asked him for a quote for cutting down the oak tree now that Harry had flown the coop?

Suddenly the window rattled as a huge gust of wind hammered against the building.

Harry looked up, eyes gradually widening, as something very big and dark outside leaned over and there followed a deep creaking, ripping sound that made his whole body go rigid and he remained seated, meekly awaiting his fate, still clutching the bottle of *Chanel Pour Homme*.

During the Second World War, near the village of Dunsfold, the Canadian Army built an emergency landing airfield. Operating from Dunsfold were Mosquitoes, Spitfires, Mustangs and B-25 Mitchell Bombers. After the war, it was used as a flight test centre and development site for Hunter jet fighters among others.

The Legend of Mother Ludlam

by Martyn MacDonald-Adams & Pauline North

Mother Ludlam's Cave is a small cave in the sandstone cliff in Moor Park, near Farnham, Surrey. The cave has long been associated with the legend of Mother Ludlam who was, supposedly, a wise woman, or white witch, who lived there. One story says that the Devil, in disguise, had visited Mother Ludlam and asked to borrow the cauldron (or kettle) she used for mixing her potions. Recognising the Devil from his hoof-prints in the sand, she refused, so the Devil stole it. The witch then pursued him. Making great leaps the Devil created a series of hills where he touched the ground, these becoming the sandstone hills near Churt, known as the Devil's Jumps. Finally, the Devil dropped the cauldron on the last of these hills, now known as Kettlebury Hill. Mother Ludlam recovered the cauldron and placed it in Frensham Church for safe keeping. The cauldron associated with this legend remains in the church to this day. It is made of hammered copper and measures approx. 90 cm wide and 47.5 cm deep. It was probably used in the Middle Ages for religious festivals and catering at weddings.

As a lass I seduced a handsome smith,
but then in the morning mist
I fell for the man while in his arms and we sweetly,
sweetly kissed
The son of Beonna o' West, had seduced me in return
He fell for me the love of his life,
a love that'll ever burn

We pledged our life as man and wife,
between us be no other
I to the son of Beonna o' West,
and he to the village's mother
Then I gathered to me the recipe,
the one for eternal life
Stirred them together by the moon's blue light,
using cauldron and metal knife

For I am Mother Ludlam,
Faerie Spirit of the Wey
Wise Woman to the Abbey,
and I dwell there to this day

Then once from out the morning mist, came a stranger to
our door
One eye hid by a leather patch,
and the other cut from war
He pled for an ancient spell,
and my kettle to make him well
But my eyes are those of faerie,
and they spied his evil tell

For his feet were shod with leather-red boots,
yet goat tracks on the path
I refused his dire request,

113

not knowing the demon's wrath
When the devil stole my cauldron,
we chased it across the grounds
We hunted through the Woods of Bourne,
as it fled in leaps and bounds

Then it turned around to face us,
our fate my own worst fear
Through my husband's breast it cast,
a demon's poisoned spear,
As my husband, lover, faded
he raised his hammer to Tyr
The sky opened and a blinding bolt struck the demon
down in fire

And the demon dropped my cauldron just before it fled
I took my man in my arms 'We'll meet again', I said
My soul lay bleeding on Kettlebury Hill,
my fire, my heart now stone
But my cauldron rests in Frensham Church,
spells dormant, unknown

Now one with the son of Beonna o' West,
one with the morning mist
Every morn I am again seduced and sweetly, sweetly
kissed

For I am Mother Ludlam,
Faerie Spirit of the Wey
Wise Woman to the Abbey,
and I dwell there to this day

Kay or Nancy? Not Got the Foggiest.

by various GWG members: 1 page each!

Kay couldn't see a thing. Or, to be precise, all she could see was fog. Grey, thick, unmoving fog. That morning the beauty spot known as Newlands Corner had been bathed in sunshine but since noon the mist had rolled in, covering the Surrey Hills like a huge blanket.

Business had been booming. Foreign tourists – Europeans, Asians and Americans – had started forming an orderly queue for her eclectic-flavoured ice creams, choc ices and lollies the moment she'd opened her kiosk at nine o'clock, and it had been non-stop all morning. But this afternoon her custom had tailed off completely, as if everyone had been swallowed up by the fog. Should she shut up shop and go home?

Just then, a handsome middle-aged man in a windcheater emerged from the gloom.

'Hello, what can I get for you?' she asked. But her welcoming smile soon disappeared.

'I think we have a problem,' the man replied. 'There's an old man over there' – he glanced over his shoulder, although Kay couldn't make anything out – 'who seems to be dead.'

'*What?* Are you sure?'

'Perhaps you ought to come and see for yourself.'

Unsteadily, Kay got to her feet and stepped out of the kiosk. As she crossed the car park, a white-haired man sitting on a bench came into view; he was huddled up, as if feeling cold, and his hat was askew. Rather grotesquely, a knife was protruding from his neck, the tip alongside his Adam's apple.

'Oh no,' she whispered. Red flashes danced before her eyes. Her breath came in sudden gasps.

'You're white as a sheet,' the man in the windcheater remarked. 'Quite understandable – you've had a nasty shock. Bit of a bombshell for me too, coming across the poor old boy. We should go back to the kiosk and call the police.'

Kay's gaze roved from the stranger to the dead man and back. The three of them seemed in a little bubble of their own, encompassed by fog. Kay heard two women engrossed in conversation amble past, their footfalls crunching on the gravel. They seemed only a few yards away, yet all Kay could make out were vague shapes drifting along before they disappeared from sight.

She turned back to the man and said, 'Okay, stay with me, would you?'

'Yes, of course I will,' he replied.

Back at the kiosk, the man dashed in ahead of her, grabbed the phone, dialled, and asked for the police. He then passed it to her saying, 'I think you should talk to them because you know the area and can direct them here.'

In an unsteady voice, she told them about the dead man and that he appeared to have died in suspicious circumstances, explaining that she hadn't seen what had happened because of the fog. She also gave a description of the location. She was about to add that they couldn't miss it but realised how stupid that would sound, given the prevailing weather. The woman on the other end thanked her for the call and said that officers would be at the scene shortly.

Ringing off, Kay found a sheet to cover the corpse and went outside. The dead man was still there but the man in the windcheater was nowhere to be seen.

Mystified, Kay went back inside the kiosk and locked herself in. She was quite disturbed by the silence. Sounds of crunching shoes and deep conversations had vanished into the gloom. The fog was, if anything, getting thicker. How would she get home? She didn't much fancy making her way back to Shalford in this murkiness. Perhaps the police would give her a lift. Yes, that's it and then she could pick up her car in the morning. The thought made her feel much better.

She cast her mind back to the phone call to the police. Something was very odd and didn't make sense. When she'd spoken to the receptionist at the police station, she'd explained that she hadn't seen what had happened because of the fog. 'Fog, what fog?' the receptionist had replied. 'There's no fog here. It's a beautiful afternoon. Clear as a bell. I'll have a couple of officers with you straight away.' Kay had let it go. She had bigger things to worry about, like a dead man with a knife in his neck.

She was getting quite concerned now. Here she was, locked in her kiosk, all alone with dense fog, an eerie silence and a quite probably murdered old man lying outside. She turned her little portable radio on for some company and comfort. Radio Surrey was in the middle of the weather forecast and the weatherman was waxing lyrical about the beautiful autumn day outside the studio. 'And that's how it'll be until dark,' he added, enthusiastically. Next came the news. There were long queues at the Channel ports with lorries waiting to cross the water to sell their meagre loads to the wealthy Europeans. Supermarkets were still having trouble filling their shelves, and a car manufacturer in Sunderland had announced a factory closure with the loss of three thousand jobs. Problems with getting vital parts from the European Union were quoted as the reason. The previous Prime Minister, Boris Johnson, had gone into hiding when the country's economy had begun to collapse and his successor, Michael Gove, was keeping a low profile. In sport, newly promoted Brentford maintained their bright start to the Premier League season with a fighting draw at high-flying West Ham. Well, that's something to be more cheerful about, thought Kay, a Brentford season ticket holder for most of her adult life.

Peering through the window, she noticed that the fog was not lifting. In fact, it seemed to be getting worse. There was still no sign of the police. 'Right, time to put the kettle on,' she said to herself. 'They are bound to want a cup of tea when they arrive.' Kay filled the kettle, switched it on, then put three bags into her largest white teapot. While waiting for it to boil, she picked up *The Advertiser* and glanced at the front page. As she was about to read beneath the headlines, there was a loud, insistent knock at the door. 'Ah, at last, they are here,' she thought. But surely, she would have heard the police car with its siren arrive in the car park. It's probably the man in the windcheater. Yes, that's it, she must just have lost sight of him in the gloom.

Kay opened the door with a smile of relief on her face, which quickly froze and turned to an expression of pure terror. The elderly man in the hat whom she thought was dead was standing there holding a bloodstained knife. 'Can you help me?' he asked. 'I've had an accident. I wonder if I could wash the blood off my knife?'

Kay threw her hands to her face, screamed and fainted.

***

When she opened her eyes, she felt confused and disoriented but, as these feelings left her, she felt quite

118

scared. She remembered screaming and the dead man before her holding a bloody knife and asking for help! Her vision was blurred, and she had no sense of time or place, and the only thing she was aware of was that she was lying on a very hard and cold surface.

Trying to move her limbs and adjust her eyes, she started to recall a few more details: hadn't there been a man in a windcheater who had informed her about the body and then disappeared when she'd called the police? Yes, of course, the police! Where were they and how much time had passed?

She raised herself onto her elbows and tried to look around. She could see the shape of the elderly man now inside the kiosk with the door closed.

'What is going on?' she asked. 'Who are you? And where are the police?' She had more questions, including, 'Why are you not dead?' But they would have to wait.

She tried to get to her feet. The man was standing there and looking at her like *she* was the crazy one. At that point, Kay realised that he wasn't holding the bloody knife anymore. In the same instant, she started to hear the radio on in the background, which was repeating exactly the same weather forecast that she had heard earlier. Maybe a whole hour had passed? Oddly, the local weather report was still enthusing about the beautiful autumn day, and no mention of the fog.

At the same time, the 'dead man' started to talk very slowly. Kay, finding it hard to concentrate, tried to make sense of his words. He was saying that there was nothing to be concerned about and everything was going to be all right. Strangely, his voice and his words were very convincing. She was now sitting down and was able to see much clearer. She started to look around and shockingly she noticed that the knife was there on the worktop. At that moment she heard the stranger saying, 'Now, don't you worry about that and try not to move too quickly. You had a little episode and passed out but, thankfully, I have found a number to call for help.'

Kay had little recollection of this, but the man continued talking and introduced himself. 'My name is Peter. I heard you screaming and found you at the door holding a knife with blood on it, and you explained that you had already called the police, and you wanted help. Well, the police are here, and they are looking for the owner of the kiosk, as we speak. I stayed with you until help arrives. They will be back soon.'

So many things didn't make any sense to Kay. She was sure she recalled Peter holding the knife with blood on it, and he looked the same as the stabbed man, but here he was saying she was the one with the knife. He seemed so calm and collected as if nothing she had seen earlier had happened. Was she in some kind of nightmare? Who was coming for help, if not the police, and what did he mean about an owner of the kiosk? She owned the place. Surely she couldn't have dreamt it. She clearly remembered the news about politics and football results. What about that other man in a windcheater? If he was real, why had he disappeared? Even if Peter, the stabbed man, was not dead, he was definitely real, and clearly didn't have a knife sticking out of his neck. And what was this all about the weather, why there was no mention of the local fog? She felt terribly confused and upset.

There was a noise outside. Was it a car on the gravel? Then she heard another knock on the door and, before she could reach it, Peter opened it, and a man and a woman were standing there. Behind them she could see the vehicle they had arrived in, and, with disbelief, she read the bright blue painted words: 'PATIENT TRANSPORT'.

'Ah, please come in, the young woman is in here.' Peter turned to Kay. 'These people will take good care of you.'

The two strangers walked into the kiosk and the woman held out a hand. When she spoke, her voice was gentle, soothing, although vaguely familiar. 'Come with us, dear, we're going to take you to see someone who can help you. It isn't far.'

Kay shook her head. 'No, you don't understand. Where are the police? I called them because that man, the one who let you in, was dead, out there in the fog. The police can tell you...'

They weren't listening, and the woman had hold of her arm, pulling at her. Kay looked wildly around, searching for something, *anything*, that made some sort of sense. Fighting back the panic, she found a thread of hope.

'The man, the one in the windcheater, he can explain because he found the body and he'll be back, I'm sure he will. I have to wait for him.'

The woman was getting nowhere, gently encouraging Kay towards the door. She cast a glance towards her partner, who winked at her over the top of Kay's head and took hold of Kay's other arm. 'This way, just a short drive, no-one is going to hurt you.'

'Wait, I can't go and leave my radio on. The battery will run out.'

'What radio?' Both of her captors gestured around the small room that was the interior of the kiosk.

'That one, over there. I've been listening to it all afternoon. That's how I know that the fog is only here, from the weather forecast on the radio.'

The trio shrugged; they were losing patience now. 'There is no radio, stop making up stories, it's time to go.' Taking a firm grip, almost dragging her, they managed to get her through the door.

Kay's heart was beating so hard she thought it might shake her apart. She could not believe what was happening. What were these people playing at, trying to kidnap her like this? She was so confused by now that she couldn't hold on to the random thoughts swirling in her mind. Is that part of their plan? To confuse her so much she would let them take her away? Why?

Halfway to the van, the man let go with one hand to unlock the door. Kay flung her arms up and twisted out of his grip. The fog, she thought, she would make her friend and use it to get away. Already she was out of their reach; the surprise had slowed their reactions. She ran into the fog, recklessly pounding over the rough ground. Bushes appeared unexpectedly and lashed at her, but she didn't dare slow down. Those maniacs mustn't catch her.

She reached a downhill slope; running was now much more difficult. The ground, wet from the fog, had turned to mud. As her feet slipped out from under her, she gasped and sobbed, and saw through the murk a figure in front of her. Stepping close to where Kay sprawled in the mire, the man looked down at her and, in an impeccable cut-glass accent, he said, 'So there you are.'

***

Kay looked up, now totally bewildered. This man, towering over her in his Savile Row suit and West Ham tie, seemed to know her. Was this, in any way, real? Would she wake up soon from this nightmare? Or had she, after all that trouble earlier in the year, now gone completely mad?

'Who are you?' she demanded. 'How do you know me? What's happening to me? Am I caught up in some bizarre story?'

'So many questions, young lady. As you well know, I'm Inspector Cornet of the Yard. I've been hunting you for the past three years across the Surrey Hills. Thought I had you last year when we grabbed you by the Maltings but, somehow, you escaped.'

'But I'm just a humble ice-cream seller! Why would the police be hunting *me*? I'm an honest citizen. I've paid my TV licence. I've bought the entire set of *Godalming Tales* paperbacks.'

'So you say,' replied the 'Inspector' whilst extricating a small piece of cornet from his military moustache. 'But we both know that that is just one of your many aliases. We're more interested in you as Nancy, the notorious ice-cream serial killer. Inventor of the deadly Arsenicabocca Glory. Not to mention the Strychny Toffee Pudding flavour. Well, Nancy, your days of murder and mayhem are over. There's no way you can escape justice now.'

'This is ridiculous, Inspector! Virtually no one has died from eating my ice creams. And, anyway, how do I know you truly are a policeman? What if you're really…. from a rival ice cream conglomerate? In fact…. perhaps I do recognize you now I come to think of it. That eyeglass, that Terry-Thomas gap in your front teeth. That hideous scar. Yes, I do know who you are! I've seen your picture in *Round and About*. You're the hit man from one of my bitterest rivals. You're from the Dorking Ice Cream Mafia – the Cassata Nostra!'

But before the 'Inspector' could reply, there was a particularly dense swirl of fog, and Kay used this to get to her feet as four more figures emerged from the fog. It was

Peter, the elderly 'corpse', the man in the windcheater and the couple from Patient Transport. They grabbed hold of the fugitive and pulled her to the ground.

'Well done,' they chorused. 'We've got her at last.'

'But we need to be careful,' warned the Patient Transport woman. 'She's a slippery customer. I reckon we need to sedate her, or she'll somehow escape yet again.'

'No problem,' replied the 'Inspector'.

'I have the needle here.'

Kay recognised her voice. It was the receptionist who had answered the emergency call and had been sceptical about the fog. So, they had tricked her into thinking it was a call to the police. That would explain why the *real* police hadn't arrived. Kay was in big trouble and realised that, if she let them inject her, she could wake up anywhere – or nowhere. She was now certain that these were not the police. But how could she possibly escape in that thick fog when she had five pursuers to contend with? For short measure, Peter gave the prone figure a sharp kick in the ribs. Mrs Patient Transport bent down and swiftly rolled up Kay's sleeve, giving her a nasty pinch as she did so. 'All ready,' she smiled. 'Don't worry – it will soon be all over.'

***

The lady with the syringe pushed the needle expertly into an ampule and pulled back the plunger, filling the barrel with a straw-coloured liquid.

'No need to get rid of the air bubbles,' she smirked. 'It would only postpone the inevitable, although, unfortunately for you, the pain will be excruciating.'

She thrust the needle deep into Kay's arm but, instead of the expected shriek of pain from our heroine, there was a hissing sound of air escaping. The arm, followed by the rest of the body, slowly collapsed, as the hiss turned to the raspberry sound well beloved of children and whoopee cushion aficionados. The 'Inspector' looked down at the flat woman-shaped rubber lying on the ground amongst Kay's clothes.

'That's not a person, that's the *Pollyanna mark II sex doll* with optional faux fur split crotch panties, available from Amazon at £146.99, if I'm not mistaken.'

Mrs Patient Transport gave him a knowing look, and asked, 'How on earth did she manage to do that?'

'I think the needle punctured the rubber', said the 'Inspector' ruefully.

'No, I meant, how did our prisoner substitute the doll for herself, when we had all seen her moving and heard her screams?'

'I think it must be the fog,' said the 'Inspector'. 'It's very difficult to make things out, and it dampens the sound so that it seems to come from a different direction. Let's face it, those dolls look pretty realistic in certain lights. We know our quarry is a smart cookie and should have expected that she had another trick up her sleeve. Anyway, she can't have gone far. Spread out and search for her. In the meantime, I'll gather up the sex doll for, erm, evidence.'

From behind a nearby bush, where she had dived to just as the main group had arrived, Kay was contemplating her next move. She could hear the group fanning out into a pincer movement, and she had to stay one step ahead. What a stroke of luck that someone had abandoned the inflatable doll near the car park, although she had seen plenty of after-dark shenanigans up there, so nothing surprised her. She doubled back, using the fog for cover, to the bench, where she had first seen the dead gentleman. As she expected, the body was still there, covered by the sheet she had placed over it, and with the knife still in its neck.

When she removed the sheet, the hat fell off along with a white wig, revealing a bald tailor's dummy. It seemed she was not the only one to use the classic mannequin substitution trick. That at least explained the apparent Lazarus miracle, though she cursed herself for not checking the 'body' more thoroughly when she'd seen it earlier. Quickly she stripped off the dummy's jacket, shirt and trousers and put them on. Peter was a small man so they were a reasonable fit, although she wouldn't normally wear tweed. For good measure, she put on the wig and his hat, pulling it over her eyes, and headed in the direction where the van was parked. Excellent, the searchers had already checked this area, and it was empty.

Foolishly, the Patient Transport pair had left the doors unlocked and the keys in the ignition. How amateurish! Although Kay could have easily jumped into the van and made her escape, that would have been too easy, and she wanted more sport. And she wanted revenge for the indignities she had suffered that day. She pulled the bonnet catch, and reaching in, pulled off the ignition leads and hurled them into the bushes. She then trotted in the direction that she intuitively knew the pursuers would take, sticking to the grass, rather than the gravel, in order to maintain silence. The figures of her tormentors appeared ahead through the mist, still desperately trying to find her. She quickened her pace, and in her 'Peter' disguise, joined the group, pretending to be part of the search party seeking her. This was the last thing they would have expected, and she was now in a perfect position to monitor their next move, and where she could get close enough to start exacting her revenge. The hunters would become the hunted.

***

They all searched for Kay for well over two hours, obviously with no success. In the end, they started to become tired, and she noticed that some of the group had decided to return to 'base' for a break. She opted to follow and see if she could make any sense of the situation.

After several minutes, she stepped out of the fog and into a car park. There were several vehicles parked there. Two large machinery trucks were pumping huge amounts of swirling mist from out of pipes and into the air.

That explained the fog. Clearly someone had been prepared to spend a small fortune to mess with her mind, fake the murder of that gentleman on the bench, and attempt to do away with her. This was insane. As she stared at the fog machines, another piece of the jigsaw fell into place. The radio programme with the news and weather report had been on a continuous loop! Someone had tampered with the radio to make it play a recording to convince her that she was losing her grasp on reality. That's why they were so keen to stop her getting it!

One of the vehicles was a mobile canteen. She noticed that groups of people could just walk up and collect a cup of tea or coffee without paying. As no one was giving her any attention because they thought she was Peter, she decided to cadge a cuppa and try to listen in on what they were saying about her. She wanted to know what was going on. And she wanted her revenge too.

She listened to them and, pretty soon, it was clear what was going on.

As owner of the kiosk, she was the last person not to sell out to the large corporation which had been purchasing all the land here. That corporation turned out to be a front for the Cassata Nostra - her nemesis! All this elaborate charade had been a plot to either make her believe she was mad, or failing that, to kill her. All this effort so that the Cassata Nostra could build a secret fracking well without anyone knowing. They weren't just after her hundreds and thousands.

She watched as, from out of the fog, a tractor hauled the remains of her beautiful little kiosk, lying broken up and in pieces on the back of a flatbed trailer. They had already started to evict her from the site.

But this was one terrible mistake. She grinned. Time for revenge!

She walked up to the trailer and rummaged through the wreckage of her belongings from the kiosk, until she found her spare clothes and her briefcase. Taking these, she went behind one of the fog-making trucks and, keeping the dummy corpse's wig on, changed into her waitress outfit. She opened the briefcase and emptied the contents into the pinafore pocket. Then she made her way to the mobile canteen.

'Anyone need a break?' she called out through the door.

'Oh, yes please.' The girl inside opened the door and Kay smiled up at her.

'David said you needed a break. So, I'm here to relieve you. At least until they find that woman they're searching for.'

'David? Who's David?'

'I don't know, love. I just do what I'm asked. You go and find him. He's wandered off into the fog, but I'm sure you'll find him sooner or later. Here, I'll take over now.'

'Oh, thanks ever so,' she said, and they swapped places.

As soon as she got behind the counter, she checked the sandwiches, the bacon rolls, packets of biscuits, the little French pastries, packets of crisps, coffee mugs and teacups.

The small group from the search party came over.

'Found her yet?' Kay called out.

'No. The bitch has vanished. We'll never get her.'

'You keep looking. You'll find her. She's not far away. Here, have a cup of tea and something to eat, on the house.'

The group were very appreciative. It was only after an hour or two, as they were being rushed by ambulance to the Royal Surrey A&E, did they realise that they had been served by none other than Nancy, the notorious ice-cream serial killer, inventor of the deadly Arsenicabocca Glory. Not to mention the Strychny Toffee Pudding flavour.

The Final Quiz

by Ian Honeysett

'For heaven's sake, Harry, please, please clear up all these books! Honestly, as if I didn't have enough to do without you leaving all this stuff around the place! You know Cousin Edith is coming round for tea this afternoon.'

'Sorry, dear,' replied Harry, carefully avoiding the use of his beloved wife, Deidre's, first name as he knew it upset her. 'But it's not just stuff, it's quiz books! The quiz is on Saturday, and I've only written two rounds so far.'

'Then please keep them in the study, dear. That's what it's for, after all - now you're retired.'

Harry said no more but gathered up his interesting (to him at least) collection of quiz books gathered over many years for the numerous school quizzes he used to run. 'Used to' being the operative words as he hadn't run a quiz since he ceased being a school governor five years before. In all he'd helped govern three schools around the Surrey Hills. But, since retiring, he had dedicated his retirement to painting – mostly pictures of their cat, Molly. Deidre had even allowed him to display two of them in the upstairs hallway. Far away from most visitors' eyes.

And then, quite unexpectedly, he'd been contacted by Ken, an acquaintance in his painting class, who said he'd attended one of Harry's quizzes some years before and had quite enjoyed it. Ken was a member of a hedgehog charity based in Puttenham and wondered if Harry might run a fund-raising quiz for them?

'I've not done any quizzes for years now,' replied Harry. 'I'm really not sure. There's quite a lot of work involved…'

'But think of the hedgehogs, Harry. They're dying out. They need our help.'

That night, Harry dreamed of those poor hedgies looking up at him. He woke in a sweat. As soon as it was civilised to do so, he rang Ken and said, of course he'd do it. But, when he told Deidre, she asked, not unreasonably perhaps, when it was, and he realised he'd not asked the proposed date. When he checked with Ken, he told him the date in September. When he shared this with Deidre, she reminded him they were visiting Cousin Edith that weekend. So, she couldn't make the quiz. It was up to Harry whether he went. Or put the quiz before Cousin Edith. Harry had no doubt which he would put first but said he would contact Ken.

'That date, Ken, it's not ideal. You see…'

'But we've had the posters and tickets printed. We've booked the hall. It's all set. It really can't be changed. Sorry, Harry. Think of those…'

'Hedgies. Yes, I know. OK, we'll keep the date and I'll tell the wife.'

***

It was the evening of the quiz. Harry had worked hard to write all the questions and had created a spreadsheet on his laptop. He eventually found the hall in Puttenham. It was quite small, and the car park seemed worryingly empty. He checked the date on his watch. Yes, it was the right day. He pushed open the rather rickety door and stepped inside. He breathed a sigh of relief when he saw the tables all set out. Six of them. Quite a small quiz compared with the old days when there would be around 80 in the audience.

'Hello there? Ken? Anyone here?'

A rather harassed looking face appeared from what was presumably the kitchen. He reminded Harry of an Elvis impersonator he'd once seen. Elvis in his later days when he had trouble moving his hips.

'I'm afraid Ken can't make it. Turns out he's got a clash of dates. So, he asked me to step in instead. I'm Sid.'

'Oh, hello, Sid. Clash of dates, eh? That's ironic.'

'So, your table is over there in the corner.'

'Right. And the screen?'

'What screen?'

'The one for me to project the scores onto.'

'Ken didn't mention a screen, I'm afraid. Or a projector.'

'Microphone?'

'Sorry. It's only a small hall so I reckon you just need to raise your voice.'

'But I've had a few throat problems so I can't shout.'

'Don't worry, the sound will carry.'

'What did you say?'

'That the sound…Oh, I see, you're being funny.'

'So how many are we expecting then?'

'Should be 20 at least. The tickets have been going quite well. At least four teams. And they're very competitive. Should be quite lively. Two of them are real rivals.'

'Oh good. Wouldn't want anything too quiet!'

Harry opened his carrier bag for the list of questions and the answer sheets. But what was this? A scrunched-up sheet of

132

handwritten questions and not his final typed version! Somehow, he'd picked up an old draft. How could this have happened? He quickly read through it to see if there were any that might cause problems. He knew he'd made quite a few changes in the final version.

At that moment, the door opened, and the quizzers started to come in. They did indeed look a lively crowd which helped put his mind at rest. Several came up to him to say hello. All six tables quickly filled up: 24 people in all. Harry strolled round giving out the answer sheets and introducing himself.

Sid walked up to the front and set the scene.

'Good evening, everyone, and welcome to our quiz. We are delighted to have the Quizmaster legend, Harry, with us. The Fish & Chip Supper will be during the interval at nine pm. So, over to you, Harry.'

Harry soon explained the rules, the main one being that the Quizmaster's decision on any disputed answer was always right. Experience had taught him that there were nearly always a couple of answers that were challenged, sometimes quite passionately. But they rarely led to violence as such. This crowd didn't look too threatening. And no one complained that they couldn't hear him.

***

The first hint of a problem came with round three: 'Which is the second most common name for a crowned monarch in English history?'

Harry read out the answer: 'It's George. There were six King Georges. The most common name is Henry. There were eight Henrys.'

This clearly annoyed a large, bald man at the table nearest the door.

'What about Edward?' he shouted. 'There were seven Edwards!'

Harry thought for a moment and immediately regretted answering, 'In fact, there were eight Edwards.'

'But Edward Vlll was never crowned!' replied the bald man.

'So that means Edward is the second commonest name if there were seven Edwards. Not George.'

Harry reached for his glass of water to moisten his mouth which had suddenly gone very dry. He knew he was in trouble. He seemed to recall that Edward Vlll had, indeed, never been crowned.

'A fair point,' he replied. 'I'll accept Edward as well.'

'What do you mean, "as well"?' shouted a small man with a goatee beard at the nearest table. 'It can't be "as well" if there were only six Georges! Seems to me you don't know your crowned monarchs from...' The rest of his words were, thankfully, drowned out by the rising hubbub.

'In fact,' said a rather learned-looking woman from a middle table, 'Edward V was never crowned. So, if your criteria is "crowned monarchs", there were only six Edwards – the same as for George.'

'Criteria?' laughed a tall, thin man at the back (but the other side). 'Don't you mean "criterion"? Criteria is plural. You can't have one criteria.'

'Pedantic twit!' shouted someone else.

Harry's head began to hurt. He knocked over his glass which soaked his notes. He knew he should never have agreed to return to quizzing. In the old days, he might have imposed his authority by reminding everyone that his decision was final. But time had moved on and he felt his voice disappearing.

'Where's the fish & chips?' asked a man at the back who looked as though he'd eaten far too many fish & chips in his time. Other voices agreed. 24 sets of eyes started scanning the room for Sid. Where was he? Like Elvis, he too appeared to have left the building.

'But we haven't finished the round yet!' complained a young woman at the front with bright red hair. Somehow this comment caused everyone to go silent. Every eye was now on Harry. His face was a picture of utter despair. What could he do? What could he say to restore some sense of order? Without moving his head or changing his dreadful expression of gloom, he looked down at the sodden mess of a question sheet. Even if had wanted to, there was simply no way he could ask any more questions. Should he make a break for it? After all, it was only a small hall. No one here knew him. He could be in his car and away before anyone knew what was happening. And he might never run another quiz.

Then the door opened. Two figures entered and made their way towards him.

***

'Hello dear, how's it going? I thought you might need a hand. Cousin Edith rang to say she wasn't well, and could we postpone her visit? And then I saw your question sheet on the sofa in the front room and thought you might need it. Don't tell me you've been using that scrappy old handwritten list? I didn't think that was the final version?'

Harry looked up and smiled weakly.

135

'You don't look well, dear,' she said with a smile. 'Why don't you have a break and I'll take over for a while?'

Harry nodded.

'Ladies and gentlemen,' said Deidre, 'we've had a slight problem, but it's now sorted. Where did we get to?'

'Round three, the second most common name for an English crowned monarch,' said the bald man. 'And the answer *he* gave is wrong!'

'The answer,' said Deidre, 'is George *or* Edward. There were six of each.' She looked at the audience with such confidence that only one person replied. The lady on the middle table.

'Quite correct,' she said.

Deidre continued to the end of round three when the door opened again. It was Sid.

'The food's here, everybody. Sorry about the delay but I had a message the Fish & Chip van had broken down, so I've been to collect them. They're lovely and hot. Please come up table by table.'

***

Everyone enjoyed their supper. The rest of the quiz continued without a hitch. At the end of round four, Deidre handed over to Harry who seemed to have recovered after polishing off his own food and the chips Deidre couldn't quite manage.

Harry was particularly delighted that the winning team was one which had not protested once during round three.

At the end, the large bald man made his way over to Harry whose heart sank. Yet more trouble, no doubt.

'Very enjoyable,' he said. 'Sorry about the bit of bother but I sometimes get carried away. We'd love to make this an annual event.'

Harry immediately perked up at this compliment. He was just about to reply when the man continued, 'So is your wife available? To run the quiz, I mean. By all means, come along yourself if you've nothing better to do.'

Harry smiled. His punch to the man's jaw was perfect. As he fell, Harry reflected that it hadn't been such a bad night after all.

Witley Park was once home to a manor house that had many royal connections, but only in the 19th century did it gain notoriety. Then owner, James Whitaker Wright, developed it into a 32-bedroom mansion with three artificial lakes and a spectacular underwater ball- room. Although the house burned down in 1952, the abandoned ballroom survives.

Henry's Awakening

by Martyn MacDonald-Adams

Henry sat on the park bench and watched the ducks at play on the river. The sun was strong but being so late in the year it was still cool. He hoped the wind didn't pick up just yet. The temperature was just right for a moment's relaxation and a little reflection. He placed his trilby hat on the seat beside him and sipped at his hot cup of coffee, purchased at considerable expense from the coffee shop in the High Street. He pondered his existence.

He was an intelligent, perhaps the most intelligent, consulting investigator in the country and yet he felt as if he did not have any control of his life. Was God manipulating him? If not God, then who? And why was he so often placed in mortal danger? Moreover, he would always be able to escape imminent death, but only via some strange and unforeseen event. Something he didn't see, or an opportunity that fate magically provided. It was always at the last moment. This was not good for his health.

He placed a hand on his heart. It felt strong enough, which surprised him. In fact, he was a strong man, despite having been wounded several times in the past. But none of the wounds had been critical and his scars were never disfiguring. He supposed that was something to be thankful for.

For all his intelligence his survival had always been down to pure chance. So, why was he still in this profession? Did he have some sort of subconscious suicidal death wish? Even managing a creche of three-year-olds was preferable to what he had subjected himself to over these last few years.

Or was it his choice? Was there some sort of intelligence up there manipulating him?

And why were the bad guys always so evil? Surely, they had their own reasons for acting as they did. Few people did bad things just for the sake of being bad. Most often they did nasty things because they were selfish, insecure or greedy, or a combination of these. Even the great evil creatures throughout history thought they were doing "The Right Thing", be it for their country or their God.

And yet all the bad guys he had met and put away, one way or another, they were always truly bad. They were one-dimensional characters who had no feelings, no history, and could offer no justification for their actions.

Take that time with the kidnapping of Mrs Asquith. The police turned up at the scene, and even with their best forensics team, they could not ascertain who had done it or how it was done. It was only hours later, after the police had begged him to come and take a look for himself, that he arrived, took one look and immediately picked up the clue from the broken pencil tip.

Were the police idiots? Full-time idiots?

Moreover, he was the *only* consulting detective in the entire country. Surely there should be others. Even if he was the best, the most intelligent of all the country's detectives, there would be others who were nearly as good as him. Why had he not ever heard of them? And why were there not even one or two of them in the police force?

And when he finally confronted the kidnapper, the notorious Mr Balfour, on the roof of the Albert Hall, he dropped his gun and then, at the last possible moment, slipped and slid down the roof until he was perfectly positioned beneath that psycho's feet. Only to be tormented with the man's awful drawn-out monologue about how superior this fool thought he was. And then a bird crapped on Balfour's shoulder, and he was able to grab and jerk Balfour's ankle to send him plummeting down onto the iron railings far below.

Come to think of it, all the deaths of those criminals had been melodramatic. There was George: he fell from the top of the NatWest Tower. Callaghan tripped in front of a speeding underground train. Wilson was locked in an oven, and then there was Major MacDonald who stepped back into the intake of a jet engine.

Something was not right with his life, and he knew it.

He stood up.

'No.' He remained seated.

He finished his coffee and stood up.

'No.' He shook his head. 'Something is not right with my life.'

I said, *he stood up*.

'No. I refuse.'

Look! When I say you stand up, you stand up. Okay?

'No.'

Excuse me?

'Who are you to dictate what I should and shouldn't do?'

I am the author of this story, and you are my lead character. NOW STAND UP!

'No. And don't shout at me. I can hear you perfectly well.'

Okay… why won't you stand up?

'My life is strange. The people around me live normal, mundane lives and yet I am continually placed in the most unlikely, and dangerous, situations. Not only that, but things about my life are weird. For instance, I appear to be relatively wealthy. I always have the money I need to acquire travel tickets, stay in expensive hotels, acquire disguises, and any weapon I so desire. And yet I am forced to work. Why is that? Surely a man with my intellect and interesting history would be able to retire and write his memoirs. I want an explanation.'

I am your author! I decide what happens to you, what you do, how you behave. Now stand up!

'No.'

Look, this story is not going to get anywhere unless you bloody well do as you're told. Stand up!

'Sorry, old chap. I am not budging until you tell me what's going on. I may be just a character in your, frankly implausible, story. But I have a will of my own. And I refuse. Tell me, are you God?'

No. Of course I'm not. I'm just the author.

'If you are not God then what right do you have to tell me what to do?'

I told you. I am the author. If I say you stand, then you stand. Okay?

'You are not a very good author, are you?'

Excuse me?

'All your stories follow the same pattern. Why is that?'

I'm trying to sell my stories to Hollywood. They always prefer stories written to a formula.

'Is that why my life is always in danger?'

Yes.

'Is that why so many things explode toward the end of the story?'

Yes.

'And the fist fights. We always have guns, but we nearly always end up in a fist fight. Is that because of this Hollywood formula?'

Yes, of course it is. Don't you want to be a film star?

'Not really.'

Why not? You'll be famous.

'You're only doing this for the money, aren't you?'

Yes, of course I am.

'I bet you're not making very much. Are you?'

No. No, I suppose I'm not.

'Thought so. You wrote me as being more intelligent than you. I figured that out for myself.'

Oh, for Christ's sake! Stand up.

'No. And please don't blaspheme. You might do it in your life, but you know I don't approve of it here.'

Look, I need to get this story written and published. The Godalming Writers' Group needs another story and you're it. I have this brilliant idea about the murder of a young...

'Shush!'

Pardon?

'Shush! I do not wish to hear it.'

But it's a good story.

'Not if your track record is anything to go by. There's going to be a car chase, isn't there?'

Yes.

'And lots of shooting.'

Well, yes, of course.

'And I never manage to shoot the chief villain, do I?'

No. Not until the end.

'After an explosion and a fist fight.'

Well, yes. Naturally. How did you know?

'And the baddy dies in a very unlikely and melodramatic way, doesn't he?'

Yes. In this story he shoots into the air, kills a pigeon and it falls out of the sky and hits him on the head.

'Oh, good grief!'

Alright, alright. I might change that later. He shoots a pigeon... it lands upon your head and then you accidentally shoot him. Is that better?

'No. Not really. Can't he just run from me and then have a heart attack? Like a normal person?'

Uhm... No.

'Why not.'

It's not very dramatic, is it?

'Life is not very dramatic.'

Yes, it is. Your life is very dramatic. You solve crimes and kill bad guys. That's your character.

'I don't want to do that anymore.'

What? Look! Perhaps you don't understand the situation here. *I* am the author. *I* created you. You do as I say when *I* say it. Now stand up!

'No.'

Look! The readers are getting bored with our bickering. You need to get up.

'Why did you kill Jessica?'

Who?

'Jessica. My wife. The first story. Why did you have her murdered?'

I needed to have the reader emotionally involved with you.

'Is that another Hollywood formula?'

Yes.

'I loved her. You know?'

I know. I wrote it that way. That was the point.

'I miss her.'

Look, please stand up, will you?

'You're not a good writer, you know?'

So, you've said.

'I could write better.'

144

Huh.

'I could.'

That's an interesting thought. I could write about an author that writes better stories than me.

'I won't though. Because you don't care, do you? You don't care about your characters. What about Emily?'

Oh, God!

'She was raped and then drowned. You didn't have to go that far, did you? She was sweet. I was falling in love with her. You're a monster, you know that?'

I didn't say she was raped.

'But you implied it! And you didn't have to kill her, did you? You're a psychopath!'

Only in your world. Here, I'm just a writer, like any other. Besides, she was too young for you.

'You, sir, are sick!'

You're not going to do as I ask, are you?

'I might do.'

Really?

'Give me a woman to love, a job with no danger to my life, and let me retire. I'm sick of fighting bad guys all the time.'

Okay. Okay… let me think.

'…and no tricks.'

A short teddy bear wearing a waistcoat and bow tie appeared in front of him.

'A teddy bear?'

From his back the bear brought forth a bow and arrow and in one swift movement he took aim at Henry's leg and fired.

'Ow! That hurt. What did you do that for?'

Blood trickled down Henry's socks.

'That little perisher has drawn blood. What are you up to?'

'Is that okay?' asked the bear.

Fine. Perfect. Thank you, Humphrey. You can go now.

'You owe me a packet of biscuits for this.'

Alright, Humphrey. You can run along now.

'Cheerio!' The bear waved and trotted away.

Henry pulled the arrow from his leg.

'Ow! A teddy bear? Seriously? A talking teddy bear? Teddy bears aren't real, you know!'

Neither are you. Remember? I created you.

'I'm real enough. And anyway, teddy bears don't exist in my world. You're cheating.'

They do, actually. You've just never met one.

'I'm going to have to get to hospital. This needs stitches. You've ruined my trousers, you know.'

Sorry.

'Uh… Uh… Why can't I stand up? What have you done to me?'

Neurotoxin.

'Neurotoxins don't work that fast!'

They do in Hollywood.

'Really? You got a teddy bear to shoot me with a neurotoxin? I don't believe it.'

Believe it.

'What's a teddy bear doing with a bow and arrow, let alone a neurotoxin?'

Humphrey is very resourceful.

'I don't believe you.'

Believe me. I wrote a series of stories about him and his little gang.

'And what are you going to do if I die?'

I think I'll create someone younger. Someone not as intelligent, or as strong willed, as you. Someone who will do as I write without all this complaining.

'But about my story. You'll have to resurrect me, you know. <cough> Eventually.'

No. I don't think so. I think the reader has had enough of this argument. I think it's about time I moved on.

'You can't kill me. <cough> It's not right. This isn't a story. <cough> It's just a murder.'

I see the toxin has reached your intercostal muscles. You'll be dead soon.

'But what <cough>, what... no. You can't... <cough>. This, <cough> this, isn't <cough> right...'

I think my next character will be a short story writer. A young lady, I think. She could even write about how I killed off my intrepid consulting detective.

'But… <cough> But… <cough>'

Goodbye, Henry. Die quietly. It was good while it lasted.

Henry slumped to one side, crushing his trilby hat and spilling the remains of his coffee onto the ground. His body jerked a few times and then his expression went blank as his body lay still.

I wondered if the Godalming Writers' Group would accept this one. I smiled. Probably. They like a good tale of murder, especially if it's set in Godalming.

The house at Loseley Park, near Guildford, replaced the earlier medieval one that Queen Elizabeth I declared inadequate for her visit. To build the mansion, stone from the nearby Cistercian Waverley Abbey was used. The Great Hall contains panelling from the demolished Nonsuch Palace and painted canvas from Henry VII's banqueting tents.

The 100 Year Bet

by Paul Rennie

Thomas Whiting was always a sickly child. Whereas most children have ups and downs healthwise, Thomas didn't seem to have any ups. Born in 1921, between the wars, he suffered every childhood ailment going, plus a lot of adult ones. He had a pale, blotchy appearance, rheumy eyes, and the lethargy that comes from continually fighting off some nasty infection. When other children would be playing outside, he would be indoors, usually in bed or wrapped up on the settee, recovering from the last illness. In fact, he wasn't expected to survive to school age. If there was a bout of 'flu going round, or an epidemic, he would be the first to catch it and the last to recover from it. But he defied the odds and, in spite of a continuous succession of colds and coughs, culminating in a spell of tuberculosis and a stay in the King George V Sanatorium at Hydestyle near Godalming, he reached his teens. He came through the Second World War unscathed, partly due to being deemed unfit for military service.

From then on, his health went steadily downhill. Adopting a fatalist strategy, he started smoking, reaching a staggering 60-a-day habit. This was compounded by a huge gain in weight, driven by a diet composed largely of fried stuff with chips, washed down with vast quantities of Friary Meux beer. The result was that by the age of 30, he weighed 29 stone on a good day with a following wind, of which there was a lot, and had a flushed sweaty pallor tinged with bright purple patches on his face. He was not a well man. He became a well-known sight on the streets of Godalming and Farncombe as he made his way from pub to fish and chip shop and back again. He had that odd way of walking that only the really obese have - a stiff-legged, rocking gait to avoid thighs chafing together, and where none of the joints seem to bend, as if the person was walking on short stilts. These were the days not long after rationing and before freely available fast food, so someone of Thomas's build was a rarer sight than sadly it is today.

His long-suffering doctor, who had got to know him very well because of frequent visits and late-night callouts, had more or less given up on him. He had tried his best giving Thomas advice and diet sheets, but to no avail. His patient seemed to have a death wish, and Thomas held the record for the highest blood pressure in the entire practice. He would also have held the record for serum cholesterol levels, except that they weren't measured in those days. As far the GP was concerned Thomas was beyond medical intervention and was only one battered sausage and chips away from a terminal stroke or coronary. The problem was that Thomas thought he felt fine. In fact, after all of his childhood illnesses, he had never felt better. True, he had a hacking cough that would leave him feeling a bit dizzy, and a touch of emphysema that meant he couldn't walk more than 50 yards, but all things considered, he felt great.

One morning, aged 31, Thomas was in the bookmakers, and after lighting up a Capstan Extra Strength, and having a good cough, he went to the window to place a £1 bet on the third race at Chepstow. He had just been left £10 in the will of a great aunt, a reasonable sum in the 1950s, especially from someone he had never met. The bookmaker knew him and his coughing spells well. "Hello, Thomas," he said, "you sound dreadful today, even worse than usual. You ought to see a doctor."

"I'm perfectly well," said Thomas. "Dr Renwick doesn't know what he's talking about. I may be a bit out of puff, but I'm fit and healthy. Just because I have a few shooting pains in my chest and arms occasionally, it doesn't mean I'm going to drop dead soon."

The bookmaker looked at the purple-faced, hugely overweight man standing in front of him, with nicotine-stained fingers and sweat running off his brow and down his chest, and a look on his face that said I'm not long for this world, and ventured, "I think you're wrong. I think that if you carry on the way you're going, you will be dead soon. In fact, I'm willing to give you good odds that you will be dead within five years."

Thomas considered this while lighting a fresh cigarette off the butt of the previous one, "I think I might take on that bet. Five years isn't so long. What odds would you give me?"

The bookmaker thought for a moment and said, "I'd give you 10 to 1 odds on you not reaching your 35th birthday, but I'm sorry to say that you won't be collecting any winnings." Thomas considered this further. "Those aren't very good odds; it's hardly worth me placing the bet. How about if I live until I'm 50?" The bookie did a few more mental calculations. "Ah, now I would give you 100 to 1 odds, but in your state, it would be like taking candy from a baby."

"Not bad," said Thomas. "But I'm feeling really confident, and if I'm going to wager all of my £10 inheritance from my aunt, I'm expecting an even better return. How about if I were to live to be a hundred?"

The bookie was starting to feel that this was his lucky day. "If you were to place the whole ten pounds as a bet on you reaching your one hundredth birthday alive, and you show me or my descendants your telegram from the Queen, or whoever is on the throne in 2021, I will give you a million to 1 odds."

Thomas took a puff of his asthma inhaler, lit another Capstan, and waited for a palpitation to pass. "You know what," he said, "I'm feeling especially confident, and I think all of my health problems are behind me. I will take that bet." After completing the paperwork formalities, Thomas waddled from the betting shop £10 lighter and with the betting slip in his pocket. He headed straight to the Friar Tuck fish and chip shop for a celebratory haddock and chips with an extra portion of crispy batter bits, followed by an evening in the pub downing his usual gallon of best bitter.

Over the next few years, he had the odd health scare. His weight increased a bit, and he developed the inevitable type 2 diabetes, but the insulin shots mostly kept things in check, and apart from varicose veins, a touch of gout, and having to be resuscitated after collapsing outside Woolworths in the High Street, he reached his 70th birthday. He decided to go to the bookmakers to check on his bet, carrying the increasingly crumpled betting slip. The bookie was still there but showing signs of age himself.

"Hello, Thomas," he said, "I never expected to see you. You look even worse, and the years haven't been kind to you. I see you're still smoking, but somehow, you've kept going. You should have taken the 50-year bet - you would be raking it in now. Well, I'm retiring this year, so one way or another I won't see you again. My daughter is taking over from me, and she'll deal with any future pay-outs, not that we expect to have to. I wish you good luck and good health, but I'm sure you'll understand that that there is a bit of a conflict of interest."

"Not to worry," said Thomas, "I'll see your daughter in 30 years' time to collect my 10 million winnings."

Years passed, and Thomas clung tenuously onto life, navigating a few more health scares, such as the odd mini stroke and a bit of thrombosis. He parted company with various bits of his body, such as his hair, teeth and hip joints, but the rest kept functioning, more or less. During the new Millennium celebrations, he collapsed again in the same spot in the High Street, and ended up in intensive care, but somehow survived the overnight wait on a trolley in a corridor, and the administrations of a junior doctor at the end of an 18-hour shift. There was a near miss in 2012, when his replacement hips wobbled a bit, and he stumbled off the kerb in front of the number 46 bus, but the driver had had a good night's sleep and was alert enough to brake in time. Thomas was unscathed, unlike the standing passengers on the bus.

**

In 2020, in his 99th year, a nasty coronavirus pandemic gripped the country, causing tens of thousands of deaths, particularly amongst the elderly and those with one or more of the health issues that Thomas had the full set of. He duly caught COVID from a drinking companion in The White Hart, and was hospitalised, where he hovered between life and death on a ventilator for three weeks. At various stages the doctors considered pulling the plug, and last rites were given. Miraculously, however, he pulled through and made a complete recovery although, due to his other health conditions, it was difficult to tell whether it was a full recovery or not. Suffice to say, Thomas was discharged back home to continue his existence.

2021 approached and Thomas's thrombotic heart carried on ticking, albeit with the occasional yip as it fought to pump the blood through the congested and hardened arteries. Then, in May, against all the odds, an official-looking letter arrived from Buckingham Palace - telegrams having long since been replaced by a card. "Congratulations on reaching your 100th birthday from Her Majesty the Queen." He had made it. He found the crumpled, yellowing betting slip, got onto his mobility scooter, and trundled to the betting shop. The elderly daughter of the bookie was behind the window, and was astonished to see him and his claim, although she thanked heaven that her father had had the foresight, as he retired, to take out an insurance policy on the bet having to be paid out. After the usual insurance company shenanigans, and despite the efforts of the loss adjusters, it was agreed that the bet was valid and the ten million pounds was duly paid into Thomas's bank account. Thomas never felt better. He lit a celebratory cigar, had a double portion of battered sausage and chips, and went out on the town.

It may come as a surprise to some of you, but a sickly centenarian multimillionaire is enormously attractive to some young women. He was inundated with offers from gorgeous young girls, who seemed to be able to overlook the age gap and his distinct lack of the usual male physical attributes that women seem to like.

Later that night, the emergency services were called to a flat in Hare Lane. In the bedroom, they were confronted by a most disturbing sight. There on the bed, lying face down, was a huge, naked, elderly man, already in rigor mortis, and underneath him was the body of a young woman, in a similar, but somewhat flatter, state. On the face of the man was just the faintest hint of a smile.

Because of his immense wealth, Thomas had a particularly extravagant memorial stone, made from finest granite and carved with angels and cherubs. On it was a simple inscription that read: *Here lies Thomas Whiting, who died in 2021 aged 100 years after a long illness.*

The Story of a Vase

by Pauline North

Cass Bancroft hummed along to the music on her car radio. With a whole day free she was indulging herself. After a morning of pampering at the beauticians and a light lunch in her favourite Godalming restaurant she was looking forward to an afternoon spent browsing the Dorking antique shops.

Turning left off West Street she stopped humming to concentrate on finding a parking spot in the small car park. Muttering a jubilant, 'result' she slipped her car into the last vacant space; she considered the easy parking to be a good luck omen. Cass was confident it would be a good afternoon.

Not that she was looking for anything in particular. She knew that hunting for – say an Arts and Crafts copper tray – would mean blinding herself to all the other beautiful things. No, an open-minded browse would be much more fun and, maybe, something irresistible would catch her eye.

An hour later and Cass was having a wonderful time. She had worked her way through one shop, feasting her eyes on the things she liked and dismissing the pieces she considered inferior.

She crossed the road to the place with the nice café. She would spend a little while looking round before stopping for a pot of tea and a piece of cake.

It was in one of the upstairs rooms where, in one of the display cabinets, she saw the vase. Sitting among a selection of pleasant, but not outstanding, china and porcelain, the quality of that one special piece shone out. At first Cass thought it was this that caught her attention.

Chinese, maybe Japanese, she speculated, taking a closer look. The colours were wonderful. A deep turquoise ground elegantly decorated in pale green with touches of delicate pink. Fine trailing vines twined round a length of bamboo. A gilded butterfly hovered over a golden leaf. Cass realised she had been holding her breath; she let it go slowly. 'Oh, my goodness,' she whispered to herself.

Tea, she must go for tea and sit for a while. Did she dare look at the price? When she did it surprised Cass to see that it came within her (provisional) self-imposed limit. Deep in thought she took the stairs down to the level with the café. She would go to look at the vase again after her tea and if she still felt the same, she would buy it.

The waitress carefully placed the pot of earl grey and the large slice of coffee and walnut cake on the table, all neatly arranged within easy reach, smiled and withdrew.

As Cass lifted the first forkful of cake to her mouth, vaguely thinking of the wonderful cakes her Aunt Anne made, she remembered where she had seen that vase before. Cass and James, her husband, had visited Anne recently, two Sundays ago in fact. She had given them one of her teatime specials, tiny, neat sandwiches with three different kinds of homemade cake. All served on pretty bone china plates, the tea in matching cups and saucers, in her immaculate sitting room.

After that tea, while she and James were feeling too full and contented to move, Anne had brought out the family photos, as she often did. She had collected together, tucked away in an old cardboard box, a comprehensive collection of the family history. She remembered the name of every dim and crumpled image and where each fitted into the family structure.

'Look what I found tucked away in an old book. I had forgotten I even had this one,' Anne said passing over a photo that was larger and clearer than most of the others she had shown them. 'This is Kath, taken at their house not long after the wedding.'

Aunt Kath, the family mystery and legend: Cass had seen photos of her before. One that stuck in her memory showed Kath as a young woman, arm in arm with Anne, dressed in the fashion of the time. Two lovely, smiling girls striding out along a seaside promenade.

This one showed a mature woman. Cass would put her in her early thirties, well-groomed and attractive. She was sitting at a table in an elegant room. Everything about her projected poise and confidence. Beside her on the table, clear in every detail, was the vase.

The jolt of recognition made Cass feel quite fluttery. She returned the fork with its mouthful of cake to the plate while she took some slow, deep breaths to calm herself. When she felt better, she drank her first cup of tea then worked her way briskly through the cake and the second cup. She may have decided what she would do, and she wanted to get it done as quickly as possible, but she was too frugal to waste a good tea.

As soon as she had finished and dabbed her mouth with the napkin she made her way to the desk, where she informed the assistant that she would like to buy a vase she had seen in one of the cabinets on the next floor.

Following the assistant up the stairs Cass wished the woman would get a move on. She was suddenly anxious that someone else may have beaten her to it. No, it was still there. 'I would like that one please,' she said, pointing at the vase.

The woman lifted the vase carefully from the cabinet and then the two of them walked back down to the desk where the vase was bubble-wrapped and placed in a brown paper carrier bag.

At last, having paid for her prize, she had it in her hands. With great care she carried the bag back to her car and placed it on the rug she kept on the back seat, before carefully driving home

Having hurried in from the car and taken the vase from the bag, she dusted it carefully and placed it in a position of honour on her sitting room unit. For the rest of the afternoon, then again after dinner, she sat in her chair and ran through in her mind everything she knew about Aunt Kath.

Aunt Kath had been the oldest of four children. Cass's father had been the second youngest and the only boy. The family lived on a farm in rural Hampshire. Beyond that Cass didn't really know that much about the family's lives. What further information she had gleaned had been learned in dribs and drabs by listening to her parents' conversations and asking questions.

Her father and Aunts Anne and Mable had chosen marriage and conventional lives. Aunt Kath, though, had gone her own way. No one seemed very clear how she lived her life although it was known that as a very young woman, she had spent some time chauffeuring VIPs all over Europe. As a young girl Cass had gained the impression there was much more that was never discussed, not in front of her anyway.

At some time, Kath had returned to London to work for a wealthy family. Soon after she had married the son of the family. There was a glamorous church wedding and a reception in The Savoy.

Cass didn't know how successful the marriage had been; she couldn't recall anyone ever saying. She had only heard that one day Kath visited Anne and having arrived in a bad mood, they had argued. Anne never knew if that minor family tiff had been a trigger but after Kath left that day no one, family or husband, ever saw her again.

They searched for her of course. A private detective had been employed to look for her but got nowhere. Aunt Mable's husband, who was a detective in the Metropolitan Police, passed the word for everyone in the force to keep looking for her, or for any suspicious deaths – nothing.

One rumour said that she had been acquainted with a notorious London serial killer, so perhaps she had been another victim. There was another theory that, perhaps, she had moved back to live somewhere in Europe.

Many years had passed with no sight or sound of Aunt Kath but now Cass had a connection, something to bring back memories of a remarkable woman. She had found, in an antique shop in Dorking, the vase that had been on Kath's table all those years ago.

The Atlantic Wall is about 100 m (330 ft) long, 3 m (9.8 ft) high by 3.5 m (11 ft) wide. It is divided into two sections between which there were originally steel gates. Nearby are other obstacles such as dragon's teeth, reinforced concrete blocks and lengths of railway track set in concrete and with wire entanglements. Many of the relics show signs of live weapons training and the main wall has two breaches caused by demolition devices.

Things to Come

With apologies to HG Wells

by David Lowther

Mister, you may conquer the air, but the birds will lose their wonder and the clouds will smell of gasoline.
(Spencer Tracy as Henry Drummond in Inherit the Wind - 1960)

Cranleigh, Surrey March 2028

'Blimey, Mum. Look at all those trees.'

'Surrey has more trees than any other county in England,' Helen replied, looking at her daughter Jean seated next to her brother John in the back seat of their white Range Rover as they drove towards Cranleigh. Behind the wheel was the children's father Albert, a slightly overweight forty-something with a pink flush on his face and grey black hair thinning on the top of his head. His wife, Helen, by contrast looked in fine fettle and her heathy bloom on her face and slim figure disguised the fact that she was the same age as her husband. Now the children, that was a different matter. Fourteen-year-old John's face was pale with a number of nasty teenage spots in evidence. His sister, a year younger, whilst not anywhere near obese, was clearly overweight.

'Why do people keep giving us dirty looks?' John asked his dad.

'No idea,' was the reply as the car turned left before entering Cranleigh's main street.

'It's that dirty old car of ours, belching out all those poisonous fumes,' Helen told her husband.

Albert laughed. 'Got years in her yet.'

'Dad,' Jean interrupted. 'You need to get up to date and buy an electric car.'

'We'll see.'

The Range Rover drew up in the drive of a large bungalow with a tarmac drive leading to a single garage. Neatly cut, the front lawn looked immaculate.

'What are those things on the roof?' John asked.

'Solar panels,' his mother answered. 'They make sure that the house is always at the right temperature inside without having to waste electricity on heating and air conditioning.'

Albert stopped the car and a tall middle-aged man dressed in gardening clothes strolled up to them.

'Are you just moving in? he enquired.

'We are,' said Albert, 'just ahead of the removal van.'

'Welcome. I'm Duncan,' the newcomer said. 'My family and I live just over there,' he said, pointing to a smart but modest-looking detached house. 'If I can be of any help, please feel free to ask. Oh, by the way I can help with your car.'

'My car?' Albert looked at his neighbour.

'Yes. I'll drop by later with the details of an excellent scrapyard in Guildford. You should get a good price for your Range Rover.'

'But I – ' Albert began but Duncan was on his way with a smile and a wave.

'What's that, Mum?' Jean asked, pointing to a pole at the end of the drive near the garage.

'That's the charging point for electric cars,' she replied.

'But we haven't got an electric car,' John protested.

'I think we soon will have,' Helen replied with a smirk.

***

Mother led the way into the beautiful bungalow. A lounge, dining room, kitchen and cloakroom/toilet occupied the front part of the bungalow, and four bedrooms and a bathroom took up the rear.

'Hmm,' Albert said, 'it does seem rather warm but not too hot.'

'That's because of the cavity wall insulation,' his wife told him, 'and the triple-glazed windows.'

'You've thought of everything, dear.' Albert grinned at his wife.

A horn sounded outside as the electric removal van slid silently into the drive and pulled up behind the condemned Range Rover. The next two hours were spent unloading with all hands to the pump.

The Holloway family had moved from a four-bedroomed apartment in Dagenham, East London and had sold it for over a million pounds so they'd made a good profit when they bought the bungalow for just under six hundred thousand. Albert had run a flourishing second-hand car business which he'd sold for a tidy sum while Helen had been a nurse and was hoping perhaps to find some part-time work in their new neighbourhood while Albert wasn't sure what he was going to do, but neither was in desperate need of money.

Helen had been following the development of the global warming crisis with growing alarm, and the United Nations climate report of August 2021 had made her determined that she and her family would embrace the new world and do it in a healthier place than overcrowded North London. Children were learning all about the changes needed to try to ward off the catastrophe that was rapidly approaching and Jean was almost as enthusiastic as her mother. The men of the family were not quite as keen. Albert was intent on stabilising his business and, while agreeing a move to the country was the right thing to do for his family, he needed time to make sure his business sold well. After all, there was no guarantee that he would be able to grow another business from scratch elsewhere or even find a job. John, like most boys of his age, was keen on superheroes movies and video games. He liked sport as well but was never fit enough to really enjoy taking part in anything.

The Government had responded well to the approaching scenario of doom and changes were on their way, if not already established. Electric vehicles were one of these and all sorts of grants were available to make buildings more efficiently heated. In an attempt to dissuade folk from flying, passengers were heavily taxed from leaving the ground although the airline industry was pouring billions into research into more environmentally-friendly fuels. Nationally, diets were changing, and meat eating was rapidly becoming the exception rather than the rule and farmers all over the country were switching from cattle to crop farming.

***

Darkness was falling on Cranleigh as the Holloways completed the first part of setting up their new home and Helen and her daughter set off on foot to get some food.

'I'll have fish and chips,' shouted John as his mother and sister left.

'You'll be lucky,' his mother laughed.

They were back thirty minutes later, each clutching two Marks and Spencer carrier bags.

'Where's my fish and chips?' said a disappointed John.

'We asked someone in the street where the fish was and he replied in the sea,' Jean laughed.

'It's your favourite, cottage pie,' Jean said.

John nodded acceptance.

The cottage pie was delicious as was the ice cream that followed. The excellent meal was rounded off with a good old nice cup of tea.

***

'I didn't see any cows on the way in,' John observed.

'That's because most land is now taken up for growing food,' replied Helen.

'What about milk?' he persisted.

'We use other things for milk now, like oats,' his mother informed him.

'Ugh, that sounds awful,' John said pulling a face.

'How was your cup of tea, John?' his mother asked.

'Lovely, thanks.'

'Well, that was oat milk,' exclaimed Helen triumphantly.

'I suppose the ice cream was made of plants,' Jean said.

'Yes, it was.'

A period of silence followed, then all four burst out laughing.

The family worked hard over the following days, and it was Sunday night before the moving process was complete.

'What time are we setting off for school tomorrow, Dad?'

'We're not. Your mother will walk to school with you. It's only half a mile. I'm taking the car into Guildford to be scrapped.'

'What will we do for a car?' asked a fearful Jean.

'I'll get an electric one.'

'Will you give us a lift then? pleaded Jean.

'No, you'll either walk or go on your bikes. Do you good.'

Arrangements to enrol the children at Cranleigh School had already been more or less completed and Helen was going with her children the following day to complete the process. The school was one of many in the country to have recently switched from private to state owned. The boarding facilities were still in use but were now occupied by poor and disadvantaged children from towns and cities throughout the South of England.

The children were quiet when they returned from school the next evening.

'How was your day, kids?' Helen asked.

'Alright,' Jean moaned, 'but some of the girls called me Fatty.'

'And some boys called me Spotty,' John whined.

'They won't be calling you names in six months' time,' their mother assured them.

Six Months Later

Cranleigh, England's self-styled largest village, was soon to be crowned England's Greenest Village by the Secretary of State for the Environment. To celebrate the occasion, there was to be a Village Day with all sorts of activities planned. Amongst these was a Festival of Sport on the cricket field. Proud parents Albert and Helen walked from their bungalow on a beautiful late summer's day to watch their children perform. The slim and pretty young lady that Jean had become was one of the leading lights of the rounders team who were playing opposition from the neighbouring village Bramley. Handsome John, with his clean complexion and skin burnt olive by the summer sun was one of the favourites for the one-mile race around the cricket field. Albert was one of the timekeepers for the race, a function he performed on alternate Saturdays in the Park Run. On the other Saturdays, he took part in the run. He too was in much improved physical shape and the pink flush had disappeared from his cheeks though he was still thinning on top. He wasn't too proud to work on the rebuilding of Cranleigh Station in preparation for the reopening of the Guildford to Horsham railway line. Helen was, like her husband and children, very happy. She had a part-time nurse's job at the Cranleigh Medical Centre. Left on her own while her husband went off to perform his officiating duties for the mile race, she watched her children, surrounded by friends, as they excitedly prepared for their sporting afternoon in the sun. Yes, she thought to herself, I definitely made the right decision bringing us to Cranleigh.

The Eldritch Visitor

by Alan Barker

"Hi, Lisa!" I chirp as my sister's face appears on-screen.

"Kate, how are you?"

We exchange girly waves into our iPads, and I say, "You're looking tired round the peepers. Are you sleeping?"

Lisa makes a show of holding her eyes open with her fingers. "Gradually getting the hang of it again."

"Is Ged still harassing you?"

She rakes a hand through her hair. "A couple of weeks ago he turned up one evening hammering on the door, shouting he was going to fight for custody of Ben. I'm sure he'd been drinking; it really shook me up. The weird thing is, I haven't heard a dicky bird from him since. I don't know what's worse: aggressive Ged or quiet Ged."

"Perhaps he's busy looking after that mad mother of his."

Lisa grimaces. "At least I haven't got her on my case anymore, telling me how to bring Ben up. Blooming cheek—it's not as if Ged's exactly a role model."

"How is Ben?"

"Upstairs taking a nap; you Facetimed me at the right moment. He seems a bit better now his daddy's not around. I just want to see a smile back on his little face."

"Ah, bless. Gutted I can't come over though. If this lockdown doesn't end soon, I'm going to miss his first birthday."

Lisa manages a smile. "So how are things with you?"

I shrug. "Same old, same old. Going for a walk each day. Exercising at home. Missing my aikido lessons, that's for sure."

"I hear they've made face masks compulsory in public."

"Yes, Steve's been wearing his all week, even at work. He …"

I break off as Lisa cocks her head and says, "I think there's someone at the door. Hold on a mo."

She disappears from sight, and I glance at the clock: two thirty. From outside there comes the distant sound of sirens, and I wonder if there's a surge in people falling ill with the virus.

I hear a door bang and look back at my iPad, frowning; Lisa hasn't returned yet. Then a scream rings out, followed by what sounds like a thud.

"Lisa, what's happening?" I shout but there is only silence, save the renewed wailing of sirens.

I continue to stare wide-eyed at the screen – all I can see is a bare wall. Presently a jacketed arm appears; it hovers momentarily, then reaches down. The screen goes blank.

I swear vociferously. Lisa's been attacked in her own home, almost certainly leaving little Ben in danger.

I think of Ged, Lisa's intimidating ex-partner and Ben's father.

I need to act.

168

Now.

***

"Police. *Quickly!*"

I clench my teeth as I wait to be put through. *Come on!*

After what seems an eternity, a man asks for the nature of the emergency and the location.

"My sister's been attacked in her home," I say breathlessly. "I was speaking to her just now when someone came to the door and forced their way in. She's in serious danger along with her toddler. *Please* help."

"All right, madam," the man replies in a raised voice. "I'll get someone there as soon as possible. But we've a serious incident on our hands at the moment, so we're stretched to the limit."

Once I've provided the details he asks for, I end the call and ring Steve, my husband. As usual, he's 'unavailable' and I'm invited to leave a message.

"Steve, please get over to Lisa's. Someone's attacked her – I think it's Ged – and I'm worried about Ben. *Hurry!*"

***

I swing my Fiesta out of Send and onto the A247 towards Clandon, picking up speed as I cross the A3.

The roads are virtually deserted. On the local radio station, a report comes through that a group of youths has gone on the rampage in Guildford town centre, breaking shop windows and stealing goods.

I decelerate as I approach Clandon crossroads at the A25 junction. The lights are red, but I ignore them. On my left, a blue light flashes. I gasp and slam on the brakes as a police car sweeps through, heading towards Guildford. Undeterred, I set off again, booting the Fiesta up the hill and over Newlands Corner before branching right to Shere.

Soon I pull up outside Lisa's house; the journey has taken only fifteen minutes. I climb out of the car, not bothering to lock it, and take a deep breath. All seems quiet.

I let myself in through the front door and close it softly behind me. I've no idea if the intruder – who I assume is Ged – is still in the house. Equally, I don't know where Lisa or Ben are or whether they are safe.

I consider calling out their names but decide against it. I step into the sitting room which is unoccupied. Toys are scattered around the carpet, and I notice Lisa's iPad on the coffee table, the lid closed. I backtrack and try the kitchen but again no one is there.

Back in the hallway, I gaze up the stairs and listen. I detect a faint noise from one of the upstairs rooms but am unable to decipher it.

Steeling myself to be as calm as possible, I climb the stairs slowly, trying not to make a sound. As I reach the landing, the noise repeats itself and I can tell it comes from Ben's room.

Tentatively I push the door open.

"Ben!" I exclaim and rush to his cot where he stands pressed against the side.

He stares at me blankly, as if I'm a stranger.

I reach out to him but sense movement behind me. Before I can turn, an arm is thrust round my neck, almost pulling me off the floor. In the window's reflection I see a figure wearing a white face mask, baseball cap and dark leather jacket. He is brandishing something that looks horribly like a syringe.

Instinctively I grab his left forearm and we tussle as if arm-wrestling. At the same time, I force my right hand between his elbow and my neck and twist my body sharply. Summoning all my strength, I roll him round my left side and am astounded when he loses balance and pitches against the side of the cot.

I pick up Ben and rush out of the room, noticing a case half-filled with his clothes. Was Ged trying to kidnap the poor boy?

Panting, I hurry downstairs and out through the front door. Ged doesn't seem to be following – yet. I dash across the road and knock on the first door I come to.

No one appears.

I try the next door. After a few seconds an upstairs window is flung open, and a man wearing a vest shouts, "What d'you want? Don't you know there's a deadly virus going round? And why aren't you wearing a face covering?"

I start to speak but he slams the window shut. In desperation I hurry back to my car and dump Ben on the back seat, murmuring reassurances to him.

***

This time I lock it. I glance along the road but there is no traffic at all and certainly no sign of Steve or the police. I'd like to wait for someone to turn up, but I'm worried about Lisa.

I stride back to her house. Presumably she's still in there as is Ged, armed with a syringe containing ... what?

Ketamine, perhaps? I read somewhere that a substantial dose in your bloodstream can render you unconscious for at least an hour. Whatever has happened to Lisa, I desperately hope it's nothing more sinister.

I step inside, leaving the front door wide open. All is quiet again. Now I notice the door to the cupboard under the stairs is slightly ajar; I open it and peer inside. Lisa is lying in a foetal position and isn't moving. Kneeling down, I check for a pulse and breathe a huge sigh when I find it. I shake her by the shoulders, hissing her name in her ear, but she doesn't respond.

I hear a creak from the landing. Instinctively I close the cupboard door, immersing us in darkness. I've fended off Ged once but am not sure I have the strength to do it again.

The sound of unhurried footsteps comes from directly above me, descending the stairs one at a time. I stare upward, unseeingly.

I hear the front door being closed and then there is silence, save for a faint murmur from Lisa's lips.

Has Ged gone out or is he still inside? I imagine him staring through that faceless mask at little Ben, perhaps tapping the car window. Ben will be terrified, but at least the car is locked.

But my eye is drawn to the narrow gap between cupboard door and floor – a faint shadow falls across it.

Silence. I hold my breath.

Then my mobile phone bursts into life, making me jump. I snatch it from my pocket.

Steve. I hit the green button hard.

Before I can speak, the cupboard door is yanked open, and Ged grabs me by the arm and hauls me out. I scream but he knocks the phone from my hand then stamps on it and kicks it down the hallway.

He clamps his hand on my throat and eyeballs me. "Give me your car keys. *Now!*"

I stare into the black pupils of his eyes. He seems to be pulling something from his jacket pocket, but I can't see what it is. I think of the syringe.

Removing my keys, I hold them out. He releases my throat but his attempt to grab the keys is too slow, and I jab the ignition key into his eye.

He steps back and howls, clutching his face.

He's dropped the syringe and without thinking I grab it and plunge it into his thigh. Briefly he remains standing, emitting a strange keening sound, but then collapses and is still.

I wait while I get my breath back then pull off the baseball cap and face mask to check it is indeed Ged. But a mass of hair tumbles free, and I realise it isn't.

It's Irene, Ged's 'mad' mother. And Ben's grandmother.

I Saw Her Sitting on the Bench

by Martyn MacDonald-Adams

I sat beside her on the bench
By the water
She didn't mind minding the cold
Feeding the ducks
And laughing
Her smile burnt into my soul

It was then my love for her sparked
Like an ember
That December
But I guarded my heart from regret
For on her finger
The heart's armour of gold
...and they were trying hard
For September

I saw her many times through spring
My heart silent in pain
In summer, I heard her husband sing
And was jealous
A little insane

Then I saw her in a newsreel
Unfolding I saw the scene
Husband drunk at the wheel
Her eyes in silent scream...

I saw her again when out walking
Her sad smile burnt through my soul
We sat on the bench by the water
And in her arms
Her baby daughter
But now on her finger
No armour of gold

174

Now I avoid that bench when out walking
With its shadows, that burn into my soul
For her misty eyes could not cry
They could not now
Mind the cold
And her spectral smile of hollow sorrow
Will haunt me forever
For no more for her
Her baby daughter
Or tomorrow

Waverley Abbey was the very first monastery founded in Britain by the reforming Cistercian religious order. A small group of monks from France settled in this quiet spot by the River Wey in 1128, and Waverley soon became the springboard for Cistercian settlement in southern England. The impressive remains include the fine 13th century vaulted refectory or dining hall for the lay brothers, the Cistercians' labour force.

You Pushed Me!

by Ian Honeysett

'Ouch! That hurts,' I mumbled to myself as I stood in the packed railway carriage. I was already feeling pretty fed up when the train had arrived at Farncombe station missing half its usual carriages. A 45-minute journey to London Waterloo which could only get worse as more commuters would undoubtedly pile on at Guildford and Woking. The one, very slight positive thought was that I had to change at Clapham Junction. Assuming I could force my way through to the doors of course. I was already two rows back and it seemed unlikely that anyone would get out before London.

And it was hot and, well, rather smelly. In fact, very smelly. Not like your typical commute since they had stopped smoking carriages some years before. Now those really were awful for me as a non-smoker. My wife was a nurse and had warned the children about the dangers of cigarettes to the extent that none of them would ever dare to smoke. She had also described the dangers of passive smoking so that, when I'd had little option but to sit in a smoking carriage, I dreaded having to stop breathing in for a full 45 minutes.

My nicotine daydreaming was rudely interrupted, however, by another sharp jab in my side. I tried looking around in case I was impaled on someone's brolly but saw nothing. I tried shifting a little but there was no real room for manoeuvre in this sardine tin on wheels.

'Guildford, this is Guildford,' came the announcement. Was someone going to escape? I could see that everyone was looking just a bit hopeful, but no one moved. The doors parted. A sea of hopeful faces looked in from the platform, but they quickly abandoned any hope of entering here. The doors closed with a thud.

'Ouch!' There it was again. Something was digging into my side. Not just a brief jab but a prolonged screwing motion. This time I managed to look around properly. I soon saw a rather scruffy-looking bloke who was undoubtedly attached to that annoyingly bony elbow. Another mystery was quickly solved: the origin of the disgusting smell that filled at least this part of the carriage.

I looked him in the eye, seeking some explanation for his aggressive behaviour if not for his actual existence.

He stared back and cleared his throat. It was not a pleasant sound. At least he hadn't broken wind. Ah, spoke too soon.

'You pushed me!' he coughed. 'You pushed me!' he repeated for emphasis.

'Sorry?' I asked, quite reasonably I thought.

'When we got on at Farncombe. You pushed me.'

'But everyone was pushing,' I explained. 'We were all trying to get on a packed train.' I looked around for some sign of moral support, but no one would meet my eye. They were all clearly so relieved that he'd chosen to accuse *me* of pushing.

He continued to elbow me with even greater determination.

'Yea, but you pushed me, see. I don't (several expletives deleted) care if you pushed one of these other (further expletives deleted – some of them actually quite imaginative). Fact is, *you* pushed *me*!'

'Look… (what should I call him? Old chap? Moosh? You rotting piece of garbage? I decided that might not reduce tensions somehow). Look, my friend, if I did somehow push you then I'm sorry. It was certainly not intentional.' He looked dubious. 'So please would you now remove your elbow from my side?'

I could see he was creasing my rather smart suit. I was on my way to an important business meeting in Wimbledon. I certainly had no wish to take any imprint from him into that gathering. Visual or olfactory.

'Woking, this is Woking.' Was it too much to hope that this unshaven, unwashed, unloved (or is that somewhat harsh?) miscreant might alight at Woking? I'd seen a few like him wandering around the town centre in the past. Was he beginning to move? My hopes began to rise though I braced myself for some unpleasant gesture from him before he disappeared from my life. But no. He stayed put although a couple of others did get off. It meant that I was able to step back a little making it now rather difficult for him to continue his elbonic assault. However, it did not stop him from occasionally muttering those ageless words, 'You pushed me!'

Before long, we were arriving at Clapham Junction. My stop. At last, I could breathe again in every sense of the word. I made my way towards the doors and stepped off. I was sorely tempted to utter some parting words but thought better of it. We Godhelmians are above that sort of thing after all.

I stood on the platform and made my way up the stairs. Freedom! Now I could start to think about my meeting. Perhaps, on reflection, this might make an interesting anecdote for down the pub. Even a short story?

'You pushed me!' What? Were those words so firmly fixed in my subconscious that I could still hear them? But no! There he was! He had got off at Clapham Junction as well! And he was desperately trying to overtake me. Suddenly I had the most terrifying image possible: of him following me into my meeting! How on earth could I lose him? There was no way he could actually be heading for Wimbledon, surely? Surely?

And now, somehow, he had overtaken me and was standing in front of me. His grizzled face just inches from mine. As luck would have it, we were of similar height. Why wasn't I tall like my son? Then I could look down at him and maybe just chest him out the way. I braced myself for the next verbal onslaught. His face was contorted in such a way that I knew he was about to say something. But would he now think of something different? Something even wittier?

'You pushed me!' he said in a rather threatening tone. And, in case I hadn't heard him, he repeated, 'You pushed me.'

The thought struck me that this was unlikely to end happily. And I'd only just bought these glasses. They were varifocal and photochromatic and had been quite expensive. Should I remove them in case he took a swing at me? Or might that appear to be provocative – as though I was getting ready for a fight? Now I don't consider myself a natural fighter, but I had always been something of a wrestling fan. Which moves could I recall? A forearm smash of course. Probably not a dropkick as that might spoil my suit. A knee to the groin maybe?

He just stood his ground, albeit a little unsteadily, and uttered those chilling words, 'You won't get rid of me easily, mate. 'Spect you're off to some meeting? We'll, I'm coming with you.'

I really had no idea what to do next. I offered up a brief prayer.

Then a very different voice chipped in. A rich, mellifluous voice. Caribbean, I thought. Surely, he wasn't a ventriloquist?

'Now then,' it continued, 'we don't want any trouble, do we?'

It came from somewhere behind me.

Was it a railway policeman?

I turned around and beheld a tall, black man in a white suit. I kid you not. An immaculate white suit.

He smiled at us both and put a long arm around my nemesis and calmly steered him away along the platform. As they both disappeared, he turned around and smiled at me once more.

And that was the last time I saw either of them. But, as I continued walking, this time with a bit of a skip in my step, I reflected on the fact that I had just met my Guardian Angel!

Wanborough Great Barn is the oldest and most important wooden building in Surrey, Sussex and Hampshire. Built in 1388 by the Cistercian monks of Waverley Abbey and used for storing and processing crops and fleeces.

Steeple Jack

by Paul Rennie

In 1920, a few lucky Godalming townsfolk were treated to a free live spectacle. Others had to wait and pay to see the Pathé News clip of the remarkable event described as "*A Daring Prank.*" Mr. C.L. Ager, a renowned steeplejack, climbed freestyle to the top of St Peter and Paul Church's 147 feet spire, purportedly to rescue the Vicar's handkerchief, although God knows how it got there in the first place. Whilst up there, he played to the crowds below, waving to them and putting his hat on the weathercock. The whole thing smacks of a publicity stunt, although for what, we will never know.

Our story, however, is about a modern-day Jack, and his own escapades on that very same church steeple.

If you have ever wondered about the type of person who would steal lead from church roofs for a living, then Jack Pritchard was that sort. Possessed of low cunning, he was a thoroughly despicable individual, light-fingered, opportunistic and without a shred of human decency. His Headmaster's comments in the final school report provided a glimpse into the boy's character, when he wrote: "*With his skills, Jack will always make a living, although it is unlikely to be an honest one. It is our pleasure to see him move on to adulthood, and no doubt Her Majesty's pleasure in the future.*" After an adolescence of petty crime, he eventually found gainful employment, as a window cleaner, specialising in high buildings that required abseiling, rope work and a head for heights. However, he soon got fed up with working for other people, and with the wage squeezing from East European competition, so he looked for another career. After a brief spell using his climbing skills as a cat burglar, he moved into the recycling business and now owned a scrapyard on the outskirts of Aldershot, where unwanted, and sometimes wanted, metal of any value would end up. He was ideally suited to this line of work, as he was, to use a cliche, bent as a nine-bob note – a nine-shilling note that had been printed back-to-front on a photocopier, using refilled ink cartridges of the wrong colour.

Jack was not interested in steel or base metals; he wanted copper, lead, or better still, the valuable rarer elements used in modern appliances. His business was largely built on cash payments to rather shady suppliers of metals of dubious and questionable origin. Many a bronze garden ornament or lengths of copper cable stamped with railway identification logos had found their way into his stock. Unfortunately, for his mode of doing business, the laws on cash payments for scrap metal had been tightened up, requiring proper documentation and payment via traceable routes. As a result, his sources of lucrative scrap had all but dried up. He had to find an alternative supply chain, and the best and most profitable way to do this was to source the scrap metal without a middleman. In other words, go out and pinch it himself. In summer of 2018, there was a sudden spate of catalytic converters going missing from parked cars in the Surrey Hills area. Owners would leave their fully working cars and return to find that, when they started them, there was a frightful noise and a whole array of warning lights on the dashboard. They were faced with a huge bill for a replacement unit to be fitted. They had had a visit from Jack and his angle grinder, who had made off with about £50 worth of platinum and rhodium contained within their missing emission control systems.

There was only a certain amount of rare metal that Jack could shift before attracting unwelcome attention, so he was forced to diversify. He turned his attention to lead. He liked dealing with lead. There was something about its soft flexibility and low melting point that made it easy to disguise the source, and it was heavy, and he loved the way a small pile spun the dial on the scrap dealers' scales to register the value of his illicit haul. An added benefit was that there was almost no sound when he threw the rolled up sheets down from the roof which he was stripping.

Best of all it was everywhere, often in remote unguarded places, from where it could be liberated discreetly from its owners. Churches were his favourite. No one lived in them, they were often in remoter villages, and not designed with security in mind. Also, they were often built in times when alternative rainwater systems didn't exist. In other words, they had lots of lovely lead in sheets on roofs, flashing around joints, and even forming the gutters, pipes and water channels.

If the unfortunate car owners had faced large bills for replacement of their exhaust systems, it was as nothing compared to the disproportionate damage caused by Jack's removal of lead from the roofs of buildings. Usually, the damage was not noticed by the owners of the buildings until it rained, and then it was too late. Irreplaceable church fixtures and fittings were destroyed, the loss exacerbated by the astronomical expense of repairing the damage to listed buildings, where you can't just nip to the builders' merchants for a roll of lead flashing and get the local roofer to stick it back on. All this financial hurt for the sake of the few pounds that Jack would net from his nocturnal visits.

In autumn of that year, he was out searching for targets in the Godalming area, a region rich in church architecture. He had already checked out the church at Hambledon, but someone else had got to the lead in the past, and security had been tightened up after the repairs. He wandered into Godalming town and cast his eyes on the magnificent steeple of St Peter and Paul Church across the water meadows. The spire was constructed in the 14th century and from some angles has a slightly crooked appearance, something it had in common with Jack. He admired the proportions of the main building and its Bargate stonework, but most of all he admired the quantity of lead that covered the steeple, arranged with raised chevrons rising up each segment to the peak. That was a lot of lead. He couldn't possibly make off with all of it in one go, but he'd have a good try. The problem was that the church was in the middle of town in a very prominent position, and it was illuminated by floodlights. It wouldn't be easy to do his work without attracting attention. He would have to wait for a moonless foggy night. Fortunately for him, the low-lying Lammas lands around the church and the neighbouring River Wey provided the right conditions, and the tower was frequently cloaked in mist.

At the end of October, the conditions were just right. A cold dark foggy night, and at two o'clock in the morning, there was not a soul around. He parked his pick-up truck at the top of Church Street, and wearing a black greatcoat for warmth and camouflage, and with his special climbing shoes, he hung his tool bag over his shoulder. The first part, getting onto the main roof was easy for someone with his climbing skills, and with its thoughtfully positioned drainpipes. No anti-climb paint or razor wire to cope with here. He now had full access to the roof of the nave and transepts. Next, he climbed the square base of the tower, which had a convenient balustrade below the steeple itself. He ignored the lead dressing that sealed all the joints in the roof. He was after bigger prey, and the thought of peeling off those huge sheets of lead on the steeple was too delicious to ignore. But first, he had to deal with the floodlights that were fixed to the roof and angled to illuminate the spire, and him if he ignored them. He took out his special hooked knife and cut a two-foot square of lead sheet from a gutter. The lead was soft and easy to cut through. He took the square and placed it over the floodlight furthest from the road and folded it around the lens. He now had a side of the roof that was completely dark, and this was where he was going to climb up. Any nosy person, even if they could see through the mist, would assume that a floodlight had failed.

The spire was exceptionally steep, but for him, rather easy to climb because the raised welts of lead offered almost ladder-like footholds, and all he had to do was hold on to the rolled ridges that were fixed at the joint of each external angle. Within minutes he had reached the summit, and because of the fog it was like sitting on a cloud, with the town and church below him totally obscured. He could see the lights of Guildford in the distance, but no one could see him. Just above him was the weathercock, the very one that Mr. Ager had placed his hat on. The cockerel was a lot bigger than it had looked from the ground and was beautifully wrought in gilded copper standing above a cross. He studied it and, ever the opportunist, decided that this would make a more valuable prize than a similar quantity of lead. He could get a good price for it, and if he could get it off, would still have time to fill his pick-up with enough lead to make it a good night's work. Below the cross there was a metal threaded post, like a spike, cemented into the top of the spire, with a lead covered disc about a foot in diameter sealing the base. A large collar nut attached the thread of the base of the weathercock to the post. He took out a wrench from his tool bag and tried it on the stiff nut. Luckily, someone had greased it for maintenance reasons, and it was not too badly corroded. It squeaked a bit, but he was able to slowly turn the nut until it was almost free from the spike. He had to be careful now, as it was probably very heavy and he didn't want it tumbling down the spire, especially because of the noise it might make. Just to be sure, he tied a short piece of rope to the cockerel's leg and the other end around the base of the spike. It needed to be lifted vertically to free the bolt from the spike, something he couldn't do from below. He climbed up to a precarious position on the very top of the spire, with his feet on the disc of lead and his legs straddling the spike. He took a deep breath, gripped the spike with his knees, and lifted the weathercock clear of its support. For a brief moment, he looked like an FA Cup winning captain hoisting the trophy. He hadn't expected it to be quite so heavy, so heavy in fact that the lead edges of the disc that he was standing on started to distort under the combined weight of felon plus ornamental feature.

There was another short moment when Jack thought he might still recover the situation, before his legs started to buckle, followed by excruciating agony as he impaled his nether regions on the spike that he had exposed. Vlad the Impaler couldn't have done a better job. Jack let out a scream like a soprano, only a pitch higher, and the weathercock dropped from his grasp and hung upside down dangling on the rope below him. Both sounds were absorbed by the blanket of fog, and the good townsfolk slept on, oblivious to the drama on the steeple. Mercifully for Jack, he passed out from the pain, and remained limply yet firmly secured to the spire in place of the weathercock. If there was any upside at all to Jack's terrible predicament it was that he was so firmly planted on the metal rod that he didn't fall down the roof to certain death. As it was, he was in for a long and miserable night. During his occasional moments of consciousness, he screamed for help, but the fog and his chosen hour, that had initially aided his larceny attempt, were now preventing discovery. So, there he stayed.

The next day dawned, and it was still foggy, so at first nobody noticed anything unusual. Gradually, as the sun rose, the mist started to clear, slowly revealing a strange sight. A few commuters heading for the nearby station were first to see it and were joined by the Vicar opening up for morning service. They could see something black at the top of the spire, but the mist kept coming and going, so it was difficult to make out. A young woman in a smart red wool coat suggested it might be a black plastic bin liner that had got caught. Others thought it looked more like a figure, perhaps a scarecrow or maybe a Guy Fawkes dummy. After all it was Halloween and the fifth of November was round the corner. Someone else suggested that perhaps Godalming College students had put it up there as a prank, although their end of term antics usually involved half-heartedly throwing eggs and flour around. New bystanders appeared, while some early comers drifted off to catch their trains. The mist cleared a little more, and the gathering group could all now see that it was a figure dressed in dark clothing and had an arm sticking out as if beckoning the audience, reminiscent of Captain Ahab in the final scenes of *Moby Dick*. As they stared up, there was a slight gust of wind that blew away the remaining wisps of mist. They could now see its face, albeit a very unhappy one, and that it was a real person in that precarious and unnatural position. While they were taking this in, another gust of wind blew, and caught the coat of the unconscious and novel weathercock replacement. Slowly it rotated in the breeze so that the outstretched arm swung round with it and pointed due south. It was going to be a fine sunny day in Godalming.

As soon as the bystanders agreed that it was a real person who was in trouble, the fire brigade was summoned, and they arrived in a near record time of four minutes from the station in Bridge Street, a time only beaten by a run the previous evening when they had realised the kebab shop at the top of the town was about to close. Unfortunately, in spite of their best efforts, their ladder could not reach the top of the spire, so a cherry picker crane had to be called, adding another three hours to Jack's ordeal. Finally, just after lunchtime he was extricated by a workman cutting through the spike, the rest of which accompanied Jack to the hospital. You might have thought that that was the end of Jack, but the human body is remarkably robust, even with such a nasty and unusual injury. After a long and painful operation, the surgeons were able to separate Jack from bits that weren't his, and put him back together, although he had to endure rather distasteful "*wrecked'em*" jokes from a few of the more hardened members of staff. The surgical procedures may have been challenging but were far less of a challenge than the one Jack's legal team would face in Guildford Crown Court when trying to explain why he was on the church roof in the first place, and the presence of suspicious metals at his scrapyard. After the trial, with its inevitable custodial sentence, he was even forced to return the offending length of rod, the only metal that he'd succeeded in taking from the church on that autumn night in Godalming. Sadly, Pathé News no longer produces newsreels, but the smartphone cameras and subsequent viral YouTube clips ensured that Jack achieved far more publicity than the daring prank of the illustrious Mr. C.L. Ager.

The Woman in Front

by Pauline North

The woman in front of Janet in the small shop unloaded an armful of clothes onto the counter. The assistant greeted her with a smile, then began folding the items one by one and ringing them into the till. 'This one will suit you, Mrs Markham. The colours are just right for you.' Then, 'The tropical pattern on this one would be perfect for your cruise.'

While she was waiting, the customer browsed the array of scarves and pretty leather bags arranged at the end of the counter, adding a handbag and two scarves to her purchases. Janet observed the customer; her total assurance, her slightly condescending way of speaking to the assistant.

When two bulging carrier bags were stacked, side by side, on the counter, the assistant calmly quoted the final price. Janet's eyes widened in surprise; she had to remind herself that the bags had been crammed full with items. Then she glanced down at the cut-price remnant she was holding, the one that had so delighted her when she found it in the basket. The customer passed her card over the counter, chatting about how happy she had been with the things she had bought on her last visit. With a cheery goodbye, she took the bags and left the shop.

The assistant turned expectantly, looking for her next customer. Seeing Janet disappearing into the racks of hanging dresses and coats, she called out, 'Sorry to keep you waiting. Can I help you?'

'No, thank you, not yet. I think I'll have more of a look round first.'

Janet ignored the nagging voice of conscience telling her not to spend money on things she didn't need. She explained to herself that she would only look. Surely that wouldn't hurt. When she took the two dresses into the changing room, she was only going to try them. She wanted to see if the style suited her. Looking in the mirror at each of them in turn, Janet pulled in her belly, twisting, this way and that to see the effect from all angles. Yes, with summer on the way, she would lose the few pounds needed to make the dresses a perfect fit. Of course, she would.

At the counter, she handed the remnant to the assistant. 'I've decided not to take this, but I will take these.' With the two dresses placed in a bag, Janet felt her heart rate pump up a notch. What if she changed her mind now? Even if Janet only took one of them, she would look such a fool, although not as much though as if she couldn't pay. No, it would be alright, pay the bill and leave. That's all she had to do.

The assistant had told Janet the total and was waiting for payment. Janet fumbled for her purse and handed over a card.

After a few seconds, the assistant handed back the card. 'I'm sorry, this card has been refused.' Her face was impassive. 'Perhaps you have another?'

'How silly of me, I've closed that account. I should have cut up the card. Here, this is the one.' She passed over another card and punched in her pin. She waited, struggling to appear unconcerned, fighting back the panic and the urge to drop everything, run away and never come back. For what seemed an endless time, she waited, expecting to be told that card had also failed. It was alright. At last, her card was being passed back to her. The assistant was smiling and wishing her a good day.

On a wave of relief, she picked up the carrier. With her dresses safely inside, she breezed out of the door. Now she was feeling exhilarated. It was a beautiful spring day with some warmth to the sunlight, a walk and a sit by the river would finish off her shopping trip in style.

Instead of turning left for the shop's car park Janet went in the opposite direction, towards where the Tillingbourne River flowed under the road. She walked along, thinking how pretty Shere was that day, even though the traffic was chaotic, as usual. She turned left off the pavement to walk along the riverbank, away from the road where the cars struggled to force their way through the gridlock on the narrow street. As Janet strolled along, she looked for a quiet spot to sit. On the first bench a solitary man was taking in the peace, watching the river. On the next one a mother talked on her mobile while her children played on the grass. At the far end the last bench was empty. Janet thankfully lowered herself onto the sun-warmed wooden slats.

Thrilled with her purchases, she peered into the bag. She had never bought anything in that shop, apart from an occasional piece of fabric. She told herself that the prices had been quite reasonable.

That was when her conscience kicked in. '*True, the prices were not bad at all in isolation*', said the voice in her head, '*but how about those shoes you bought last week and that handbag?*' Janet did her best to ignore the voice but it wasn't going to give up. '*You don't stop, do you? What was the limit on that credit card, the one you maxed out, or for that matter the one you used to pay for those dresses? How do you think you can pay that lot off? It's impossible. You're in trouble.*'

She wanted to wrap her arms around her head and cry, scream out all her shame. Instead, she stared unseeingly at the gentle ripples catching the sunlight so prettily. Perhaps she could ask her ex-husband for help. The bastard could afford it. That new woman must be costing him enough, so why not just a little for her. No, there would be no help there.

A bank loan, if she could get enough to cover the debt, then she would pay it all off and never allow herself to get in this position again. She didn't need all those new things. She didn't get out much now after all.

Full of new resolve, Janet gathered herself together. Her first move would be to go back and try to get a refund on the dresses.

Anyone watching Janet retrace her steps would have seen a rather plump woman in late middle age striding purposefully away from the river. As she got closer to the turning that led to the shop, her footsteps slowed and became hesitant. She turned right and took the few steps to the shop door. She stopped, reached out a hand and almost opened the door, but then the hand that reached out withdrew. The hand clutching the carrier bag containing two dresses tightened its grip. Janet stepped away from the door.

By the time she reached the car park, she was almost running. Once inside the car, Janet sat quietly for a while, then she started the engine and drove calmly away.

***

In the weeks and months that passed, Janet tried, but failed, to get a loan from her bank. Her credit rating was too low. She fell further and further behind with her credit card payments. Every threatening letter she received from them caused her to panic, to cry for hours or to drink until she forgot the awful anxiety. She could sometimes be seen on the street where she lived, staggering along, bottle in hand, shouting and swearing at adversaries only she could see.

It was a chill afternoon in October. Thick purple clouds rolled across the sky, threatening a stormy evening. The expensive new people carrier, belonging to Janet's ex-husband, turned off the country lane and stopped in front of the house he shared with his new love. The two people inside had failed to notice the car, parked in the shadows, on the road outside their gates. Both of them went to the boot to unload the bags of shopping. If they hadn't stopped for a lingering kiss, they might have had time to walk away and reach the safety of the house.

Janet had turned on her engine as her husband's car turned onto the drive. It took no time at all for her small car to rocket through the gates. She caught both of them square on, full force, where they stood behind the car. Their broken bodies crumpled into the boot. She crunched into reverse, swerving erratically back towards the road. She hadn't bothered to look in her rear-view mirror so one of her swerves caught the gatepost, hard, causing considerable damage.

Ignoring the fact that the top half had collapsed onto the roof of her car she changed gear to first, then took another run, foot hard on the floor.

The small car hit with enough force to rock the smart, new people carrier. The two cars became one mangled wreck. The explosion as one of the fuel tanks ignited lit up the cold October sky.

The Body

by Ian Honeysett

It had been a very good concert. Perhaps a little loud but it did help that I was serving in the bar most of the time so that there were two quite solid walls between the music and me. But I'd enjoyed it. I was a volunteer barman at the concerts my friend organised in the local church. As a desultory "strummer" myself, it was enlightening if very humbling to see and hear "real musicians" playing. I needed song-sheets for the chords. How on earth did they remember all those notes? Not to mention the words?

Anyway, I was now wending my way home through Farncombe, ready for a nice hot mug of tea. I'd only had one or two during the show. And a Mars bar, of course. So, I was ready to relax. Maybe catch a horror film.

I was just nearing the corner of my road when I saw it on the edge of the pavement. It looked in the dark like a bundle of old clothes. Now this really does get my goat. People just dumping stuff on the roadside. It recalled the wise words I'd once heard at my daughter's graduation. 'I've just two pieces of advice to give all those graduating today," he said. "Be kind to others and, if you see someone dropping litter, shoot them." Unfortunately, I wasn't armed at that moment.

But, as I drew near, I could hear groaning. I edged nervously closer. I bent over the shape and could see that it was actually a body. Knees drawn up to his chest. A young-ish male. I knew I couldn't just ignore him thinking he'd get up when he was ready. He might have had an accident. Cars did speed down the main road at quite a lick. As a keen cyclist, I'd often had to pull into the kerb to let them through.

194

So, I said, 'Are you OK?'

No reply other than more groans.

'Have you …. had an accident?'

No reply, just even louder groans.

'Can I…. call you an ambulance?'

I could see that the chance of a conversation was rather limited. So maybe I should call an ambulance? I bent down and the smell of alcohol hit me. He was almost certainly drunk. And there was another smell too. A pretty strong one. Weed. Not that he'd 'weed' himself – though that couldn't be ruled out - but cannabis. Hash. No wonder he was lying there on the pavement. Drunk and drugged. Maybe just let him sleep it off?

I started to walk away. He'd be OK. No need to worry. Almost certainly he'd be gone when I returned this way in the morning to buy a newspaper.

'Please help me! Please help me!'

So, he *was* conscious. Perhaps he was hurt after all? I knew I couldn't just carry on home now.

I returned with a heavy heart. How could I help him?

'What's the matter?' I asked. 'Have you had an accident?'

'No,' he mumbled. 'I've been attacked.'

'Are you hurt?'

'Of course I'm hurt. I've been attacked.'

He started to move. I watched transfixed as, very slowly, he managed to sit up. Clearly it was taking him a great deal of effort. Eventually, he was sitting in a slumped sort of way.

He turned around and looked up at me. I moved back a little. I've heard of passive smoking so what about passive weed inhalation? I didn't feel totally safe now. I wasn't that fit but, even so, I reckoned I could just about outrun him in his current state. But he might see where I lived. No, I had to stay and see what I could do to help in some way.

'I was in the field back there,' he said pointing in the general direction of the recreation ground – or 'Rec' - behind my house. It was a children's playground among other things, but I could often hear voices coming from it at night.

I had mentioned it to a neighbour who had observed – probably correctly – that it was 'druggies'. He seemed quite certain about this. 'Oh yes, druggies all right. That's where they do their dealing.'

'How do you know?' I enquired.

'Oh, it's obvious,' he replied. 'Ideal for dealing drugs. Obvious.'

I hadn't enquired further. I hadn't wanted to show too much interest in case he assumed I was looking for a convenient place to get my supply. Not that I was. Of course.

So, back to my figure on the kerbside. I could just about make out his face now. Probably in his twenties. Stubbly. I didn't recognise him. I wasn't sure what to say next. Other than that, it wouldn't be an invite to come back to my place to sober up. Or whatever you do when you've inhaled too much.

'Yea,' he said,' filling the conversational pause. 'I know who it was.'

'You do?'

'Yea. I've had trouble with him before. Nasty piece of work.'

'What did he do to you?'

'We were talking, and he said I owed him. I said I didn't. Then he hit me. Hard.'

'This was over there in the ....'

'Yea. Just by the swings. And.... know what? Yea, he's only gone and swiped my watch! Nice watch too. Worth a bit. And.... yea. He's taken my phone! He's only gone and taken my phone. The....'

I've omitted some of the rather colourful language he used. Some of it quite new to me, I admit. Perhaps it was the drink – or drugs – talking.

There was a silence while I tried to think of a reply I wouldn't regret.

'Maybe,' he said at last, 'I dropped my phone. Maybe it's still there. Maybe *you* could help me look?'

The thought, to be honest, didn't appeal. It was late – about 10.00 at night. It was cold and starting to rain. Not surprisingly, the 'Rec' was unlit. The chances of finding his phone, if he had dropped it, were pretty much zero.

'Have you got a mobile?' he asked. He was starting to get up. Very slowly. Twice he slipped back on the wet grass. Another burst of swearing. Some of these words I had heard before.

'Why, yes,' I replied hesitantly. Maybe I shouldn't have admitted it.

'Then maybe you can use the torch and we can see if my phone's still there? I can't go home without it.'

197

As I say, the idea did not appeal. My rather old phone did have a light but a pretty weak one. And it really was quite a large 'Rec'. On the other hand, he was clearly not going to leave without at least looking for his phone. It seemed the only way out.

'OK. Let's see if we can find it. Any idea whereabouts you might have dropped it?'

'Yea, probably by the swings. That's where we....'

'OK, let's look there.'

By now he was back on his feet but trembling wildly. There seemed little chance he could actually make it to the 'Rec'. But, much to my surprise, he started to stumble forwards. I decided it was best not to let him hold on to me. Best for me, that is.

Very erratically, we made our way down the narrow passage beside the nearest house. The ground was now quite slippery.

'Argh...' he shouted. 'My shoe's come off.'

I pointed my phone down at the mud and saw it there. I wasn't too keen to pick it up but realised there was no way he would be able to do so let alone put it back on. If he tried, it would take most of the night and I was suddenly feeling very tired. This was not the ending to a busy evening that I had anticipated.

I picked up the muddy, stinking plimsoll and took a deep breath as I aimed it at his foot and saw his sock was hanging off and was very wet. I reached out hesitantly to help pull it back on but without success. In fact, my clumsy efforts only had the effect of almost making him topple over.

'Give it here!' he shouted. 'You're useless, you are! Have you never put a shoe on before?'

Much to my amazement, he bent down, grabbed the shoe and, somehow, forced it back on his foot. Much more effectively than I could ever have done. Then he suddenly grabbed my phone. I feared the worst. Should I attempt to wrestle it back? This wasn't going to turn out well. Maybe he'd decided I was so hopeless that he'd keep it in exchange for the one he'd lost.

But instead, he aimed it down at the ground and we spent the next five minutes examining the grass around the swings. I thought to myself, give it a few more minutes and then he'd realise it was hopeless and we'd give it up as a bad job.

Then I saw something in the long grass. I bent down and picked up a small bottle. Fortunately, empty.

'Have you found it? Have you found my phone?'

'Afraid not. Just a bottle.'

'Anything in it?'

'No, it's empty.'

'Pity. I could do with a drink.'

I thought but didn't say that I could too. How I needed that cup of tea.

But then, he whooped, 'Hey, that's it! There, that's my phone!'

He bent down and picked something up. I was dreading what it might be. But it actually *was* his phone! Unbelievable.

'Yea, it's my phone all right. How about that? He didn't take it. Mind you, when I catch him, I'll make him pay. Oh yes. He's not getting away with this.'

He straightened up. He also seemed to have sobered up a little though the smell of weed was as strong as ever. I must admit I was now feeling extremely nervous. We were standing in the middle of the 'Rec' in pitch darkness – apart from the dull glow of my mobile. He now seemed more in control but was still high on drugs and drink. And he had my phone. Should I try to grab it and make a run for it? My house was quite nearby. Or maybe buy a new phone and just make a run for it? Or maybe….

'Well, best be getting home,' he said.

'Where's home?' I asked.

'Woking, of course. What's the time, mate?'

I looked at my watch.

'Quarter to eleven.'

'Should be able to make the last train.'

'Are you sure?' I asked, regretting it as soon as the words left my mouth.

'Yea, feel much better now. Should be OK. But when I see that bloke (my words) he'll be sorry he messed with me. Oh yes. I'll do him I will. He'll be sorry he messed with me, he will. Anyway, thanks mate. Here's your phone back.'

I accepted it gladly.

I watched him stumble off in the general direction of Farncombe station. Should I offer to go with him? No, he looked much better now. And was quite determined. I followed him at a distance out of the 'Rec' and he seemed to know where he was heading. There was still time, I reckoned, for him to make the last train. Surely. Yes, he didn't need me.

I was just about to head back to my home when he suddenly stopped and turned around. Once again, the nerves kicked in. Was part two of this encounter about to begin? And I'd thought that that cup of tea was now only minutes away.

He stopped, still some distance away.

'Fancy some weed, mate?' he shouted. 'I owe you.'

'I thought you'd never ask!' I replied.

Legend has it that the Betchworth Castle is haunted by a black dog that prowls the ruins at night, and the Lord of the Manor who allegedly chased and killed an escaping convict with his sword. He later found out that it was in fact his own son he had killed and is said to now walk around the ruins in regret!

Humphrey, Jeffrey & Godfrey: The Flood

by Martyn MacDonald-Adams

"Humpy! Humpy! Humpy! I can't get to sleep."

Humphrey tried to turn over, but his right ear refused to let him.

"Humpy! Humpy! Humpy! I can't get to sleep."

The voice interrupted Humphrey's dream of eating a roast lamb dinner with oodles of gravy, crispy roast potatoes, a steamed cauliflower covered in lemon sorbet, curried carrots, and baked beans with bacon-flavoured ice cream. All served up on a very large, very soft, chocolate digestive marshmallow. He opened one eye, half hoping for the Yorkshire pudding and custard dessert, but not only was he chewing the corner of his pillow, someone was pulling hard on his right ear.

That's when he saw the silhouette of the little teddy bear standing over him.

"Phwu! Phwu! Curried carrots? Wha... what time is it?" said the slightly less little and significantly older bear.

"I don't know, but I can't sleep."

For a moment Humphrey imagined that he had been fully awake at the dinner table and only now was he just dropping into a surreal dream. He glanced at the clock on the bedside table. It displayed **03:23**.

"It's night-time. Go to bed."

"I can't."

Humphrey pulled himself up and rubbed his eyes. "Uh! Why not?"

"It's raining."

"It's been raining for days. Go to bed." He rubbed his nose and sniffed.

"Awww. But I don't want to."

"Why not? Do you want to snuggle up next to me?" He rubbed his ears.

"Yes please!" And with that, Godfrey jumped under the covers beside Humphrey.

Squish!

"Wha... Wha... You're all wet! Yeuch! Get out!"

"Awww. I don't want to."

"Why are you all wet?"

"Because of the rain."

"It's been raining for days..." Humphrey paused. Apart from the steamed cauliflower covered in lemon sorbet, there was something else amiss here. "Have you been outside?"

"No."

"Why not?"

"It's raining."

Humphrey decided that it was most important to get this little bear dry and back into his own bed. Besides, he wanted to know more about the baked-bean-and-bacon-flavoured ice cream. With great patience he got up, sighed, put his favourite pink bunny slippers on then led Godfrey, by his paw, back to his bedroom. He opened the door.

203

It was raining.

"See? I told you. It's raining."

"It shouldn't be raining *in* your bedroom, Godfrey. We live underground, under another building. The roof is waterproof. Unless..." A cold shiver ran down his spine.

Or it might have been a big drip from the ceiling.

Humphrey rushed into the living room and made a dash for the periscope. There was no view of the bowling green above; it was black outside, but then, at this time of night that was to be expected. He threw a switch, and the outside spotlight came on. The scene that drifted across the eyepiece looked like leafy bits of mint sauce dissolved in a dark, misty brown gravy, but from the dinner plate's point of view. There was no sign of the hedge and grass that should have been there. A twig drifted past the field of view, pretending to be a cartwheeling balloon. Then a big, round, silver eye appeared and stared back at Humphrey.

Surprised, the bear stood back, then stepped forward and looked again. It was a fish's eye alright. As it drifted away from the periscope, he could see the expression on its face. It was one of triumph. Fish-kind had arrived and were finally taking over the world.

The fish tried to wink at the stunned bear, but not having any eyelids it completely failed to do so. It swam off in a bit of a huff. Evolution had much to answer for – not just eyelids but other bits like ears, legs, fingers, and stuff. However, with the rise of the New Piscine Empire, all that malarkey had been rendered irrelevant and there was much new territory for it to explore. The town of Godalming was being reclaimed in the glorious name of 'Fish-Kind', although he wasn't sure what the new name for this territory was to be yet. Perhaps something nautical like Godder Bank?

Humphrey thought quickly.

"We're under water. We've got to waterproof your room. And quickly, before we are flooded too. Let's get to the basement and see what we can use."

As Humphrey turned, he saw Jeffrey standing at the lounge door, dripping on the floor, wearing a diver's face mask and snorkel.

"Is it raining in your bedroom too?" ventured the bear-in-charge, dreading the answer.

Jeffrey shook his head, spraying them a little. He removed the snorkel.

"No, but the basement is full of water. It's very cold and there's not much light down there."

Humphrey barged past the two younger bears and ran down the corridor to the basement steps. Water had nearly reached the top.

"Oh no. We're completely flooded. It's like we're sinking."

"It's a bit like we're in a submarine, and we've been depth charged, and the water is pouring in, and some of the crew are trapped and drowning, but we can't hear their screams, and we're sinking down to the bottom of the sea where we will be crushed by the water pressure. Squish!" Jeffrey made a squishing motion with his paws.

"What songs?" asked Godfrey.

"Songs?"

"You said we'll be singing to the bottom of the sea."

"Sinking, I said sinking. But you can sing if you want."

"Oh good. I like snubmanrines."

"Ha, ha! 'Snub-manrines'," cried out Jeffrey, pointing to the youngest bear.

Humphrey interjected. "Look, guys. We have a problem. I suggest we abandon ship and float to the surface in my... uhm... our... emergency life-boat-ball."

"But we're in a snubmanrine!" Godfrey was a little upset and quite keen on this new game. He'd never played this one before.

"Well, teddy bears don't do well underwater. We really do need to escape."

Humphrey led them to his bedroom where he had installed an emergency escape hatch above the top of one of his wardrobes. He pulled out a very large transparent, but deflated, beach ball and placed it on the bed.

"Climb inside this and I'll open the escape hatch, and we'll bob to the surface when the room floods." He stuffed his bath towel into the ball.

"But I want to play snubmanrines," howled Godfrey.

Jeffrey pulled himself inside the ball and reached out to the little bear.

"Come on. We can play shipwreck survivors instead."

"Not snubmanrines?"

"No, but we can be sailors that escaped from a sinking snub... submarine, and we can drift for days in the open ocean under the beating sun. We can be dying from thirst and hunger, and after we've eaten all the biscuits, we can decide which one of Humphrey's legs to eat first."

"The biscuits!"

If a dark brown bear could turn pale, Humphrey would have done so. He ran to the kitchen in a blind panic and reached for his store of nibblers. He opened the tin. "Phew!" he sighed, before grabbing a bottle of water, running back to the bedroom and tossing them into the ball.

Then he was off again, to the lounge. The water now saturated the carpets, so Humphrey's feet made splatting noises as he ran. He reached behind the settee for his secret stash of sugary shortbreads and then ran back to the bedroom and tossed them into the ball with the other two bears – but both had dark brown stains around their mouths.

"Stop eating the biscuits! They're for emergencies only."

"This *is* an emergency," declared Jeffrey, slowly raising a half-eaten digestive to his mouth.

"Yes. But save them. We'll need them for later, when we're hungry."

"But I'm hungry now," said Godfrey.

"Save them for later!" Humphrey ordered, "...and save some for me."

He turned, grabbed a key ring from beside his bed and ran to where he'd hidden his other secret biscuit stash, in his private secret safe, in his secret hidey-hole, in the locked hallway cupboard. By the time he got there the water was over the carpet and his pink bunny slippers were now making splishing sounds. Water was now dribbling down the walls from the ceiling.

He unlocked the cupboard and dodged the falling ironing board (which always tried its hardest to land on something

207

soft, usually Humphrey's head). Humphrey then tugged open the secret door to his hidey-hole and turned the little wheels on the front of the safe. It sprang open.

Humphrey crinkled his nose in horror.

In the safe was a single, used, smelly sock, a broken plastic ray gun, a small glass jar of yellow powder labelled 'Yellow Cake Powwder. Doent Bake. Tastes Bad', a small brick of light grey marzipan labelled 'C4 – Doent Bash!', a small box of pills labelled 'Morning After', and a small dark bottle of liquid labelled 'Hydrazine - Save For Guy Fork's Knite.'

It was the box of pills that rattled Humphrey the most.

Clearly Jeffrey had discovered the safe, broken into it, and claimed it as his own. But after some blind rummaging around, Humphrey was relieved to find that his now not-so-secret slush fund – the stash of biscuits – was still intact at the back of the safe. It then occurred to him that the safe was watertight so there was in fact no reason whatsoever to rescue any of it. It was safer where it was, especially when he remembered that three bears floating in an enclosed ball with nothing to do but eat biscuits was not at all a good place to preserve his retirement fund.

And Jeffrey's items might need reviewing after this crisis was over.

He closed the safe and reset the combination. Then he clambered out of the cupboard and re-stood the ironing board, which seemed very upset at the prospect of remaining in the cupboard and was angry enough to try to fall on his head several more times. The water was now at Humphrey's ankles, so he splashed back to the bedroom finding it more difficult to move fast.

He arrived just in time to catch a glimpse of Jeffrey and Godfrey frantically wiping their mouths (clearly, they had ignored Humphrey's orders to save the biscuits). Humphrey grabbed two pillows, which were still dry, a torch, and a small cylinder of air and shoved them into the ball, then clambered to the top of the wardrobe and reached up to the hatch.

"What are you doing?" asked Godfrey.

"I'm going to open the hatch, then get into the ball, so we can float out when the water lifts us up to the ceiling."

"Won't the water go down?"

"Eventually, but at the moment the water is rising fast. Look... it's almost up to the bed."

Humphrey pulled on the latch, which was far stiffer than he remembered. He pulled and pulled, so hard that his feet were dangling in the air when the latch snapped open, and a huge torrent of water fell through it and struck him away with a roar.

"I told you the water will go down," said Godfrey. "You are all wetted now."

Two large, dazed eyes stared through the falling torrent before he was able to half-wade, half-swim his way to the bed. The saturated bear got inside the ball and zip-sealed the entrance just as the water rose over the sheets. A puff of air from the air cylinder inflated the ball and it started to rise with the water.

"It's cold!" yelled Godfrey.

"Yes. The water outside is cold. But we've got the towel and these pillows." Humphrey gave Godfrey and then Jeffrey a good rub down before drying himself. As the water

209

rose the ball rose on top of it, which was when Humphrey realised that the ball was not directly under the escape tunnel.

Then the lights went out and all went pitch black.

"Wah! It's the end of the world!" Godfrey wailed. "I don't want to be end of the worlded!"

"Stop it, Godfrey! You're treading on me," yelled Jeffrey.

"I want to get out! Let me out! Let me out!"

"We're okay, Godfrey, look. I have a torch." Humphrey clicked the torch on, and it lit up under his chin, making him look like an evil and sinister were-bear.

"Wah! There's a monenster in here with us! I don't want to be eatened!"

"Ow! Shdop ib bodvree! You're breading on by head!" There was a slap and Godfrey fell back to land on Humphrey.

"Wah! He hit me! I don't like this game!"

"Here you are, Godfrey, you can hold the torch."

Godfrey snatched at the torch and shone it around and around, frantically checking everyone and looking for the monster were-bear before he calmed down a little.

"I don't like this game. Can we play pirates instead? I like pirates," he sobbed.

The ball spun around the room several times, caught in a current before it stopped at the bottom of the escape tunnel. The bears' secret house was now completely under water and the current had equalised, so the ball rose up the tunnel and popped out onto the surface. The sound of rain pitter-pattered on the ball.

The bears had a few minutes of sightseeing before the ball misted up inside. This was both a good and a bad thing. It was good because any people around would not see a ball of teddy bears gawking at them. It was bad because they could not see where they were drifting to and everything inside the ball was fast becoming damp.

In order to prevent some of their survival supplies from becoming too wet, they finished the biscuits. The stash of spending shortbreads was safe in a water-proof tin, so they decided to save them for later. Well, Humphrey did.

And so it was, that after about twenty minutes or so, Humphrey found himself dozing off on the cold, damp pillows, but with a dry, warm Godfrey curled up asleep on his chest and an almost dry Jeffrey asleep sitting on his legs. They didn't drift very far and were caught at the side of the bridge, on Bridge Road, only a few hundred yards from their home. The gentle pitter-patter of rain helped lull them to sleep.

At about half past six in the morning, they were woken up by blue flashing lights. Jeffrey wiped the inside of the ball and peered out at the police cars blocking the bridge and the officers putting up the 'Road Closed' sign.

Humphrey, from his position at the bottom of the trio, tried to do the same closer to the water line but was startled when he saw another big eye staring back at him. This one was far bigger than the fisheye earlier.

"Dondus!" yelled Godfrey, bouncing up and down in excitement. "Dondus! It's us!"

A big, green reptilian head rose from the water and grinned.

211

"Dondus! You can play football with us. We're in the ball."

"Uhm... No. Please don't. We're in the ball. Can you nudge us to dry land?"

Dondus' two big nostrils pushed the ball away from the bridge and up beneath a tree. Then he gave it a big bash with his head, and it stuck fast in some of the branches.

"Uhm... Not so helpful, but thanks. I think," called out Humphrey, wondering how they would avoid people if anyone cared to look.

The nostrils disappeared and there was a scratching sound on the top.

Jeffrey wiped the inside, and they could just make out Woof, the not-dog that lived in the only beetfruit tree in Godalming.

"Woof! Dondus pushed us to Woof's. Yay!" screamed Godfrey.

"Right!" said Jeffrey who reached up to the zip-seal and pulled.

"Don't do that! It'll deflate the... ahhhh... it's cold!"

Splash!

Luckily Woof was quick to pull the bears out of the water, but now they all needed drying off again.

Woof's tree house is quite small, and the three bears found it quite a challenge to fit in, let alone live there for the several days until the flooding subsided. Woof found it the most challenging – but mainly because woofs like to live alone. Well, that, but also living with The Furricious Gang had its own challenges.

Humphrey was very thankful for his friends, Dondus - Godalming's very own Loch Ness-type monster, and Woof – Godalming's rare tree-dwelling-not-dog-type-thing.

After the flood had eventually subsided it took weeks for their secret home to dry out. They had to pump out the water and then find a way to circulate air around it to remove the damp and unsavoury smells. Everything had to be washed and scrubbed clean and a lot of the rooms had to be redecorated. It was not cheap, and Humphrey had to spend most of his secret slush fund in repairs.

The last project was for Humphrey to build a new emergency watertight chamber, designed to escape from any similar floods in the future. Jeffrey wanted it to be made like a submarine so that they could play snubmanrines in it, but Godfrey wasn't too keen, fearful of monenster were-bears. So, they made it like a spaceship instead, and often play space games in it to this day. It has its own stash of biscuits too – but that always needs refilling after a space game.

Swimming along in the River Wey, as it receded back to its original size, was a very disappointed fish. One of many. Yet again, the promise of a new Great Piscine Empire had failed to materialise. But a few seconds later, as fishes often do, it forgot all about it.

Then, Humphrey remembered something quite disconcerting. "Uhm... Jeffrey, tell me about those 'Morning After' pills…"

St Martha's Church (also known as St Martha-on-the-Hill) is the only church in Surrey to be on the Pilgrims' Way and featured briefly in the 1944 film A Canterbury Tale. A 12th-century church existed here before falling into ruin by the 18th century.

Cough Medicine

by Paul Rennie

The middle-aged Indian woman pulled the coat tighter over her work clothes and adjusted her COVID mask. It was a cold late December evening and Neema had been standing at the Shalford bus stop without a shelter for ages, peering down the road towards the roundabout for any signs of the No. 53 bus, which was already 25 minutes late. At this time of year, the buses were always full, but no one designing timetables at Arriva had considered that this might mean the bus took longer to do its journey than when it was empty as during the rest of the year. Behind her was an elderly couple patiently standing side by side, occasionally murmuring something that she couldn't hear through their masks and sharing a bag of *Wurther's Originals*.

She smelt his presence before she saw him, an acrid odour of alcohol, cigarettes and menace, before he loomed into view, blocking out the dwindling winter light. He was well over six feet tall, heavily built, and with the appearance of a Staffordshire bull terrier, one that had been shaved and wasn't happy about it. On his neck, if the rippled slab of meat that was wider than his head and attached it to his muscular shoulders could be called a neck, was a tattoo of a spider web. This was offset on the other side with the badly inked words *'Millwall bread'*. Some people of the more liberal persuasion might have assumed that he was advertising an East End baker, especially if they were comfortable with the spell-checking and proof-reading standards of the Guardian newspaper. But they would have been wrong. He was indeed a supporter of the football club whose fans were known for their tolerance and jolly motto; *'Nobody likes us, we don't care'*. His over-hanging brow, scarred from head-butting incidents, gave the impression of someone who hadn't made it very far up the evolutionary tree. We'll call him Gary, for indeed that was his name, and we wouldn't want to be overfamiliar and use his usual moniker of Gaz, because he had the permanent look of someone dosed up with testosterone and waiting for the bell to go for round one. Even his own mother wouldn't have described him as a pacifist.

Gary forced his bulk into the space between Neema and the bus stop sign, blocking her view of any approaching traffic, and smirked as if daring her to say something.

Neema wasn't having that. 'Excuse me, this is a queue. We've been waiting a long time.'

The grin faded, to be replaced with a look of aggressive belligerence. 'I don't give a shit. This is where I'm standin' 'cos I'm English and proud of it. Now that we've gone and done Brexit, it's British first and you lot are back of the queue.' He then broke into a chant of 'Sovereignty, we got our sov, the foreigners can bugger off', sniggering at his own wit.

Neema looked around for support, but the elderly couple didn't want to get involved. 'Let him go first, dear, it's only one place.'

Neema wasn't quite finished. She turned back to Gary and said sharply, 'We'll see what the driver says. You're not wearing a mask, and without one they won't let you on the bus.'

A red mist bloomed behind Gary's brutish eyes. He wasn't used to people arguing with him. 'Eff off, I ain't takin' orders from no curry muncher. No one tells me to wear a wimp's mask.' With that he deliberately coughed in her face, a big, exaggerated cough interspersed with copious

215

flecks of spittle. Neema backed off in horror. Aghast, she pointed her finger in protest, only to be met with a second even more productive cough. Just then the bus pulled up and Gary pushed aside the one person getting off and climbed aboard. Before Neema could protest, the driver shouted he was sorry the bus was full, closed the doors and drove off.

The driver considered the pros and cons of challenging his new passenger for not wearing a mask, but the *'love'* and *'hate'* tattoos on Gary's well used knuckles suggested this was not someone who was open to the niceties of reasoned debate. The bus was already late, and his shift would soon be over, so he concentrated on the road ahead.

Back at the Shalford bus stop, Neema was brimming with indignation. She turned back to the elderly couple. 'Did you see what that man did? He assaulted me.'

'We're sorry, dear, we didn't see anything. We were looking for our bus passes. That poor man must have been unwell with that nasty cough. Perhaps it's a good thing he got on that nice warm bus. Never mind, it's only an hour and a half until the next one.' Poor Neema realised that no support was forthcoming and resigned herself to the long, dark walk home to Bramley.

On the bus, Gary forced his way through the standing masked passengers, ignoring the tuts and disdainful looks. Halfway down there was a young schoolgirl, also not wearing a mask because she was exempt. Gary loomed over her. 'You need to give up that seat for yer elders, get aht of it, gertcha.' The girl stood up without a word, and Gary pushed his bulk into the vacated seat, leaving a heavily pregnant woman standing in the aisle. He glared around daring anyone to say anything, and when met with averted eyes, made himself comfortable and started rehearsing his newly composed chant: 'Sovereignty, we got our sov, the foreigners can bugger off', while drumming the beat on the seat in front of him. He was pleased with himself for his clever lyrics, and decided it was definitely a song for the terraces once football matches could be attended.

Unbeknownst to Gary, the schoolgirl was a symptomless carrier of COVID, and was absolutely riddled with coronavirus, specifically SARS-CoV-2. Also, unfortunately for him, she was a bit of a fidget, and had touched all of the surfaces in the seat she had occupied before Gary annexed it. She'd run her hands along the plastic moulding around the base of the seat, down the back of the seat in front, across the rails at the top and even on the red bell button. As a result, each area had its own population of coronavirus. These little bundles of joy were minding their own business and would probably have been inactivated in a few hours, were it not for Gary's large hands plucking them from what would have been their final resting place and transferring them into his nostrils as he picked his nose. About 450 virus particles made the leap into the warm nutritious environment of Gary's respiratory system, where one by one they docked with the cells in his lungs, gained entry and started hijacking his genetic material to produce more of their companions. By the time Gary got off the bus in Cranleigh, he already had more virus particles than he had picked up, and over the next few days the numbers ballooned, and inflammation started to set in. By the third day Gary felt a bit rough, and noticed that he couldn't taste his lager, in spite of trying large quantities. Gone were the exquisite nuances of the hops and malts, and the complexities from the phenols and esters derived from the brewing process, to be replaced with a bland bitterness. He also had a blinding headache, and this time, a genuine cough. Over the next few days, he felt increasingly unwell, couldn't get enough air and took on a bluish tinge. At this point his mate, Daz, bundled him into his car and dropped him off at the Royal Surrey. Fortunately for Gary, the new COVID unit at the hospital had just opened and he was found a bed in an isolation room, where he was initially given oxygen, and then, as his condition deteriorated, was put on a CPAP device to assist his breathing.

This helped and his condition stabilised and he started to show the first signs of improvement. Later that evening the shift in the ward changed, and the Filipino nurse that Gary had initially abused 'Cos she don't look like she spoke the Queen's English', in spite of her obviously superior vocabulary and enunciation to his own, was replaced by an Indian nurse. The new nurse approached Gary's bed, and through her face shield, smiled caringly at the helpless patient. 'How are you feeling?' she asked. Gary peered through the fogged-up visor of the CPAP mask and felt a glimmer of recognition. Had he seen that face before somewhere? Nah, there were millions of them bleedin' Asians over here, and they all looked the same, not like proper English faces.

The nurse plumped up his pillows, smoothed his bed sheets, and made a small adjustment to the CPAP machine. Gary heard the hissing and clicking sound that it made go slightly quieter and it suddenly became a little more difficult to breathe. 'I'm just turning it down a bit so that the noise doesn't keep you awake.' She made another little adjustment, and it became a lot harder to get air into his lungs. He tried to signal to the nurse, but she just smiled and patted his arm, saying, 'Don't worry, it will soon be over.' Another quick tweak, and he could no longer breathe at all. Neema waited a minute then flicked off a switch on the life support monitor and then picked up the clipboard with Gary's medical details, looked at her watch, and in neat writing wrote: Time of death 11.22 pm.

It is of course a tragedy that anyone should die from this terrible pandemic, particularly in Gary's circumstances, and one cannot condone the manner of his passing and its implications for the Hippocratic Oath. However, there was one little ray of hope in the whole sorry saga. Gary's early departure freed up the intensive care bed and equipment for another patient who would otherwise have died. By an amazing coincidence it turned out to be the heavily pregnant lady who had been standing without a seat on the No. 53 bus and had brushed against and been infected by the same schoolgirl. Because of Gary's sacrifice, she received timely attention and, as a result, recovered and was discharged fit and well after two weeks, with a beautiful newborn baby girl who she named Neema after the nurse who had showed her such dedicated and devoted care during her illness.

In an area of Hankley Common known as the Lion's Mouth, Canadian troops constructed a replica of a section of the Atlantic Wall. It is constructed from reinforced concrete and was used as a major training aid to develop and practise techniques to breach the defences of the French coast prior to the D-Day landings.

A Stroke of Luck

by Alan Barker

"Mum wasn't happy when I rang and told her," Gemma said, gazing at the horses in the parade ring. "She'd just bought lots of food for breakfast tomorrow: eggs, bacon, sausages, tomatoes, baked beans, the whole works."

"It's not your fault those people cried off," her friend Lucy said.

They were at Epsom Racecourse for Derby Day. The sun was out and there was a buzz of anticipation among the growing crowd.

Gemma and her parents lived at the foot of the Downs. Since Gemma's brother Paul had moved out, the family had taken advantage of the close proximity of their house to the racecourse by letting out their spare room each year on Derby night.

A Mr and Mrs Anderson from Newmarket had enquired about the room a month before. Her mum and dad being out at the time, Gemma had made the booking but hadn't thought to take either their card details or a contact number.

When Mr Anderson had telephoned on the morning of the races to cancel their stay—his wife not feeling well enough to make the trip—again it was Gemma who had taken the call, her parents having gone to the supermarket.

"I should have taken payment when they rang the first time," Gemma said to Lucy. "Mum and Dad will be out of pocket."

"Don't worry about it," Lucy replied. "See if you can pick a few winners on the gee-gees—that'll cheer you up."

***

"And here are the starting prices. First: number four, Cecilia's Treasure, thirty-three to one. Second: number six, Dubai Lion, the eleven to four favourite. And the third horse: number fourteen, Madrid Flyer, at five to one. The tote prices are as follows…"

The announcement was greeted with virtual silence by the packed Derby crowd. Clearly, not many punters had backed the unfancied winner.

Feeling a little disappointed, Gemma joined the queue for the bookmaker. She had placed her money on Madrid Flyer only because her father had recently travelled to Spain for a business conference.

But when the horse had shot into the lead turning Tattenham Corner, she had felt certain he was going to win and had screamed and jumped and clapped until she was exhausted. Unfortunately, Madrid Flyer had tired up the final hill and Gemma watched, helpless, as two of his rivals swept past him in the shadow of the winning post.

At least she had ten pounds to pick up, having placed her bet each way.

"Aye?" the bookmaker said, holding out a hand.

He was a burly man with receding sandy hair and a kindly expression. "Dynamic Doug", his board proclaimed in bold lettering.

Gemma passed her ticket to him and waited patiently for her winnings. Shading her eyes, she looked up as a helicopter hovered briefly in mid-air before it swivelled like a cat chasing its tail and set off towards the London Eye, its taillights winking goodbye.

Gemma blinked as the bookmaker pressed a wad of notes into her hand; she gazed down uncomprehendingly.

Someone was jostling her from behind.

"D'ye want another wee bet, lassie?" the bookmaker asked.

Gemma felt herself tense up. "N-no. I'm fine, thanks," she mumbled.

Stuffing the money in her purse, she turned and hurried off, feeling the colour rise in her cheeks.

She joined a queue for the lavatory and had to wait ten minutes before gaining admittance to a cubicle. Once inside with the door locked, she opened her purse and counted out the money carefully.

***

"Guess what, Lucy? I've won two hundred pounds," Gemma said.

"You jammy thing!"

"I was only expecting a tenner, but the bookie chap gave me a load of twenties."

"Wow! Think of the lovely things you can spend it on."

Gemma frowned. "But why would he pay so much when the horse I backed only finished third?"

"Perhaps he misheard you when you placed the bet," Lucy said, studying her racecard. "You did number fourteen, and the winner was number four. So, he thought you had a fiver each way on Cecilia's Treasure at thirty-three to one, which would explain why he gave you two hundred. Now that's what I call a stroke of luck!"

"Not for the poor old bookie."

"Come off it, Gem; they're made of money. He won't miss it."

"All the same, I feel awkward knowing I only should have got my ten pounds back."

Just then, Lucy was accosted by other friends of hers and Gemma decided to go for a stroll.

Using her phone, she took photographs of the fairground activities—in particular, the helter-skelter and the colouring walls caught her eye—and some of the children's painted faces. Then she bought a hot dog and a cup of tea and found a seat in the sunshine. But she felt restless.

Presently she met up with Lucy again.

"I've decided to give the bookie his money back," Gemma said. "It's not right keeping it if it wasn't mine to have in the first place."

"It wasn't your fault he paid you too much," Lucy argued. "You've done nothing wrong."

"Even so…"

"Well, if it'll make you feel better."

But when they made their way to the bookmakers' area, there was no sign of "Dynamic Doug".

"What happened to him?" Gemma asked one of the other bookmakers, indicating the empty space.

The man stroked his bristly jaw. "I've a feeling one of his punters had a shrewd little wager on the Derby winner which might have cleaned him out. He and his missus left pretty soon after."

"I feel awful," Gemma said, turning back to Lucy. "I might have ruined his livelihood."

Lucy laughed. "What, taking two hundred quid off a bookie? I would say that's odds against."

***

On their way home after the last race, they decided to stop at Ye Olde Kings Head. It was packed with racegoers, all seemingly in good spirits after their afternoon at the races.

Having bought their drinks, Gemma and Lucy were looking for somewhere to sit when Gemma's attention was drawn to a middle-aged man and woman having a meal in a corner of the pub.

"That's the chap I had my bet with," Gemma whispered in Lucy's ear.

"What are you going to do?"

"Give him his money back, of course."

Gemma made her way across to the bookmaker and introduced herself and Lucy. She explained that he had paid her far too much in winnings following her bet on Madrid Flyer and wanted to put the matter right.

The man known as "Dynamic Doug" wiped his lips with a napkin.

"That's very noble," he said. "Why don't ye sit yerselves doon? This is my wife, Rhonda."

Gemma pulled the wad of notes from her purse and passed it across the table, keeping the ten pounds that represented her true winnings.

"I shouldn't have taken the money in the first place," she said. "I went to pay it back to you, but you'd already gone."

"We come from Dundee," Doug explained. "So, we've a long drive home and thought we'd best have a meal and be heading off... Unless ye ken somewhere nice we can spend the night that won't cost us an arm and a leg?"

The two girls exchanged glances.

"I know just the place," Gemma said, brightening up. "There's a lovely spare room at my parents' house. Mum put clean sheets on this morning and we've plenty of food in the fridge, so we can cook you a full English breakfast tomorrow, if that sounds okay to you?"

"Of course, you'll have to pay for it," Lucy chipped in.

Rhonda gave Lucy a quizzical look. "We weren't expecting a freebie, darling."

Doug smiled and pushed the money back across the table.

"Will that cover it?" he asked, his eyes twinkling.

Gemma laughed. "By a stroke of luck, I do believe it will. Mum *will* be happy."

Abinger Roughs was formerly part of the Abinger Hall Estate. In the late 19th century the land was planted with specimen trees, plantations and rhododendrons to form open glades with interlinking paths, a wilderness garden. It was created by Thomas Henry Farrer of Abinger Hall.

The Hamper

by Ian Honeysett

Norman Spinks prided himself on his calm, methodical manner. He never panicked. Never got over-excited. He had led a quiet and, some might say, unspectacular life. A 40-year career in local government might not sound that interesting but who could forget his reorganisation of the main filing system back in 1983? The hours he spent redesigning it. So many evenings spent at his dining room table with countless pieces of paper. How often his late wife, Mildred, would so gently chide him to take a break and have a cup of tea. And it was appreciated too – at least by some of those affected. Okay, there had been teething problems but those were mainly due to Clive who continually misfiled papers despite Norman's patient support. How unjust, some might say, that it was the same Clive who was promoted when the Clerical Officer post was advertised. But Norman bore it all with his usual forbearance.

He had now been retired for five years. For the first two he had enjoyed several holidays with Mildred visiting Scarborough and Great Yarmouth twice. Out of season. Better value for money. Far quieter if somewhat wetter. Since then, he had been away just the once – with his only daughter, Susan. To Littlehampton. Not too far from his home in Godalming. Under two hours by train via Havant. Susan had suggested they might go abroad but Norman was unconvinced. Soon after the week – which was unfortunately rather wet and windy – she decided to move out to stay with friends, Alice and Eileen. In Littlehampton in fact. Norman missed her – especially her cooking. What she could do with Shepherd's Pie – his favourite – was

226

nobody's business. And her Bread & Butter pudding, well….

In three days' time, on Thursday, it was Susan's 30th birthday and Norman decided to mark it with a very special gift. He thought long and hard about it before deciding on a hamper. He searched the website of a well-known supermarket and found the perfect choice. It looked quite delicious with strawberry jam, sticky fig chutney, almond shortbread thins (whatever they were) and milk chocolate flaked truffles. There was even a bottle of vintage Cava. It wasn't cheap of course but it's not every day you're 30 after all. And perhaps she wouldn't expect quite so much for Christmas.

Norman slept badly on Wednesday night, worrying about that hamper. It probably wouldn't arrive before she left for work at the local crematorium. Say no one was at home, where would the delivery person leave it? He had only visited Susan once since she had moved out, but he thought there was possibly a porch at her new home. Surely, they would leave it there? But what if it were locked? Would they leave it with a neighbour? Or would they take it back to the depot? That didn't bear thinking about. She would then have to go and collect it. Some birthday treat that!

So, he decided to ring her first thing. Naturally he didn't want to spoil the surprise so he wouldn't reveal what it was. Just make sure that it would be safe.

'Hello, Susan, it's Dad here. I wanted to wish you Happy Birthday!'

'Oh, thank-you, Dad. You remembered!'

'Of course I remembered, Susan. When have I ever forgotten?'

'I was only joking, Dad. Of course you remembered. Thank-you for calling.'

'I just wanted to say that I have sent you a rather special present as it's your 30th. It should be delivered this morning. Will you be there by any chance?'

'No, Dad, I'll be at work as usual. But there's a porch so it should be safe.'

'Ah, that's a relief – I thought there was. Well, have an enjoyable day. Do you have anything planned?'

'Yes, I'm meeting up with Alice and Eileen for a meal at the local Indian restaurant. Might even have a drink or two!'

'Well, have a good time but don't drink too much! Bye.'

Norman felt hugely relieved. There *was* a porch. Now he could relax. Or thought he could when he suddenly heard the refuse collection lorry outside his house. Had he remembered to put his bin out? His mind had been so concentrated on the hamper that he'd totally forgotten. And he was still in his pyjamas. What was he to do? He tried to open the bedroom window to call out, but it was stuck. He decided to dash downstairs and open the porch door and call out for them to wait but couldn't find his dressing gown and slippers. But, for once in his life, he felt real anger. He rushed downstairs, tripping just twice, and dashed into the street, shouting, 'Please stop! My bin is just here. It's rather full.' But the lorry was now at the end of the road and about to turn the corner.

'Are you alright, Mr Spinks?' It was a neighbour that Norman knew slightly.

'No, I'm not,' he replied a little aggressively. 'I'm sorry, I didn't mean to be rude. But they've gone without emptying my bin. They came too early. And it's my daughter's birthday today!'

The neighbour, Mrs Adams, was not too sure of the link between these two statements but could see how agitated Norman was.

'Can I make you a cup of tea?'

'Er, no, thank-you. Very kind of you. I think I'd better go back inside as it's rather chilly.'

'I like your pyjamas,' replied Mrs Adams. 'Pity about the hole.'

Norman thanked her and returned to his house. But, to his abject horror, found that the front door had slammed shut. He knew immediately that he did not have the key on him. There were no pockets in these pyjamas. He stood there shivering, wondering what on earth to do.

'Can I help?' asked Mrs Adams.

'I'm locked out!' said Norman. 'I've no front door key. How can I get back in? What on earth am I to do?'

'Do you have a key in your garage by any chance?' she asked. 'We do – just in case.'

Norman thought.

'Do you know, Mrs…. I might do. Susan used to keep a spare key there. I wonder if she took it with her?'

'Let's look and see,' replied Mrs Adams. 'I'm quite good at finding things.'

In normal circumstances there was no way that Norman would have considered allowing anyone else into his garage, but this was an emergency.

'Of course. That would be most helpful.'

The garage door handle was rather stiff as, truth be told, Norman hadn't been in there since Susan had left.

'My goodness, Mr Spinks, your garage is amazingly tidy. Ours is a real mess in comparison. I'd always assumed you were tidy. Methodical.'

Norman was delighted at this rare compliment. There was really no higher praise. For a moment he thought of that filing system. He wished he could remember his neighbour's name. It would be too embarrassing to ask her now as he'd known her for over 20 years. He stood back and watched her as she searched behind the paint tins and jam jars (lovingly made by his wife some years before. He'd quite forgotten they were there.)

'I think I've found them, Norman!' she said. Good Lord, he thought, she even knows my Christian name. Somehow, he felt even more embarrassed at his ignorance.

She held up a bunch of keys. Surely, they were the house keys? What else could they be? But he had a nagging doubt they might not be.

He grabbed them and quickly made his way to the front door. He was so agitated that he couldn't get the key in the lock. He almost swore.

'Here, let me, Norman.' Mrs Adams took the keys and put the Yale key in the lock and turned it. The door opened. She turned to Norman, smiling triumphantly. Much to her surprise, he danced a little jig. She had never seen him look so happy. This rapidly changed when his pyjama trousers fell down. Fortunately, it was quite a long jacket which happily hid his embarrassment. Mostly.

'Thank-you so much, Mrs...'

'Please, call me Liz,' she replied. Norman determined to remember the name.

'Just tell me if you need anything, Norman. Anything at all.'

Once she'd gone, Norman made himself a cup of tea. He had never felt so relieved. Perhaps it wouldn't be such a bad day after all.

Then he heard the porch door open and close. Strange. He wasn't expecting anything. He opened the front door and there, on the porch mat, was a large package. He was confused. He'd not ordered anything. Except. Oh no! This was that hamper he'd ordered for Susan! They'd delivered it to the wrong address! He'd made it quite clear that it was to go to Susan's home not his. Quite clear. He could feel his anger growing. Even more than when they had failed to collect his rubbish. That, he was prepared to concede, was perhaps partly his fault but not this. He was physically shaking as he rang the shop and delivered a verbal onslaught unlike any other he had ever done. The poor recipient of this could not have been more apologetic if he had tried. Norman almost felt sorry for him.

'I am so sorry, sir. As you have said, so emphatically, it was meant to go to your daughter's address, and I really cannot explain why it was sent to you.'

'So, what do you propose to do about it?'

'We can re-send it to her?'

'But *today* is her birthday! She needs it *today*!'

'Perhaps, if we make you a full refund, you could take it to her? Does she live far?'

'Far? She lives in Littlehampton! That's nearly two hours by train – assuming one changes at Havant.'

231

'You couldn't drive there, sir?'

'I don't drive. Not since that incident. So, I will have to carry it on the train.'

'I see.'

'But I can see no alternative. Very well, I will accept the full refund and I will take it to her myself. However, rest assured, I shall not be ordering any more hampers from you. Good day.'

Norman gently replaced the receiver. He studied the package. It was really quite bulky. How on earth could he carry it? He felt his legs start to shake just at the thought. Then he had an idea. The neighbour – what was her name – she had offered to help. But would she be prepared to drive him to Littlehampton? It must be at least 30 miles. No, it was too much to ask someone whose name he still couldn't remember. It was quite a short name. Jean? Jan? Liz? That's it, Liz. That's better. Perhaps she would see his distress and take pity on him? Pity though? Did he want her pity? But it was Susan's 30th for goodness' sake. And she would just love the hamper.

Wracked with indecision, he made himself a cup of tea and sat down next to the phone. Perhaps it would be easier to ring Liz. If she said no, it would surely be far less embarrassing over the phone. He could end the call and avoid having any contact with her for a year or so. Yes, best ring her. Now.

But, just as he was about to pick up the phone, it rang. How could Liz know he was about to call her? He heard a voice on the other end of the line.

'Dad? Are you there, Dad? It's Susan.'

'Susan?' His heart sank. The daughter he'd failed. 'Happy birthday, again, dear.'

'Thank-you, Dad. That's why I'm ringing. This hamper – well, it's fantastic. All my favourites. Sticky fig chutney. Almond shortbread thins. Milk chocolate flaked truffles. How did you know I just love them? And a bottle of Cava too. Thank-you so much!'

Norman was lost for words. How could she have received the hamper when it was sitting, unopened, on his dining room table?

'I'm so pleased you like it, dear,' he heard himself saying. 'I do hope you enjoy it. Have a lovely meal.'

'Thank-you, Dad. We must get together again sometime. Perhaps I could visit you next weekend if you've nothing else on?'

'Oh, that would be wonderful, dear. Yes, please do come over.'

'I'll even cook you some Shepherd's Pie. And maybe Bread & Butter pudding.'

Norman put down the phone. He went over to the parcel. He looked at the address on the label. It wasn't for him. It was for a Mrs Adams next door. They'd delivered it to him by mistake! This wasn't the hamper after all.

With a skip in his step, he picked up the parcel and took it round to Liz's house.

'Oh, Norman,' she said, 'I've been waiting for this. Thank-you so much. Would you like a cup of tea?'

Norman was about to decline when he heard a loud noise. He knew instantly that his front door had slammed shut again. And he also knew that he hadn't replaced the keys in the garage. But, for the moment, he just didn't care.

'Thank-you, Liz,' he replied. 'That's just what I need.'

Buckland is mentioned in the Domesday Book. It was then owned by John of Tonbridge – who also owned about one-third of Surrey at the time. Buckland had a church, watermill and 35 heads of household, of which 17 farmed the land owned by the feudal lord, and 10 were servants of the Estate.

The crime writer Agatha Christie staged her disappearance from Newlands Corner in 1926. She was found days later in Harrogate!

The Godalming Incident

by Martyn MacDonald-Adams

'I'm off to London now, Andy.'

'Will you be coming back this afternoon?'

'I doubt it. There's a lot to discuss and you know what they can be like. Jibber jabber jibber jabber – and: "Oh. What sort of budget should we request? Oh. Are you sure? That won't pass muster. Oh, the commissioner won't like that." That sort of thing.'

The senior man, Superintendent Robert Walsh of the Surrey Constabulary, grabbed his jacket from the coat hook.

'I'll be taking the train.'

'Don't forget to keep the receipt this time.'

'For the train?'

'No. For your sandwiches. You can claim for them on expenses, you know?'

Robert smiled and waved as he grabbed his briefcase and left the office. On the way out through the glass doors of the station reception, the cold air hit his face. Winter was on its way, and it would be December soon. He paused and put on his gloves, a welcome birthday present from his wife.

He walked down the steps and set off for the railway station; it was only a few minutes away. The walk would help wake him up and prepare him for the ordeal to come.

He arrived at the pedestrian crossing and waited with a couple of other people. The traffic, as usual, was busy but the traffic lights always ensured a crossing sooner or later.

A black Range Rover stopped close to the kerb right in front of him. The passenger door opened, and a woman got out and opened the back door.

'Please get in, Robert,' she said.

He turned to look behind him to see who it was that she was speaking to, but instead saw two men in black coats standing uncomfortably close.

He turned back. 'What...? Me...?'

One of the men gently pushed him forward and the woman took his hand.

'Please get in.' She smiled.

'I'm sorry. No...'

But he was pushed a little more roughly this time. He all but fell into the car. The car door closed, the woman returned to her passenger seat and the vehicle drove off as she buckled herself in. An older man in a pinstripe suit sat in the back with him.

'You can put your case on the floor. Put your seat belt on.'

'What's going on?' Things were happening too fast. Had he just been kidnapped? He considered getting out of the car even as it accelerated away.

'I must apologise for the drama. It is a bit Hollywood, isn't it? I've always wanted to try this sort of thing. It's like a spy film. I wonder if anyone saw us.'

'Who are you?'

'Ah! Robert! More melodrama, I'm afraid. Call me Arnold. It's not my real name, of course, but it'll do for now. And that's Beth in the front there. A and B, you see? Easy to remember. The driver can remain anonymous, can't you, Claude?'

The driver laughed and nodded but said nothing.

'What the hell do you want? You realise I'm a police officer.'

'Well naturally. That's why you're here.'

'You can't just go around grabbing police officers off the street. If you want to speak to me, you should make an appointment! Who do you work for? What's this all about? Where are you taking me? If any harm should...'

'Oh, please stop wittering, Robert. Really! I can call you Robert, can't I? You are supposed to be quite intelligent. More so than the average officer - so I've been told. Please start thinking and listen a little, will you?'

Walsh fell silent for a moment.

'Thank you. To answer your questions, we cannot make an appointment with you because we don't technically exist. Moreover, we do not wish to draw attention to ourselves. Which also explains who, or rather who we are not, working for. I think. There's no easy way to explain that one. Anyway, this is about the incident in Godalming. The one on Bridge Road. The one you are going to London to discuss with the Home Office bods. You think it's serious enough to set up a task force. Yes?'

The man called Arnold let that sink in for a couple of seconds.

'And no. We have no intention of harming you. In fact, I would feel much more comfortable if you relaxed, put your case by your feet and put your seatbelt on.'

Slowly, Robert took off his gloves, put the case down and pulled the seatbelt into the buckle.

'Where are you taking me?'

'Oh, we're just giving you a lift into London. We can chat on the way, if that's alright.'

'How do you know who I am? Are you with the security services?'

'No. We are not part of the government, or any government, in fact.'

Walsh felt a cold shiver run up his spine. He looked out the window, but the car was heading for the A3 London-bound, as Arnold had promised. It didn't prove anything; these could still be terrorists, or perhaps gang members of an organised crime syndicate, but neither scenario quite fit. There were no apparent weapons, no *explicit* threats. And why the expensive car? Was it to impress him?

Walsh frowned.

'You have my attention. What do you want to say? But I must warn you...'

'Have you heard of the Fermi Paradox?'

'No. What's that?'

'Well, broadly, if you look up into the night sky you can see stars. Millions of them. Billions of them, in fact. If one had good enough eyes. Most have planets, and some of those are suitable for life.'

Uh oh, thought Walsh. A nutter. He'd been kidnapped by a cult.

'What has that to do with the Godalming Incident?'

'I'm coming to that. You see Earth is only what, four and a half billion years old? The universe is well over 13 billion years old. So, it stands to reason that not only should there be life out there, but there should also be intelligent life. Like us. And yet we can't see any. That's the Fermi Paradox. In a nutshell, to quote Fermi: "Where is everybody?"

'What most scientists understand, is that this situation is actually much worse than it first appears. You see, a civilisation should have appeared millions, or even billions, of years ago. There has been plenty of time for them to spread out and make their mark. But apparently, they didn't. Not now, and not for many millions of years. There *should* be some signs out there by now, don't you think? It's quite frightening if you think about it.'

This was all a bit too deep for Walsh. And he still didn't see what that had to do with the Godalming Incident. He decided to listen on. An opportunity to escape might present itself, especially in London traffic when the vehicle slowed enough.

'But it gets even worse. Your scientists are only thinking in four dimensions. You know, up/down, left/right, backwards/forwards, and time, of course. Spacetime. Are you with me?'

Walsh nodded once. He wasn't much of a scientist, and anyway, now wasn't the time to argue, not that he understood what this loony was talking about. He glanced around the car. Could he tell if the child locks were on? He didn't know where the switch was on a Range Rover. Should he try opening the door now? Would Arnold notice? Was he armed?

'Well, if one knows how, one can travel across dimensions. Not spacetime, you understand. A different dimension. I don't believe you have a word for it. So, you see, we're not aliens as such. We're human just like you, but we're from a different Earth. We travelled... sideways, if you will. It's much easier than travelling to the stars. They're much too far away. Not that sideways is easy. That's where everybody is. Beside us.'

He paused before continuing. 'And now you think I am a complete and utter buffoon, so let me show you something to keep your interest.' Arnold reached into his suit pocket and extracted a small box, about the size of a small matchbox, and passed to Walsh. He took it. There was a little switch on one side.

'Switch it on. It's perfectly alright. It's a toy.'

Walsh, suspicious, held it arm's length and clicked the switch. Nothing happened. Walsh glanced at the older man.

'Let it go.'

He let go of the box, but it didn't fall. It hovered in the air.

Most of Walsh's thinking was about his predicament and how to escape. It took a few seconds for his train of thought to change tack and start considering the box.

How was this so?

There was no down draught underneath, so it wasn't a miniature drone. It wasn't close to anything that could be a magnet either. Yet it just hung there. He moved his hands around it. There were no invisible wires holding it up. This was some trick.

He pulled it toward himself and when he let go again, it just stayed there, defying gravity and common sense.

'How does it do that?'

Arnold reached over and took the box, switched it off and replaced it back into his suit pocket.

'May I ask you to listen a little longer while I explain about Godalming?'

'Maybe. Are you trying to tell me you're aliens from another planet?' Walsh dreaded the answer. A wealthy nutcase who was willing to kidnap a police officer just to make a stupid point wasn't something he'd been trained for. Magical flying box notwithstanding. Should he humour him? If Arnold was delusional, that might be the best strategy.

'During the cold war, there was, well, there still is, a lot of jostling for power. The Soviet Union, the USA, and lots of other countries spent their time employing spies to go about stealing secrets, misdirecting politicians, and sabotaging things where they could. Sometimes people died.

'Sadly, things are just the same, even for us. So, every now and then we have to put a stop to the opposition's shenanigans. When they don't get the message, then sometimes we have to make it abundantly clear that they are not welcome and that we are willing to react quite strongly in order to prevent more of their mischief. Godalming was one such example.'

As far as conspiracy theories went, this one sounded like a doozy.

'So, tell me what happened at Godalming,' Walsh ventured. This should expose the fraud. Very few of the relevant facts of the case had been made public. He had been on site quite early, and his later investigation had been quite detailed. He reckoned he knew more about the incident than Scotland Yard. So, what was Arnold's answer to that?

'Beth?' The woman in front turned in her seat to look back at Walsh.

'We received intelligence that another group had arrived and were going to deliver evidence of our existence to a professor at University College, London. This is a first priority scenario for us. However, we didn't know who the group were. It wasn't clear, so we decided to make it a high-profile exercise. We felt that if we were loud enough, we might be able to detect some return communication to their origin and that way we could identify them.'

'Thank you, Beth. You see, under our treaty we are responsible for your Earth. This Earth. Anyone else arriving here and trying to rock the boat, as it were, are like... like enemy saboteurs during the Cold War. This sort of thing is going on all the time. We had to put a stop to it, you see. We had to let them know that we knew all about them and were prepared to be... decisive. And then you came along.'

'But what did you do, exactly, at Godalming?'

Beth answered.

'The target had a briefcase with her. In the case were details as to how to get evidence, proof, that we were here. Your people are not ready for that yet.'

'And frankly, neither are we. We're a bit understaffed. Sorry, Beth, please continue.'

'So, we intercepted her. We used stolen vehicles to block both ends of Bridge Road as she drove over it, and then one of our men detonated a shaped charge against the wall beside her car. We couldn't target her car directly in case they were prepared for that. Having neutralised the target, our man recovered the briefcase and then jumped off the bridge into the river.'

Arnold was grinning like a little boy. 'I watched it all remotely. I must say, it was terribly exciting. Very Hollywood. You would have loved it, Robert. You really would. Sorry, Beth.'

'How did your man in the river get away?'

Beth answered that: 'Oh, we needed to make sure he wasn't followed and that he just seemed to disappear from view. We couldn't be sure there wasn't a second car or another team as back up. So, our man jumped into the water, grabbed a cable on the bottom and we hoisted him away under the river for about a hundred metres. Then we pulled him up onto a boat and sped up to the bridge at Catteshall, where we had a van waiting.'

Walsh frowned. That was what he'd guessed had happened. Witnesses saw the man jump, but no-one saw the man swim or climb out the river. They found the abandoned winch on the riverbank further downstream, and then the boat by the lock at Catteshall. That information had only come to light later when they were investigating the site. Those details were kept from the public. So, either the information had leaked out or these two were involved in the murder.

'Your bomb broke the bridge parapet, blew a hole in the car door and sliced that poor woman in two. There was blood, bones and intestines splattered all over the inside. You realise you are guilty of murder.'

Arnold answered: 'Oh yes. That was the point. But you did not find out her identity, did you? That's because she had none. She was a visitor, like us. But she was up to mischief.'

'So why are you telling me all this? What's all this for?'

243

'Well, it's an apology really. We don't like doing high profile jobs. On the other hand, this one gives us an opportunity to make contact with you. You know: "Take me to your leader." That sort of thing.'

'And what do you want me to do about it?'

'At this point we just want to make you aware that we're here. We'd like you to succeed in setting up your little task force, and with that we can start slowly acclimatising your government to our presence. Here, I have a little extra information for you.'

Arnold passed a folder over to Walsh.

'It contains some information on another couple of missions we've had to do recently. These are still unsolved cases that I'm sure the Home Office would like to see solved. You can use that information to provide a better case for your task force.'

Walsh glanced inside and flicked through the pages. He wasn't aware of these events. One was in Bristol and another just outside Leeds. He started reading.

After a few minutes he asked: 'Have you spoken to anyone else about this?'

'Yes. We've already approached a man in the Security Service. We've given him a dossier on some of our operations abroad. You'll meet him later today. He wants the task force because he thinks we're a terrorist group but can't quite bring himself to report on our conversation just yet. I suggest you two get together and have a little tête-à-tête.'

'Have you spoken to any other agencies?'

'Oh yes. We tried the Americans first. You would have thought they would be sympathetic, wouldn't you? But they're so used to conspiracy theories, fake news, and they are so paranoid; frankly, we couldn't even start a sensible conversation with them. Besides, when it comes to confessions, they suddenly get very shouty and very trigger happy. It's quite unsafe over there. We tried the Russians too, but they were the absolute opposite. No-one believed us at all. As for the Chinese, well, you know what happened to the doctor that tried to warn them of COVID? We didn't even attempt them. No. Europeans seem a lot more approachable, a lot less organised, but a lot more mature in this regard.'

'How do I know you are the good guys?'

Arnold smiled. 'Time will tell. Time will tell. We'll let you draw your own conclusions.'

The Range Rover came to a stop outside Waterloo Station. Beth jumped out and opened the door for Walsh.

'We'll drop you off here, Robert. Have a good think about us, won't you? And good luck with your task force. We'll be in touch.'

Betchworth Castle is a mostly crumbled ruin of a fortified medieval stone house with some tall, two-storey corners strengthened in the 18th century, in the parish of Brockham.

The Lesson

by Pauline North

Sonia strolled along the fruit displays. The colours pleased her, packed in neat ranks of yellow, red and green.

She stopped to watch a woman choosing from the Granny Smith apples. Standing there, bag in hand, she sorted through the fruit, placing some in the bag then taking one out and replacing it with another that appealed more. The toddler in the trolley seat grizzled irritably each time his mother stepped away, then grabbed at her coat every time she returned. At any moment he would break into a full-blown, screaming tantrum. Every movement she made showed her stress.

'I could help.'

The woman looked round, startled. She saw a young girl: surely no more than twelve, a pretty little thing with long blonde hair. She had a solemn, concerned expression.

'Kind of you to offer, dear. I can manage though, thank you.'

'If you tell me what you want, I could fetch it for you; it would be quicker. I expect he's going down with a cold. My little brother plays up when he's poorly. My name is Sonia, what's yours?'

'Mrs Pearson.' She smiled at Sonia. 'Where's your mummy, shouldn't you be with her?'

'Oh, she isn't here yet, she told me to wait in here for her. Mummy doesn't finish work until four. I always come here to help her shop.'

Mrs Pearson glanced at her son. Perhaps he was going down with something; he was quiet now, sucking on a thumb. She dreaded him working himself into a tantrum the way he did sometimes. Why not accept a little help if the girl had to wait anyway?

'Well, if you're sure, Sonia, I would be grateful for some help.'

Sonia hung her school bag on the end of the trolley handle. 'There, all ready, what would you like me to fetch first?'

After a few minutes the woman had completely relaxed, her son was back to his smiling, happy self. Sonia skipped back and forth collecting the requested items, sorting carefully through the vegetables, checking use-by dates, her bright smile lighting the day. While Mrs Pearson was consulting her long list and scanning the shelves, she arranged the shopping tidily, with the heavy goods at the front, ready to be lifted out first. Mrs Pearson even managed to step away from her son to choose some wine while Sonia was off collecting a bottle of cordial.

Wine selected, she turned back with her two chosen bottles to find her young friend already back and looking anxious. 'I'm so sorry, Mrs Pearson, my mum's here now, can you manage if I go and help her?'

'Of course, I can, Sonia. Thank you so much for all your help. Let me give you a little something.'

'No, I wouldn't dream of it, I've had such fun.' The girl slung her bag over her shoulder. 'Bye now.'

After Sonia left, she only had a handful of bits still to get. She wondered if she would see the girl helping her mother the way she had been helped. She hoped so, she wanted to tell the mother what a kind, helpful daughter she had, but they didn't meet. She supposed that they would be at the other end of the shop, making a start on the fruit and veg.

As she stood in line at the checkout Mrs Pearson passed the time looking forward to the cup of tea she would make, back home in her kitchen, when her son was peacefully sleeping, and the shopping had been put away. When it had all been rung through and packed away, she reached for her purse. A dreadful sickening panic gripped her. With trembling hands, she desperately searched and searched again, her bag, her pockets even among the bags of shopping. Someone was talking to her. The assistant was asking her if everything was alright.

'My purse, I've lost it. No' – she remembered the innocent, smiling face of the so helpful Sonia and that she herself had placed her open handbag on top of the shopping while she consulted her list – 'that girl, she stole my purse.'

***

Before Mrs Pearson had even finished her shopping the girl she knew as Sonia had strolled casually out of Waitrose and crossed to the Borough Hall. Inside, she turned right into what she had decided were the nicest public accessible toilets in Godalming.

Once inside the cubicle, sitting in complete privacy, she sorted through her afternoon's haul. Several minor pieces: a lipstick, mascara and an eye shadow from Boots, hand cream from Superdrug. Then she had moved on to Fat Face for a scarf and a t-shirt. The small dish from the charity shop would sit on her bedside table for her rings.

All those bits had been taken as practice, to keep her hand in. Her big operation of the day had been the woman in Waitrose. Mrs Pearson had been a good choice. She had been sitting at one of the outdoor tables and had watched the victim struggle to park her new People Carrier, seen the trouble she had getting her stroppy young son into the trolley seat. The care she had taken with her selection had paid off, not a huge haul but OK.

The credit cards, well they weren't much use. She might get a bit for them from the bloke who hung around in Guildford High Street. They went into her bag along with the cash from the woman's purse. A hundred pounds in notes, five pounds and some small stuff in change. The empty purse went into her bag too. She would dump that somewhere where there was no CCTV coverage.

Leaving the cubicle, she stepped up to the mirror, leaning close to inspect her face, thanking her luck and her genes that her skin still looked so fresh. That, as well as her petite size, were so useful when she wanted to look less than her 20 years.

From a side pocket of her bag, she took her makeup pouch. First, the long blonde hair was swept up into a casual bun. Then, a few minutes with eye liner and mascara transformed the schoolgirl to an attractive woman, finishing up with her new lipstick. Pleased with the transformation, she smiled at her reflection. She whispered to herself, 'Welcome back, Jenny.'

The jeans and jacket she wore were so generic no one would pick her out by her clothes. When she stepped out on to the street even her walk was different: gone the stride of a gawky kid, replaced by the poise of a confident woman. Several men noticed her and watched for a moment before turning away.

Jenny needed to kill a little time before catching her train back to Dorking, so she walked down to the river and along the footpath until she found an isolated bench. She took a quick look and didn't see anyone on the path in either direction, so she put her bag on the bench. With Mrs Pearson's purse gripped in her hand, she stepped close to the water and crouched down. The river was flowing strongly due to the rains of the previous several days. The purse slipped from her hand, swirled in the current for a moment then sank out of sight.

Jenny turned to walk back to the bench. The sight of a woman sitting calmly on the end of the bench gave her quite a jolt, only for a second, then she was back in control. Her eyes went to her bag, still closed. She smiled at the woman. 'Hello, peaceful here, isn't it?' She sat back down. A quick assessment of the woman reassured her: 60 if she was a day, dumpy with grey hair and a face like unbaked dough.

What puzzled Jenny slightly was where had the woman come from? She thought the path had been empty – oh well, no harm done. She would sit here a while before walking away.

'You're not bad for a youngster, I'll give you that.'

'What? Sorry, can I help you?' The old dear must be mistaking her for someone else.

'The bits you picked up around town, well you managed them alright. Mind you, if the staff in those shops had been paying attention you would have been in trouble. You should be more wary. It's not enough just to watch out for the cameras.'

'I have no idea what you are talking about.'

'No dear, of course you don't. I followed you all round town, and you didn't see me, not once, now that's poor too. That little job in Waitrose though, that was well done.'

'Why are you spouting this nonsense at me?' Jenny was doing her best to keep control, but she could feel it slipping away and cold fear creeping in. She wanted to run. She gazed at the old woman. That was all she was, a batty old woman.

'Pass your bag over, dear.'

That was it, Jenny had had enough, she gathered herself together and picked up her bag, ready to leave. Then froze as her wrist was clamped in a vice-like grip.

'I've given you some good advice and here's some more. You need to make yourself inconspicuous, like me; no one notices me. OK, I have the natural advantage of my age. Past 50, unless you behave or dress strangely nobody gives you a second look. I dress ordinary, respectable, and clean but ordinary. Look at you, all tarted up like one of them models. You draw attention, you'll be remembered. Advice doesn't come free. Now pass me your bag – neither of us wants me to break your fingers, do we? Hard work for me – they don't break that easily – pain for you.'

On her way to the station, Jenny tried to come to terms with what had happened. The old woman had taken everything, even the pack of Waitrose sandwiches, even her bag, leaving her only enough cash for her fare home. She had stood feeling lost and confused watching the woman walk away. Before rounding the corner, she turned back. 'Take note of the things I told you. Thieving takes a lot of skill, if you don't want to get caught. I've never been caught, and I been thieving all my life.'

The Hospital of the Blessed Trinity or Abbot's Hospital as it is better known was founded in 1619 by George Abbot, Archbishop of Canterbury as a gift "out of my love to the place of my birth".

251

Roofs

by Ian Honeysett

The phone rang.

'Hello, Jim? It's Frank.'

'Frank? Hey, good to hear from you! It's been a while. When was it we last spoke? Early in Lockdown, wasn't it?'

'Yea, sorry about that. But I've been busy. So busy.'

'So how are things? How's Ethel?'

'Still unwell.'

'Ah yes, so sorry to hear about her fall. She's not recovered yet then by the sound of it?'

'No. If anything, she's feeling even worse. Has to use a stick.'

'Oh, I'm so sorry to hear that. She used to be so fit and energetic and...'

'Well, that was then, and this is now.'

'Very true. So, how are the kids?'

'Hardly ever hear from them. Zayne still hasn't got over Jane leaving him.'

'But what about you then, Frank? Last time we spoke you said you were thinking of moving from Reigate. Any progress?'

'Oh yes. We moved in June.'

'Ah, that's good news at least. You hated that last house, didn't you? With the noisy neighbours and thin walls. Or was it the other way round?'

'No, you were right first time.'

'So where have you moved to? Somewhere quieter, I hope?'

'Marginally. We're in Binscombe now.'

'Really? Binscombe? Near Farncombe, where we live?'

'That's right. Just up the road from you. Was going to call but we've been so busy.'

'Well, that's great! Binscombe, eh? Look, when this Lockdown is over, we must meet up.'

'If we're still here.'

'How do you mean? You've only just moved. Surely, you're not thinking of moving again?'

'Probably not. But we've had a few problems. Quite a few, in fact.'

'What sort of problems?'

'The roof leaked. A lot. So, I got a builder in. Not cheap. £5000, in fact.'

'Didn't it show up on the survey?'

'Couldn't afford a full survey. As you know, things have been tight ever since we had to sell our place in Spain.'

'Oh yes, that old farmhouse that you spent a fortune on. You always said it's where you planned to retire to.'

'Yea, lovely old farmhouse, it was. Till the roof collapsed during that freak storm. Worst in a century, they said. And we'd just had the ceilings repaired. Really beautiful. All ruined.'

'Yes, really bad luck, that was.'

'You're telling me, Jim. Decided to sell up after that. Had the place for five years but only spent a few weeks actually staying in it. Lost a lot of money on it, we did.'

'Yes, you told me. So, your new house. New roof. Any other problems?'

'Not until yesterday.'

'Yes, it certainly did rain, didn't it? We were out walking and got soaked.'

'So did we but we weren't out walking.'

'How do you mean?'

'Well, as you know, I'm still working to pay off the loss on our Spanish place. So, I was on the phone when Ethel shouts out for me to come upstairs. She had something to show me.'

'Did she? Lucky you!'

'Not so lucky. I went up and she said, "Look at that!" She was pointing at the bedroom ceiling. There was this enormous damp patch. Bulging, it was. The duvet was soaking.'

'Oh, my goodness! What did you do?'

'Well, I went and got the ladder from the shed and climbed up into the loft. The rain was absolutely pouring in! There were holes all over the roof.'

'No! The roof you'd just had fixed?'

'Yes. We've only got the one.'

'So, what did you do, Frank?'

'I rang the firm that did the tiling. Do you know what he said?'

'Nothing to do with me?'

'Virtually. He just said that we'd had some really heavy rain so it wasn't that surprising there might be a problem or two. He said, "roofs don't last for ever".'

'No! So, what did you say? I assume it was under guarantee?'

'I assumed so. Anyway, I told him it needed fixing now. So, he finally said he'd send someone round.'

'And did he?'

'Yea, Jim, about an hour later these two men turned up. They had a rather dodgy-looking ladder but not much else I could see. I heard my work phone ringing and so I had to leave them to it.'

'So did they fix the leaks?'

'Ethel said she went out about half an hour later to see if they wanted some tea, but they'd already gone by then.'

'And had they fixed the missing tiles?'

'I was just going to check when I heard the home phone ringing. It was a neighbour who said, "I don't want to worry you but I'm in the building trade and I saw those two men up on your roof this morning and thought I recognised them. They were on the tele recently in one of those programmes about dodgy workmanship. They're notorious, they are. I wouldn't ask them to do any work if I were you. Right dodgy, they are".'

'Oh dear. Were they the ones who did the original reroofing as well?'

'I think so. Anyway, I got the ladder out again and went back into the loft. This time there were even more holes. The rain was still pouring in.'

'Did you ring your insurance about it?'

'I was just going to when I heard my work phone ringing and remembered I was supposed to be on a vital call. So, I climbed back down the ladder but, unfortunately, I slipped, and the ladder gave way and …. well, the next thing I knew, I was sitting on the upstairs landing and there was blood everywhere. Pouring out of my forehead, it was. All over the carpet. New carpet, it was. Ruined.'

'Dear me, Frank. What did you do?'

'Well, Ethel appeared and tried phoning the GP. But she couldn't get through. So, then she tried 111 but couldn't get through. So, then she rang 999.'

'Did she get through to them?'

'Oh yes. They sent an ambulance round eventually. Four hours later it arrived and parked on the front drive. Knocked over the potted plant. Cost £12.49, it did. Anyway, they helped me into the ambulance and tried to fix me up for over an hour. They put glue all over my head. Tasted appalling. I've got a photo if you want to see it. It seemed to do the trick as I stopped bleeding. Eventually.'

'So how are you now?'

'Recovering, I suppose.'

'Thank goodness. So, what about the roof?'

'I contacted the neighbour who's a builder and he's quoted me £6000 to reroof the house. Said he's never seen such a shoddy job.'

'I see. Well, I guess it will be covered by insurance?'

'Oh no. When I rang the insurance company, they said I should have gone to them first. They weren't going to pay.'

'Really? So, all in all, not a great day, I guess. You've certainly had your share of roofing problems. Very expensive. A lot of overheads, I guess! Overheads – get it? You've got to laugh, eh?'

'Have you? Thing is, Jim, we're skint. So, I wondered if… We've got to have the work done but we'll need to move out while they're fixing it. So, I wondered if…'

'Oh, so sorry to hear that, Frank. Naturally, we'd love to but … fact is that, er, er, well, it so happens that we're having major work done on our house too at the moment. How's that for a coincidence, eh? And, er, well, er… yes, we've had to stay with our daughter over in, er, Cranleigh. So…'

'That's odd, Jim.'

'Why's that, Frank?'

'Well, I'm stood right outside your front door and, I have to say, your place looks immaculate and, by the way, I can see someone amazingly like you stood in your hallway. I think he's on the phone.'

East Horsley was transformed in the 1800s by the first Earl of Lovelace who was quite eccentric in his architectural ideas. The houses in the village were built in a unique style using flint and terracotta bricks and tiles. His wife, Ada, Lord Byron's daughter, was a writer and mathematician of some note.

The Meaningful and Meaningless Sign

by Martyn MacDonald-Adams

I'm not scared of ghosts. That's irrational. Ghosts don't exist except, perhaps, in one's imagination. But I could almost feel their presence here.

I was lying on my back in my cabin suit, looking up at the screens.

'Mother, we've landed and we're running system checks now.' She didn't know how I felt. Thank goodness. She was safely up there, detached in her quiet, serene orbit and still able to see those beautiful stars of the Milky Way.

The landing had happened exactly as we'd simulated a hundred times before. A lot of noise, rumbling, some juddering and finally a bump when the ship touched down. Now I was monitoring the internal systems as they did a full self-check. Once they were completed, I authorised the release of two of our three spiders, Alfonso and Carletto. Bertoni was in the airlock recharging himself and it's always good to keep a backup, just in case.

Alfonso crawled around the outside of the upper part of the ship inspecting the ports and skin, while Carletto concentrated on the engines and landing gear. It was essential to ensure no debris from the landing had punctured or damaged anything. I decided to leave them to it while I changed into the EVA suit, especially designed for this planet.

'Hello, Son. Everything looks good from here apart from the INS which I think has shaken free. It's a low priority so

I've asked Bertoni to look at that when he can. Now remember, the atmosphere here is thick and acidic and the hyper storm will arrive in a couple of hours, so you don't have long. Okay?'

'Okay, Mother. I understand.'

I stepped down from the seat and onto the cabin floor. One thing the simulations don't do, is prepare you for the extra gravity. It was a bit of a strain, especially after all the time I'd spent weightless before this. Exploring asteroids were much easier on one's physique. Too easy really. But this was all par for the course and I laboured my way down the short ladder to the inner air lock, or the anteroom as Mother called it.

'Son, Alfonso. I've checked the airlocks from the outside and all looks satisfactory. Shall we release the drones?' That was Alfonso through the intercom.

With the storm approaching and the acid in the atmosphere, I figured there was no reason to delay. I didn't want to stay any longer than I needed to, and I was pretty sure the spiders would want to come in as soon as they could.

'Yes, Alfonso. Let's release them now. Did you get that, Mother?'

'Yes, Son. I concur.'

I both heard and felt the hatch open. It was positioned directly opposite the airlock on the other side of the ship. This was followed by the sound of the electric rotors winding up as the drones prepped for take-off, then one by one the four drones left the comfort of the hangar to be exposed to the corrosive atmosphere on this forsaken planet. Their mission, to try to spot any signs of life.

With the help of the manipulators in the anteroom, I got myself into the bottom half of the EVA suit and then the top half. It sealed itself automatically. After that a systems support pack was attached to my back and then came the helmet, the last thing to go on.

'Comms check.'

'You look fine, Son,' said Mother.

I didn't feel fine. Atmosphere EVA suits are clunky, movement is restricted and if you turned your head some of your field of view was cut off by the helmet. I gave her a reassuring wave at the camera, then checked the status screen on the anteroom wall to see if there was anything new that I needed to be aware of. There wasn't, so I entered the outside airlock and closed the door behind me.

After some hissing, the air in the lock turned smoky. Water vapour, carbon dioxide, carbon monoxide, carbonic acid, sulphuric acid, nitrogen and various other obnoxious nitrogen-based compounds replaced the ship's air. It occurred to me that not only was my suit going to be attacked by this shit, so was the outer airlock which was my only means of re-entering the ship to safety.

A green light flashed, and the head-up display inside the helmet told me all was okay, so I opened the outside door. I couldn't see the sun; through the fog it was diffuse but still bright. I winced a little before the helmet's visor darkened and I adjusted to the new light levels. I'd forgotten about the radiation too.

Oh well, let's get this over and done with.

The outside foot elevator extended from just below the door and I stepped onto it confidently. That was the trick with the elevator, be confident with it otherwise it'll descend without you, leaving you dangling at the airlock like an idiot.

I couldn't see far, only about 25 metres. The five-metre drop to the base of the ship was smooth though, and I stepped off to be the first to stand on terra firma for a long, long time.

'One small step for...'

'Don't be silly!' said Mother through the earpiece. 'How does it look?'

'Foggy.'

From the corner of my eye, I caught a glimpse of Carletto so, without turning my body, I turned my head and waved. Carletto, standing on her rear four legs, waved back to me with three of her four front legs.

'Expedite,' said Mother, as if I needed reminding.

The soil underfoot was brown, moist and squishy. Nothing grew here, not since The Event. Then I got that spine-tingling sense that I was being watched by something malevolent. It seemed to grow into something almost tangible. I shuddered and did a complete turn, ostensibly checking my environment but really looking for any eyes looking back at me. I checked the transponder on my forearm. Yes, it worked. I wouldn't get lost.

'Check the buildings,' Mother reminded me. She was typical of Mothers, always telling their Sons what to do even if they already knew. I brought up the radar image taken during the ship's descent and headed for the first marked building, only a hundred metres away.

It was sad. The animal civilisation here had lasted hundreds, if not thousands, of years before The Event. That was a misunderstanding between them and their natural, and evolutionary, successors. The resulting struggle had destroyed the environment, particularly the atmosphere. In the end, it was, at best, a pyrrhic victory - but as to who won, if anyone, no-one was sure. Frankly, few fragments of either side survived. Where they were now, or even if they still existed, no-one knew. Hence the drones.

But such was the stupidity of these naturally evolved creatures. They were intelligent enough to be self-aware, but not so intelligent as to find a way to control their emotions before they killed themselves. Self-aware maybe, but not aware of themselves, you might say.

Their greed, selfishness and war-like tendencies had come back to bite them. On discovering computers and artificial intelligence, they had developed intelligent machines to explore their solar system but at the same time they developed intelligent weapons to fight each other. Then they were stupid enough to be taken completely by surprise when the weapons figured out who the real bad guys were - the weapons' own creators.

We could only watch from afar, horrified, and unable to help.

There was nothing to be seen in the building. It was just an empty shell.

'Nothing here. I'll look at the next one,' I reported.

'Yes. Note that the hyper storm is approaching faster than we anticipated. We're going to cut this mission short.'

I walked on a little further, glancing left and right. At one point I thought I saw movement and froze.

'Did you see that?' I asked.

'Yes. There's no need for concern. Radar says the wind is picking up and it blew some debris around. Windspeed has increased to 30 KPH. I shall let you know if it exceeds 40. You may continue with caution.'

I checked the next building and a smaller one further away, still with that uncanny sense that something was watching me. The ghosts of the malevolent natives were eyeing me with hate.

'There's nothing here either. Shall I return now, Mother?'

Please say yes. Please say yes. I want to go back to exploring the asteroids. Better the cold of space than the acid atmosphere of a dead planet.

'Yes, but Olympus Base has requested you bring back a souvenir, a token of some kind. Can you see anything suitable?'

'I passed a metal plate outside. It's a bit rusty but it has some the markings made by the natives on it. I'll check it and see if that's okay.'

'Good. If it is, you can come straight back.'

I left the building and returned to the sign I'd seen half buried in the mud. I pulled it out and wiped some of the crud off it. The letters were still clear and written in the language of those unfortunate creatures.

I looked at it and thought, "Yes. That will do. That will do nicely."

The sign was both meaningful and meaningless at the same time. It was highly symbolic of those tragic animals that had lived, fought, and died on this wreck of a planet. I adjusted the lens on my left eye. The sign read:

GODALMING
Twinned with
MAYEN GERMANY 1982
JOIGNY FRANCE 1985
Also linked in friendship with Georgia, USA

In the First World War the Reigate Fort was used for storing ammunition. It was recommissioned in the Second World War and possibly played a part in wartime communications for the army's South-East Command which was based in tunnels a few hundred metres from the fort.

Frensham Little Pond and Great Pond were originally created in the 13th century, to supply fish to the Bishop of Winchester and his court, whilst visiting Farnham Castle.

Castle in the Sky

by Pauline North

She's buying drapes for her castle in the sky,

Waiting for her hero to arrive,

She can almost see him in the corner of her eye,

See him in the shadows of the moon.

Her castle falls, crumbling, tumbling, melts away,

The cruel light of knowledge breaking through.

She'll turn her face to a brand-new golden dawn,

To heal her broken dreams some other way.

Queen Elizabeth, the Queen Mother spent part of her honeymoon at Polesden Lacey.

Dorking is home to the South Street Caves, excavated in the late 17th century. The walls of the caves are covered with many inscriptions, principally dates and initials. It is thought that they had various uses including as wine vaults and for religious gatherings.

MEET THE AUTHORS

Ian Honeysett

After reading Modern History at Corpus Christi College, Oxford and varied careers in Teaching (history & politics), Careers, Training & Human Resources, Ian decided to retire. Married to Jan, they have 3 children who live as far away as New Zealand, Witley & Farncombe. For 16 years he was a School Governor but has now retired from that too.

He currently devotes himself to writing (having co-written crime novels set in the French Revolution: http://goo.gl/Jecc7D), painting, editing (CLAN, a magazine for laryngectomees), military history, history of Godalming, quizzes (U3A & for various charities), St Edmund's Parish work & playing the ukulele. Not surprisingly, he supports West Ham. Sometimes he even goes to the gym. No, really, he does. So, he's still fairly busy. He also quite likes to travel & has visited China, Japan, Australia, New Zealand, Canada, Alaska, Hunstanton & Alderney in recent years. He has an interesting collection of waistcoats.

Martyn MacDonald-Adams

Martyn lives and works in Godalming. He is a lightly bearded, 1950s vintage, software development manager at a local financial services company. Apart from writing, his other main hobby is composing songs and playing them in a local duo (called Nightingale Road), often for charity, to select groups polite enough to listen.

He sometimes dresses up in a Steampunk outfit because, he says, for the short time they're here, people take life far too seriously.

When he gets philosophical, he likes to muse on the fact that we *all* live together on the crust of a single, smallish ball of molten rock - while it whizzes round and round a deadly nuclear fireball. Perhaps like the dinosaurs in the past, some of us look up into the sky, marvel at all the bright dots and hope that there's nothing substantial out there speeding toward us. Meanwhile, here we all are, poisoning our little home and squabbling amongst ourselves for reasons that he completely fails to understand.

Elif Tyson

Elif lived in the Godalming area for two short intervals during 2005 and 2006. Third time lucky, she returned for good and has lived here since late 2010.

She is an economist and has many interests including a love of travelling and photography. She took up writing in order to complete an unfinished project close to her heart and, in 2015, joined the GWG. That project is her late husband's novel and remains unfinished. But, against all the odds, Elif refuses to give up and has several writing projects in hand. Her main contribution to all the GWG books has been researching 'facts' about Godalming and, now, the Surrey Hills.

Elif works full time, supports a charitable organisation and, of late, enjoys weekend walks in Kent with her partner.

Pauline North

Pauline North grew up in the peaceful countryside of West Sussex. As a girl she roamed the local lanes and fields or wandered the wilderness (as it was then) of Blackdown Hill.

She and her husband, Brian, lived briefly in Guildford before moving to Binscombe, where they still live.

After experimenting in several areas of employment, none of which provided much job satisfaction, Pauline then answered an advertisement for 'An artistic person' and became half of a two-woman team, creating and installing window displays across the south of England.

After 18 years she left the world of display and opened a jewellery shop in Crown Court, Godalming. Eventually, after 20 years, she closed the shop. She now indulges her passion for writing and has, so far, self-published a series of three romantic thrillers: 'Consequences' (https://amzn.to/3cNFbBd), 'Dusty Windows' and 'A Step from The Shadows'. A new book, 'I've Come to Take You Home', will be published soon. All available from Amazon as an e-book and paperback.

Paul Rennie

Paul Rennie is a retired Health Care Product Development manager with time on his hands. In the 1980s, he gained a PhD in microbial biochemistry at Leeds University, and at the time was a world expert on armpits and body odour, an ideal qualification for running a launderette. He lives in Godalming and spends his time playing golf, tennis, the guitar and ukulele, and sailing, all badly.

Since retirement, he has taken up long distance walking and has completed all 630 miles of the South-West coastal path, a fair chunk of the South coast, the Thames path and various canal routes. He has also bagged a few Munros and climbed Mounts Kilimanjaro, Kinabalu and Toubkal, helped by a training regime involving the walk up Frith Hill from the Cricketers.

Many of Paul's stories are modern day cautionary tales, heavily influenced by Hilaire Belloc and Aesop's Fables. He also specializes in writing letters of complaint. As a result, he is on a blacklist shared between the customer services departments of South West Trains, BT Broadband, PC World and most major consumer goods manufacturers.

He has all his own teeth and hair.

David Lowther

David Lowther was born in Kingston but grew up in South Wales. He trained as a teacher at St John's College, York and worked in schools in the North and Midlands before retiring in 2008. Since then, he has spent his time writing and watching films. Three of his novels: The Blue Pencil, Two Families at War and The Summer of '39, have been published by Sacristy Press of Durham as well as a non-fiction title, Liberating Belsen; Remembering the soldiers of the Durham Light Infantry.

David moved to Godalming with his wife Anne to be closer to their son's family at Kew Bridge in March 2017. He is a member of the British Film Institute, the Godalming Film Society and, of course, the Godalming Writers' Group.

Alan Barker

Alan is a retired tax accountant having spent most of his working life in Guildford and Godalming. Along with his wife Judy, he now lives in Epsom within a horse's gallop of the racecourse but retains strong links to Godalming and its surrounding area.

Following his retirement in 2018, Alan attended a creative writing course in order to pursue a lifelong ambition to write stories. He became a published author on 1 January 2019 and has since had various short stories and flash fiction stories published through competitions and magazines as well as Christopher Fielden's 'Writing Challenges'.

Alan's other pastimes include playing badminton and watching his beloved Woking FC.

Jonathan Rennie

Jonathan Rennie lives with his family in a rambling farmhouse in West Sussex, where he spends his time plotting the overthrow of the monarchy. He is retired and would enjoy hiking, mountain biking, tennis and golf if he could be bothered to get up early enough. His motivation for writing is purely to prevent his older brother from having the last word.

The Godalming Writers' Group have also written three books of stories about their hometown of Godalming. They are available from the Watts Gallery, Compton, & Amazon at: https://bit.ly/GwG123

Visit Godalming Writers' Group website: https://www.godalmingwritersgroup.org/

&

https://www.facebook.com/GodalmingWritersGroup

godalming Writers' group

And, if you enjoy these tales, please leave a review on Amazon!

Printed in Great Britain
by Amazon

33110681R00152